W9-AAT-339

Upper Darby Public Libraries

Sellers/Main
610-789-4440
76 S. State RD

Municipal Branch
610-734-7649
501 Bywood Ave.

Primos Branch
610-622-8091
409 Ashland Ave.

Online renewals:

www.udlibraries.org
my account

Connecting you to literacy,
entertainment, and life-long learning.

SPRING AWAKENING

Center Point
Large Print

Also by T. J. Brown and available from
Center Point Large Print:

Summerset Abbey
A Bloom in Winter

**This Large Print Book carries the
Seal of Approval of N.A.V.H.**

SUMMERSET ABBEY
BOOK 3

SPRING
AWAKENING

T. J. BROWN

UPPER DARBY
FREE PUBLIC LIBRARY

CENTER POINT LARGE PRINT
THORNDIKE, MAINE

This Center Point Large Print edition
is published in the year 2013 by arrangement with
Gallery Books, a division of Simon & Schuster, Inc.

Copyright © 2013 by Teri Brown.

All rights reserved.

This book is a work of fiction.
Names, characters, places, and incidents either are
products of the author's imagination or are used
fictitiously. Any resemblance to actual events or locales
or persons, living or dead, is entirely coincidental.

The text of this Large Print edition is unabridged.
In other aspects, this book may vary
from the original edition.
Printed in the United States of America
on permanent paper.
Set in 16-point Times New Roman type.

ISBN: 978-1-61173-845-2

Library of Congress Cataloging-in-Publication Data

Brown, T. J.
 Summerset Abbey : Spring Awakening / T. J. Brown.
 pages cm
 ISBN 978-1-61173-845-2 (library binding : alk. paper)
 1. Sisters—England—Fiction.
  2. Social classes—Great Britain—History—20th century—Fiction.
  3. Great Britain—Social life and customs—20th century—Fiction.
  4. Historical fiction. 5. Large type books. I. Title.
 PS3602.R722893S94 2013
 813′.6—dc23

2013024272

I dedicated this book to my mother,
Carol M. Foreman.
Thank you for always being there.

1514162

ACKNOWLEDGMENTS

There aren't enough props in the world to give Molly Glick for her spot-on career guidance. Literary agents just don't get any smarter, savvier, or more supportive than she is.

Heartfelt thanks to editor Lauren McKenna and assistant editor Alexandra Lewis, who earned the title Editor Extraordinaire for answering panic-stricken e-mails all hours of the day and night. I'd also like to thank associate director of copyediting John Paul Jones, and the rest of the Summerset team at Gallery Books, most notably Lisa Litwack for the stunning cover and publicist Kristin Dwyer for her enthusiastic support.

And as always, I want to acknowledge and thank the people in my life who give their never ending love and support: Hubby Alan, son Ethan, daughter Megan, soon-to-be daughter-in-law Megan, and someday-to-be son-in-law Chris. I love you all.

CHAPTER ONE

For anyone else, this place would have fostered a sense of serenity if not pure bliss, but Rowena Buxton felt nothing but a sad sort of detachment.

The musical notes of a nearby stream were accompanied by the occasional burst of her friends' laughter. In July, the Suffolk countryside shone with a tapestry of different greens, spotted generously with yellow and pink flowers in the grass. Rowena sat alone on a low rock wall watching her friends, also known as the Cunning Coterie, enjoying the impromptu picnic out of sight from the watchful eyes of society's gossiping matrons.

Young women wearing pastel muslin and carrying lacy, white parasols moved indolently among young men in their light suits and straw hats. Occasionally, a summer breeze would lift the ribbons or stir the flowers on the women's hats, but it did little to relieve the heat that buzzed around them like bees. Visiting Summerset Abbey had been a treasured part of Rowena's childhood and contained dozens of memories just like this one . . . excepting the inevitable pairing off, imbibing of alcohol, and smoking of expensive Turkish cigarettes that hadn't arrived on the scene until recently. Perhaps the prior generation hid their vices better, or perhaps Rowena just hadn't noticed.

"Do you think he'll ever win her heart?" Sebastian asked, coming up next to her.

She startled, almost falling off the wall, and he put his arm around her waist to steady her.

"Who? Oh, Kit and Victoria?" She glanced to where her younger sister sat with her back against the trunk of a beech tree organizing flowers into piles while Kit read to her from the latest E. M. Forster novel. Kit's dark-red head was tilted close to her sister's fair one. No doubt Victoria was sorting herbs while Kit ardently hoped his dedication would pay off next time he asked her to marry him. "Poor sot. He has her heart. It's her hand in marriage she won't give."

"What about your heart?" Sebastian's eyes were grave.

Rowena turned to look at her fiancé. "My heart is my own."

"Is it really?" he asked, his voice casual.

She twirled the flute of champagne in her fingers before draining the glass. "Of course. And you have my hand in marriage, my dear, so all is well." She ignored the pain that tightened her chest and banished her former lover from her mind.

She held her glass up, signaling to the servant keeping careful watch by one of the wagons that she needed another. He was there in moments with champagne that had been kept chilled in the stream.

"Would you like some, sir?" the servant asked Sebastian, after filling Rowena's glass. She frowned at the white gloves he wore, thinking about how ridiculous it was to have a servant wear white gloves in such heat. And on a picnic no less. The servant kept his gaze on the ground, and Rowena wondered what his name was. Like so many others in the grand estate, this serving man was anonymous. She tried not to think of her and her sister's former home in London, where the servants were a valued part of the family. Perhaps when she was the mistress of Eddelson Hall, she could really get to know her servants.

Sebastian waved a flask. "No, thank you. I have my own."

"Very good, sir."

The man left and Sebastian turned back to Rowena. "Kit's pretty stubborn."

To Rowena's relief, Sebastian returned to the topic of his best friend and her little sister. Lately, he'd begun pressing her for more affection than she was ready to give him. Their engagement was more one of convenience than love—both had had their hearts broken and neither wanted to risk their feelings again. They were dear friends and their marriage would be a partnership based on mutual respect and friendship. Why was he suddenly pushing her? Not that she didn't enjoy his physical affection—her body tingled at his touch, but that disturbed her as well. What kind of woman was she that her body would react this way with two very different men, only one of whom she truly had loved?

Tired of her own thoughts, Rowena hopped down off the wall. "Let's play some cricket, shall we?" she called to the others.

Annalisa, a vivacious young woman with light brown hair and dark eyes, groaned from where she reclined against a pile of soft pillows. "What is it with you Buxtons? You're all just so active. Always busy doing something."

"Idle hands are the devil's playground," Victoria quipped.

Cousin Elaine jumped up with surprising eagerness. "It's because our tolerance for boredom is so low. Isn't that right, Colin?" She looked to her brother, who hadn't budged.

Rowena knew he hadn't moved because he had a perfect view of Annalisa's décolletage from where he was lying. "Oh, come on, it isn't that hot and we have plenty of cold water. Don't be so bloody lazy," Rowena said.

A servant brought the necessary equipment and there was a lot of good-natured wrangling over who would be on whose team. Victoria's asthma, though much improved, still prevented her from playing any kind of sport, and she was conscripted to keep score.

In spite of the protests, the heat, and their only having seven people on each team, the group played with a surprising zeal. *And why not,* thought Rowena as she waited for her turn to bat, *they'd grown up doing little else besides going to school and playing games. It was what their set did.*

She glanced up into the sky, longing for her aeroplane. Only when she flew could she forget about her heartache, the unfairness of the world she was born into, and her grief. Only in the air was she truly happy. But her aeroplane, a Vickers biplane given to her by her uncle, was almost a day's journey southwest. Now that she was one of a select few women in England to have been awarded her pilot's license, her uncle wondered why she didn't bring the Vickers to Summerset to be stored in the barn her friend Mr. Dirkes used for his test planes. She couldn't tell her uncle the truth.

She was afraid of running into Jonathon.

"Rowena! It's your turn!" Colin yelled. Her muslin skirt had a slit up one side, but running was still problematic. Rowena enjoyed sports and was good at them. Had she been born into a different sort of family, she might have been on a team of some sort. But upper-class girls didn't involve themselves with team sports. Besides, she would rather fly than chase balls.

She hit the ball with a crack and heard Victoria

and Elaine whooping behind her. Pulling her skirts up, she ran with all her strength while Sebastian, Kit, and Daphne looked for the ball in the long meadow grasses. She'd run twice before Kit yelled surrender.

"That's the win anyway!" Victoria yelled, jumping up and down.

"It can't be," a handsome young man Rowena didn't know well protested. "It hasn't been nearly enough runs."

"Oh, don't be a sore loser, Edward," Lady Diana drawled from the corner of her mouth. Lady Diana was commonly believed to be the most beautiful of the Coterie and the most adventurous, though a small but discriminating group considered Rowena to be far prettier. "Your competitive nature is rearing its ugly puss."

Edward grinned. "But like Puss in Boots, my competitive nature has held me in good stead. It allows me to woo one as lovely as yourself, Lady Manners."

Diana tossed her head and Rowena smiled.

Victoria nodded as the rest of the Coterie came in from the field and gathered round. "Rowena's team did win. Look, here is the score sheet."

Edward pushed them aside playfully. "Why should I take the word of a jailbird?"

Rowena froze. For a fraction of a second no one moved; then in a blur of movement and with

14

a loud smack, Kit punched Edward square in the jaw. Edward went hurtling backward, falling against Rowena and knocking her to the ground.

"Bloody hell!" Edward muttered from where he lay several feet from Rowena. Shocked, Rowena stared at Kit's scowling face and clenched fist.

Victoria grabbed Kit's arm. "What is wrong with you? He was only teasing me! He always calls me that. Why are you such a brute?"

Another hush fell over the group. Rowena winced at the pain in Kit's eyes when Victoria knelt down beside Edward.

"Are you all right?"

Stone-faced, Kit reached his hand out to Edward. "Sorry, mate. I guess I overreacted just a bit."

Edward rubbed the side of his face. "Not at all. I enjoy the occasional bash on the jaw."

Victoria stood abruptly, scowling at Kit. " 'The injustice they warrant. But vain is my spite. They cannot so suffer who never do right.' "

Elaine blinked. "What?"

"Jane Austen," Victoria explained. "I thought it appropriate."

Rowena laughed in relief. For a moment she thought there might be a fight with her sister in the middle of it. Released, the others joined in Rowena's laughter and the tension lessened.

Sebastian helped her to her feet, then held her waist possessively until she shrugged away, complaining that exerting herself in such heat had given her a headache. But she worried as she helped pack up the picnic. How much longer could she put him off?

Victoria dressed for the evening with the lack of enthusiasm of someone who had done it all too many times before. There would be entertainment in the grand salon—a small quartet her aunt Charlotte had imported from London for the house party—a late supper that would take far too long, and then the usual games of bridge or whist in the drawing room.

Usually the Coterie begged out of the game playing, preferring their own amusements, but lately various and sundry relatives had been applying pressure, urging them to take their rightful place in society.

Fretfully, Victoria tossed the pearls onto her dressing table. The walls of her lovely blue-and-white bedroom seemed to close in on her. Her uncle, the Earl of Summerset, had promised that she would be able to return to London as soon as she regained her health. Victoria leaned forward and stared into the mirror. Her face had filled out since her stint in prison. She was never going to be as healthy as Elaine and Rowena, but between Cook's puddings and her friend Nanny Iris's concoctions, she had improved a great deal. And she had always been small and pale—no amount of fattening up would change that. She would corner her uncle tonight.

Resolve buoyed her and she reached for her pearls again.

"Oh, you look lovely, poppet. Are you ready to go down?" Elaine came in behind her, ravishing in a rose silk gown with short, lacy sleeves. Her cousin, with her soft brown hair and pretty blue eyes, was a Coterie favorite, but to her mother, Victoria's aunt Charlotte, her daughter was little more than an afterthought. Elaine had spent her childhood trying to please her mother and had been a ninny while constantly angling for the woman's approval. It was funny what a year away in a Swiss boarding school could do for a girl.

"I will be in a moment." Victoria struggled with her choker until Elaine intervened.

"Oh, let me do that." Victoria's blond hair was swept back with combs, and Elaine clasped the pearls around her neck. "That's a lovely dress. Is that one of the ones we'd had made up before . . ."

"Before I went to Holloway Castle?" Victoria's eyes met Elaine's eyes in the mirror. "That's what we called it, you know. The castle on the hill."

Elaine looked away.

Victoria stood, sighing. "I'm not ashamed of going to prison, you know. Many brave women have gone to Holloway Castle because they believe in the suffrage of women. I'm humiliated because I wasn't incarcerated for bravery, but stupidity. I was duped like a child into being at the wrong place at the wrong time."

"I'm so dreadfully sorry," Elaine murmured.

"Oh, don't be." Victoria forced a cheerfulness she didn't feel into her voice. "Because of my time in prison I can now quote the life works of Edgar Allan Poe and Walt Whitman. Would you like to hear?"

Elaine laughed. "Some other time, perhaps." Her cousin leaned toward the mirror and fixed a curl in front of one of her small, delicate ears. "So what is going on between you and Kit?"

Victoria's fingers fumbled, sending the pearl bracelet she was clasping around her wrist to the floor. Avoiding her cousin's eyes, she knelt to retrieve it. "Whatever do you mean?"

Elaine laughed. "Oh, come now, Cousin, the man is besotted with you, and everyone knows it. Remember, we've known Kit longer than you have and have never seen him so completely infatuated. The both of you can natter on all you want about being friends, but we know better."

Victoria's face flamed. She hated being the focus of idle gossip. It was bad enough already with her colorful past. Besides, her relationship with Kit was too confusing and no one else's business, though she did wish she could talk it over with someone. Rowena had been preoccupied with her own heartache and her flying lessons, and Prudence lived in London.

Elaine touched Victoria's shoulder gently. "It's all right. Not everyone is talking about it. Just those of us who love you. You can trust me, you know."

Tears stung Victoria's eyes and she turned and hugged her cousin. "I don't know what to do with him," she said, choking a bit. "He wants to marry me. Thus far he has only mentioned it when teasing me, but I suspect he is serious, and it comes up more and more frequently."

"Don't you love him?"

"Of course I love him, but love has nothing to do with it!" Victoria whirled around, looking for something to vent her frustration on. She chose the footrest and gave it a satisfying kick. "Ouch!"

Elaine's brows arched and she calmly bent to right the abused stool. "But I thought love had everything to do with it."

Victoria hobbled over to a wingback chair and threw herself into it. "Oh, bother. That's not what I mean at all."

Elaine pulled up a footstool and sat in front of Victoria. "Then what do you mean, poppet?"

Elaine's voice was gentle, and Victoria took a deep breath. "I don't know if I love him in that particular way or not. I enjoy being with him, but I enjoy being with you and Colin, too, and I am certainly not going to marry either one of you. I miss him when he isn't around, but I miss my father all the time, so what does that say?"

Elaine shook her head, setting her curls in motion.

Victoria leaned forward. "I'll tell you what that says. I was not meant to get married. I'm not like other girls. I've never been like other girls. I don't want to get married and have babies. I want to do something important. I want to travel and meet people and have adventures. Make a real change in the world. Have an impact in some way."

"And you can't see yourself doing that with Kit?"

"Kit is great fun, but he would change after marriage. All men do. He would want to have children, and it's hard to have adventures with nappies and nannies. No."

Elaine's nose wrinkled. "I don't see Kit changing all that much."

Victoria snorted and stood up. "That shows how much you know. When I first met him, he was as set against marriage as I was; now it's all he talks about. How can I even trust him? Shifty bastard."

Elaine stood and linked arms with her. "Trust me, my dear cousin. I'm as against marriage as you are, but for very different reasons. We can become old spinsters together."

Victoria felt a surge of relief at having confided in someone. "Why are you against marriage?" she asked as they walked down a hallway lined with the portraits of disapproving relatives.

Elaine waved her free hand. "It's a long story, poppet. Remind me to tell you when we're old and gray. Just know that I'm on your side."

They entered the downstairs drawing room, laughing. A much subdued Coterie was in force, surrounded by their wealthy and eagle-eyed relatives. Most of the members of their strange little club were set to inherit large sums of money and property, but as most were well under thirty, they were dependent on the goodwill and the annual stipends of their elders. Though they were a randy, irreverent lot behind their benefactors' backs, they attempted to keep up appearances in their presence.

Edward raised a glass in mock salute as Victoria moved to greet her aunt and uncle. She liked Edward, who was handsome and smart and, most important, completely in love with someone else. He was uncomplicated, unlike Kit, who was becoming more complicated by the day. "Good evening, Uncle. Good evening, Aunt. You're looking smashing this evening."

As always, Victoria resisted the urge to curtsy before her aunt as if she were the Queen. The impulse made her voice brisker than it would have been with someone else of her aunt's peerage and status. Aunt Charlotte rather intimidated her, and Victoria detested being intimidated by anyone. Even though she knew all too well that her aunt was a woman to be feared, Victoria couldn't help the disrespectful edge in her voice whenever they conversed.

Her aunt offered a cheek, which Victoria kissed dutifully. "Really, darling, is that how you spoke to the wardress?" Aunt Charlotte asked in a whisper as Victoria leaned close.

Victoria stiffened, then whispered back, "No, Auntie, I reserve it just for you." She drew away and her aunt Charlotte gave her a lovely smile. Those who didn't know Charlotte would think her sincere. Those close to her knew that her genuine smiles were rare and reserved for her husband and son.

"Lucky me," Aunt Charlotte answered, her eyes amused.

Aunt Charlotte unnerved Victoria, who hastily kissed her uncle's cheek and joined the Coterie in front of the fireplace.

"Where's Rowena?" Victoria asked, looking around.

"She has a headache," Sebastian answered. "She won't be joining us this evening."

"If I had five glasses of champagne and ran about like a madwoman in the heat, I would have a headache too." Annalisa grinned.

Victoria frowned. Rowena had good reason to want to drown her sorrows.

"Well, good for her," Kit said, then drained his glass. "A body has to do something to dull the boredom."

"If it's so boring here, why do you even bother?" Victoria flashed.

"Sometimes I wonder," Kit snapped back.

Stung, she stared up into his clever blue eyes, then tossed her head. "I know I certainly do."

"Oh, stop it, you two," Colin ordered. "You're both becoming boring, and we have far, far better things to talk about."

Victoria took a deep breath and let it go. "Like what, dear cousin?"

"How about . . . the fact that I've officially joined the army?" Colin answered quietly.

Next to her, Elaine gasped, and Victoria couldn't believe that around them people continued drinking their tea and gossiping just as if the phrase he'd just uttered were completely common-place.

"Mother's going to kill you," Elaine said flatly.

No mention of how their father would feel, but everyone knew that even though Lord Summerset could be a cold, hard man, it was Lady Summerset who could make a person wish she had never been born with a single disapproving glance.

"What the hell did you do that for?" Kit barked.

Colin glanced at the Dowager Countess of Kent, who had wandered near to the group. Everyone went still and smiled at her, which caused the old lady's brows to fly upward toward the old-fashioned lace cap she wore on her graying head.

"Lovely day, isn't it Lady Barrymore?" Victoria

asked sweetly. "A perfect Little Red Hen day!"

Lady Barrymore's pale eyes blinked rapidly. "You're quite mad, child."

" 'Oh, we're all mad here. I'm mad. You're mad . . .' "

" 'How do you know I'm mad?' " Kit asked, his voice affronted.

" 'You must be or else you wouldn't have come here,' " Victoria finished out the quote from their most treasured book. Apparently Lady Barrymore hadn't read Lewis Carroll because she merely shook her head and walked away, clucking her tongue.

"Old bat," Annalisa giggled.

"Mind your manners," Edward said. "The Dowager Barrymore is a paragon of virtue and too good for the likes of us, so sayeth my mother."

"Never mind that!" Elaine snapped. "I want to know why my brother would do something so . . . absurd. Father will kill you. He's been waiting for you to finish at the university so he can start training you to take over Summerset."

Elaine's normally mischievous eyes were as serious as Victoria had ever seen them.

Colin shrugged. "Perhaps that's why I joined. Perhaps it was the boring years I have ahead of me playing lord of the manor instead of having fun like the rest of my peers."

"Good grief, man, one doesn't join the army to have fun," Sebastian said.

Victoria shook her head. "When are you going to tell Auntie and Uncle? Because I want to return to London before you do."

"You can take me with you," Elaine murmured.

"You two ladies worry overmuch," Colin said. "They will fuss a bit, but will no doubt give in. It's not as though we're at war."

"We would be if the Germans had their way," Sebastian said.

Victoria shook her head. "It won't get that far. The Kaiser is related to the royal family, for goodness' sake."

The butler announced that dinner was now being served, and the ladies and gentlemen found their partners to go in for supper.

Victoria had been partnered with Kit so many times that she was surprised when Aunt Charlotte came up behind them in the line going out the door. "I'm so sorry, but because Rowena is missing dinner, I had to juggle the order a bit. Victoria, you are going in with Colin. Kit, could you please escort Annalisa?"

"Aren't I the lucky one," Colin said, taking Victoria's arm. "Shall we go in, Cousin?"

A frown crossed Kit's handsome features for a moment, then he shrugged. "Actually, I think I'm the lucky one. Be careful of her tongue, Colin, old boy. It's as sharp as an ax."

Victoria waited until her aunt Charlotte had moved past them before sticking her tongue out at

Kit. He winked back, and she couldn't help but smile. He was such good fun. If only he would forget all that marriage nonsense.

"So do you really think they are going to take it badly?" Colin asked with a worried frown.

Victoria didn't have to ask whom he was referring to. "You were in OTC all through university, weren't you? And they didn't object to that."

"Every wellborn young man goes through the Officers' Training Corp. It's expected. That doesn't mean they want me to actually become an officer."

Victoria tried to give Colin a reassuring smile as they walked through the door to the massive, formal dining room with its long, shining mahogany table, which was actually several tables pushed together. She could see the burden of his secret in the tight, tense line of his shoulders. For a moment, she conjured up an image of her cousin as the tormenting tease that he had been so long ago. "Don't worry so. I'm sure they'll be reasonable."

But even though her voice was carefully confident, neither of them believed it.

CHAPTER TWO

Rowena stared out the dormer window of her bedroom, watching the lights from the house splashing out onto the garden. The Coterie must have managed to extricate themselves from the card games because Rowena could hear low echoes of illicit laughter as it spilled out into the night from the billiards room.

Earlier, music from the drawing room had wafted up to her open bedroom windows—sweet classical airs drawn from the masters that had little in common with the music now pulsing out of the gramophone's lily-shaped speaker. Ragtime's primal rhythms filled her with a restlessness that pulled on her heart and tugged low in her belly. Music that made her think of stolen hours spent in a London hotel room with a man she could never have and would never forget.

The room, already warm, seemed unbearably stuffy, and the dark softness of Summerset's manicured grounds looked cool and inviting. Restless, Rowena snatched up her light lawn dressing gown and, after tying the ribbon at her throat, padded across the room in her bare feet. Once she'd made sure the coast was clear, she hurried like a wraith down the dim, deserted hallway, her pulse racing. She hadn't felt this good since the last time she'd taken her plane in the air. Slipping out through the conservatory, she ran across the lawn, her nightclothes billowing out behind her.

She ran past the rose garden her father had redesigned as a young man and through a gap in the hedge that boxed in the kitchen garden and the cutting garden. Out of the sight of the house, she slowed, catching her breath. The grass pathway was velvety soft beneath her feet, and the scent of fresh flowers perfumed the air. She followed the footpath past the massive kitchen garden, which provided the family and the staff of Summerset Abbey with fresh fruits and vegetables during the spring and summer and root vegetables during the autumn.

Taking a right, she moved away from the garden toward the lily pond. The frogs croaked a summer's hymn in the night, and a sense of peace washed over her as she took a seat on a small knoll overlooking the inky, moon-splashed water.

Chilled, she pulled her legs up under her nightgown and rested her arms on her knees. Purposefully, she kept her mind away from Jonathon and focused on Sebastian, whom she would be marrying in weeks. They had originally planned to wed the first of July, but had moved the date to mid-September to make sure Victoria had recovered enough to be Rowena's attendant.

She'd avoided thinking about the wedding, even

though everyone around her could talk of little else. To escape, she'd employed tricks such as staring off into the distance as if considering something important and then agreeing to everything with a little "Mhmm." This led to her having orange blossoms in her hair instead of her father's favorite lilies, six bridesmaids instead of three, and beef Wellington for her wedding supper instead of the game hen that was her and Sebastian's favorite.

She let herself be carried upon the wedding wave because the less she thought of it, the less real it seemed. Now she brought it into sharp focus. Not the wedding. She could not care any less about the actual ceremony; it was the marriage she needed to think about.

Marriage to Sebastian. Not Jonathon. Her chest ached and she clenched her fist. Sebastian. She pushed the image of Jonathon away and let Sebastian fill her mind. Sebastian, who was so handsome and kind. When gossip about Rowena's behavior with Jonathon reached her aunt, Lady Summerset had automatically assumed the man in question was Sebastian. Sebastian gallantly agreed to go along with a false engagement to save Rowena's reputation. He was a good man with heartache of his own, and when he asked her to make their engagement a real one, there was no reason not to. After all, Jonathon wasn't coming back. Her uncle had stolen land from Jonathon's family, thereby setting into motion the events partially responsible for the death of his father. Her name and her fortune and everything that they implied were, in the end, too much for Jonathon.

But she had neglected to think about giving herself to Sebastian the way she had given herself to Jonathon. Could she do that?

A warm breeze ruffled her hair and she closed her eyes imagining what it would be like to kiss Sebastian the way she had Jonathon.

"Rowena," a man's voice said softly.

She jumped and glanced behind her, red staining her cheeks when she realized that Sebastian stood there as if she had conjured him. "You alarmed me!"

"I'm sorry," he said, joining her on the bench. "There was no way to let you know I was here without startling you."

"It's all right." She knew she should be ashamed—sitting with a man in her nightclothes all alone—but she wasn't. She also knew she should be concerned about being alone with Sebastian, but she wasn't worried about that either. The night was made for lovers, but her lover had gone away. The man who was to be her husband was here instead, and she needed to make her peace with it, once and for all.

But what if she couldn't fulfill her physical responsibilities to her husband? What would happen then? Shouldn't she find out before they were wed? Butterflies circled in her stomach. She should. "It's a beautiful night," she finally said. "It's hard to believe how quickly summer is passing."

"It was an interesting spring." His voice sounded neutral and she wondered what he was thinking.

She put her knees down and turned to look at his profile in the darkness. Like her, Sebastian Billingsly was the product of hundreds of years of good breeding. In contrast to some of the other young lords of their generation, his features were even and strong. His jaw was firm and his nose and teeth were both straight. The darkness of his hair and eyes reflected the light of the moon.

He turned to look at her and she smiled. Resolutely, she moved closer to his side, and though his eyes widened, he said nothing. She leaned against him until he slipped his arm around her shoulders.

It was strange being pressed so close to a man who wasn't Jonathon, but it wasn't unpleasant. She laid her head against his shoulder, and his arm reflexively tightened about her. The longing, aching need she felt with Jonathon wasn't there, but warmth nonetheless spread through her body at Sebastian's proximity.

She closed her eyes for a moment, gathering her courage before turning her face up to his. He looked down at her, a smile curving his well-formed lips.

"By the time autumn comes, we'll be married," she said, her voice quavering. She cleared her throat. *Courage,* she told herself.

He nodded, his face thoughtful in the darkness. "Are you still satisfied with our arrangement?"

She searched his face wondering if he still was, but he had turned away and didn't meet her eyes. "Why do you ask?"

His eyes were distant. "You're very guarded. I wanted to make sure you weren't having second thoughts. So when I saw you running across the lawn, I decided to gird my loins and just ask."

Her pulse increased. She knew he would let her out of their arrangement if she wanted. She only had to say the word. But was being alone and pining away for a man who had walked away from her any way to live? Was it any better? At least she and Sebastian were honest about their feelings. They could make a good marriage, she knew they could. If only she could get past her hesitation about making love to him. Impulsively, she reached up and pulled his head down, pressing her lips hard against his. Startled, he didn't move, but then his hesitation disappeared and he pulled her close.

Their kiss deepened, and for a moment Rowena almost pulled away, but then she focused. If she could just get to know him, get to know the way his mouth felt against hers, she wouldn't feel so strange in his arms. Already her lips were matching his, and a hesitant, buttery warmth invaded her lower belly. She pressed her hands experimentally against his chest, feeling the hard muscles underneath. He pulled away and buried his face in her hair, his breath ragged.

"Rowena?" His voice was a question. In answer, she moved until she was in his lap and resumed kissing him. She pushed off his light summer jacket and linked her arms around his neck. His kisses were slow and languorous, almost chaste, as if he was holding back. Then she realized why. He thought she was a virgin. She stiffened in his arms, but when he tried to pull away, she drew his head back down.

He was going to find out sooner or later for they already had too many strikes against their marriage to play games. If they had any hope of making a real partnership, they would have to be honest with one another. So, her heart in her throat, she untied her dressing gown and slipped it off her shoulders. Then in one smooth movement, she pulled her nightdress over her head and discarded it on the grass next to the bench. Without waiting for an answer, he picked her up in his arms and lay her down in the soft grass.

"Rowena," Sebastian groaned "What are you doing?"

She shivered as the cool summer air hit her body. She let herself fall on top of him, burrowing into his warmth. No, the body she lay against wasn't Jonathon's, but the lingering pulses of the music, the exultation of her flight from the house, and the feeling of his skin against hers had broken through her reserve. It had been so long, so very long, since someone had held her like this, wanting her. "I'm not an innocent," she murmured against the base of his throat. He groaned as she unbuttoned his shirt and pressed herself against him.

He ran his hands down the velvety length of her back and she held her breath. He rolled them over until he was on top, and she could feel him fumbling with the front of his trousers. She arched against him, willing him to hurry. "Please," she whispered, "please . . ." But it was Jonathon's name that suddenly came to her mind.

Shock, like a bucket of cold water, washed over her. Suddenly, she was aware of the strangeness of the body on top of her. The feeling of a twig poking her back. What was she doing? How had this gotten so out of hand? "No. Please stop."

She reached out her hand and grabbed her discarded nightclothes and pulled them against her chest.

Groaning, Sebastian fell alongside her. She could hear the sound of his labored breathing, and tears stung her eyes. She was simply hopeless.

He put his arm over his eyes and she hurriedly dragged her nightgown over her head and pulled her dressing gown on. He didn't move. Taking a deep breath, she touched his shoulder. "Are you all right?"

"I'm fine." He sat up next to her. Handing him his shirt, she looked away until he had pulled it on. "But I don't know if I understand what . . . what just happened . . ."

"I'm sorry," she said, her voice small. "I don't know what came over me. I just wanted to . . ."

"Don't." He put a finger to her lips. "Don't apologize. We got out of hand and you rightfully stopped us. We should wait until our marriage."

She wanted to tell him the truth. Tell him she had wanted him, but was confused. That she still ached for Jonathon every night. But looking at his kind, handsome face, she knew she wouldn't. He'd suffered enough heartache. She wasn't going to add to it.

But underneath her confusion and her disappointment in herself was relief. If nothing else, she knew from the intensity of their embrace that she could one day share a marriage bed with Sebastian . . . just not yet.

Impulsively, she leaned forward and kissed him softly on the mouth. "Now, my dear future husband, how are you going to sneak me back into the house?"

Prudence Wilkes hurried up the stairs of her Camden Town flat, wondering how time had gotten away from her. She liked to have dinner already cooking when her husband got home from the docks. Hauling pallets tired him out so much that he could barely keep his eyes open through dinner as it was. If she didn't have his food on the table early, he barely made it through his meal.

He'd been working steadily ever since he had passed the examinations for the Royal Veterinary College. He didn't say it, but she knew it rankled him to live off her money. He was working hard and saving so that when he started school in the fall, they wouldn't have to lean so hard on her small inheritance.

She put her key in the lock, entered the stuffy flat, and hurried to turn on the fan she had splurged on. All it really did was move the hot air around, but it helped. A little. She had left all the windows open, but Andrew didn't like her leaving the door open while he was gone. The flat was so long and narrow that the air never seemed to circulate from the front room to their back bedroom, and the windows didn't help at all.

She had gone down to St. Pancras Gardens and sat in the shade to read. At least hearing the water in the fountains made her feel as if she should be cool, even if she wasn't. It was better than sitting in the sweltering flat all day. She tried not to think about the cool, spacious rooms of the Mayfair house where she'd grown up. That way of life had died when Sir Philip had. This was her life now, and for all intents and purposes, it wasn't a bad life. Just a different life.

Prudence went to the small counter next to the sink and set the block of ice she had just purchased into it. Pulling up a corner of the burlap, she chipped off a chunk of ice and put it in a glass before wrapping the burlap tightly around the block and placing it in the small icebox. She filled her glass with water and drank deeply before refilling it and starting supper. There was no way she was going to light the oven. Andrew would have to be grateful for the bangers she had bought and would serve with a small, and blessedly cool, plate of fresh, sliced tomatoes.

While she worked, she remembered that Victoria's letter was still in her pocket. She put the bangers in the pan, sliced the tomatoes, and then arranged them prettily on a plate. She wasn't much of a housekeeper or cook, but at least she tried.

Taking her cool glass of water, she sat at the kitchen table and opened her letter. She could almost hear Victoria's impudent, breezy voice as she read the scrawling words.

My dearest Pru,

How I wish I were sleeping on your tiny window seat rather than living in a place where everyone watches me as if I am going to collapse at any given moment, regardless of how fine a mansion it is! The doctor has given me a clean bill of health, my asthma is better thanks to Nanny Iris's concoctions, and still everyone fusses over me so!

But on a happier note, I've finally pinned Uncle Conrad down as to a date when I can move out. He did promise, you know, and has been dreadfully remiss in keeping that promise. I, however, have not forgotten that he promised me a flat in London, and Eleanor has started looking already.

The wedding is over a month away, but that's all I hear tell of day and night. I think Rowena is as sick of it as I am, at least that is how it seems. And poor Sebastian disappears every time Aunt Charlotte and his mother appear.

I am so happy I made the decision never to get married. I think Seb and Ro should just do what you and Andrew did: a week to plan, a day to get married, and you're off!

Well, I hope to see you soon. I plan on

coming up in a week or so to see the flats Eleanor has found. I will send word as soon as I know what day. Why don't you just get a telephone? They are so convenient!

All my love,
Vic

Prudence set the letter aside, mixed emotions warring in her chest. The thoughtless comment about the telephone stung a bit—but Victoria had little concept of money and would have no clue that Prudence didn't have a telephone because they couldn't afford one—so Prudence couldn't fault her much for that.

If she was honest with herself, it was Victoria's talk of the wedding that settled in her stomach as if she'd eaten a bad pudding.

She had thought she was over Sebastian. She *was* over Sebastian. It wasn't as if they'd actually had anything more than a flirtation. She pushed their one and only kiss from her mind. That certainly didn't count.

If she was completely honest with herself, she would have to admit that her biggest peeve about the entire situation wasn't that Sebastian was getting married; it was whom he was getting married to.

Rowena.

Rowena, whose thoughtless bargain with her uncle had led to Prudence's being treated like a maid for weeks. Rowena, who'd lied and covered her tracks and who said she meant well, but always seemed to do things that hurt people. Rowena, who had been like her sister and then betrayed her.

That needled.

Suddenly she became aware of a thick, acrid smoke wafting toward her from a fry pan.

The bangers!

She leapt up from the table, knocking her chair over backward. Snatching up the hot pan, she tossed it into the sink and turned on the tap. Thick smoke billowed up from the pan, and her eyes stung. How could she have forgotten them when she'd been only a few feet away?

Tears ran down her face. Stupid bangers. She hated to cook. And right now, she couldn't help but feel a seething hatred for Rowena.

She cried harder and didn't notice that the door had opened until it slammed shut.

"I do hope this isn't over my supper." Andrew set his lunch pail on the table and gathered her up in his arms.

Prudence laid her head against his chest and gulped back her tears. "I'm such a ninny. I'm just so bad at all this." She waved her hand, indicating the entire flat.

He understood. "You weren't brought up to be a housekeeper. All this is new to you, just as working the docks and living in the city is new to me. Have some patience with yourself, my love."

She hiccuped and her tears slowed and stopped. She tilted her head back to look into his pleasant hazel eyes. Even though they looked tired, they twinkled at her and held no disappointment at their ruined supper. "I just wish I were better at it, for your sake."

"I just wish I could afford to hire a maid to come in and do the hard work. But I can't, so we may as well not cry over it."

Tear welled in her eyes again, as much for the tone of his voice as for the words.

He shook her lightly and begged her to stop the waterworks.

She giggled and wiped her eyes. "But what about our supper?"

He shrugged. "It's too hot to cook anyway. Let's go down to the pub for some beer and kidney pie. Let someone else slave over a hot cooker."

Giving him a rather watery smile, she kissed her husband and went to make herself presentable. On her way to the bedroom, she picked up the letter from Victoria and tossed it into the stove. She would give no more thought to a wedding taking place miles from London. She loved her husband, and it was no matter if her life wasn't exactly what she thought it would be. Sebastian and Rowena were in her past. It was up to her to make sure they stayed there.

CHAPTER THREE

Victoria followed Eleanor through the narrow hallway and into the spacious sitting room of the first flat they were scheduled to look at. She turned a circle in the middle of the room, considering. The sitting room was important because it would be where they would do most of their day-to-day living.

The wood floor could use a good refinishing, she thought, but some pretty rugs could cover the worn areas. The windows were narrow, but tall, and the light streaming through emphasized the bits of plaster falling off the walls and the burned-out bulbs.

Her heart sank. "I'll take it!" she said even before her friend had a chance to show her the rest of the flat.

Eleanor laughed. "This is the first one we've seen."

Victoria didn't care.

Mr. Barry, her late father's solicitor, sniffed in disapproval. "I do believe this was the address your uncle liked least, Miss Victoria. The young lady is right. We still have other, more suitable flats to show you."

Mr. Barry didn't approve of lady bachelors at all, and for Victoria, with her youth and family connections, to choose to live on her own was a disgrace. Victoria knew that if it weren't for Mr. Barry's loyalty to her father's memory and his hope of obtaining the patronage of her uncle, the Earl of Summerset, he wouldn't be showing her and Eleanor flats at all.

"What do you think?" she asked Eleanor as they walked through three more rooms. The flat consisted of seven rooms: a sitting room, kitchen, two roomy bedrooms, a chamber for the live-in maid, a bathroom, and a small study with an enchanting bay window that overlooked a small park. A layer of grime lay over everything, as if the home had been vacant for quite some time, but according to Mr. Barry, an old woman had lived here until she had gone to live with her son. Apparently, she hadn't thought to clean after vacating the premises.

Eleanor's blue eyes widened and she put her hands on her hips. "It's enormous. Do we really want to clean a flat this big?"

Mr. Barry grimaced at Eleanor's East End accent, and Victoria wondered if the good solicitor realized that she had met her friend in prison. Eleanor had been Victoria's nurse, and her kindness had been the one bright spot during those dark days. She had kept Victoria's family informed of her well-being, and the only reason Victoria's uncle had consented to her moving to London on her own was because she would have a nurse living with her.

Victoria blinked. "That's why we'll retain a maid."

Eleanor giggled. "Ah. A maid. Of course. Silly me. Well, the location is closer to my job and the settlement house where you wish to work than the other flats on the list."

Even Mr. Barry's mustache quivered with disapproval. "Really, Miss Victoria. I think the place near Bond Street would be more appropriate and—"

His obvious condemnation of the flat made Victoria dig in her feet. "No. Eleanor and I have decided on this. It's perfect for us. We can both get to work easily from here, and its closer to Eleanor's family in Whitechapel."

Mr. Barry's mouth fell open for a second before snapping shut, and a little burst of triumph erupted in Victoria's chest. They would hire a maid and make the house their own.

She would be *free*.

After Mr. Barry promised to have the papers sent to her uncle to sign, and Eleanor ran off to her job, Victoria was at liberty to explore her neighborhood. Telling the driver she would be getting some air, she set out on foot. She couldn't be gone too long . . . she had promised Kit she would meet him for tea at his house.

The streets were busy and she spotted a dry-goods store, milliner's, a tea garden, and a bookstore, all within walking distance of the flat.

She noted that most of the people she saw milling about were dressed in nice, if not particularly stylish, clothing. She strolled to the corner and saw the tube just down the street.

Victoria was eager to get on with her life. Her desire to be a botanist had been little more than a desperate attempt to stay close to her deceased father. She loved botany, but now realized that the real draw for her had always been the much more pointed study of herbs and their medicinal uses. And more than anything else, she had an overreaching desire to do good in the world, to somehow make it a better place. Teaching at the settlement house would suffice for now. Kit called her a do-good, but who cared what he thought?

Her chosen neighborhood had a homey feel, she thought, looking around. Not like the Mayfair neighborhood where she had grown up, but it seemed the kind of place she could be happy. The thought of her beloved home depressed her, and she turned back to where the driver waited. Her uncle, in all his wisdom, had moved the girls out of their childhood home and let it out, so now the bright and lovely house where she had been so happy was filled with Americans, who were, no doubt, loud, careless, and completely unappreciative.

She fell into a pensive mood and was quite out of sorts by the time she reached the Kittredges' Belgravia mansion, which was not the way she wanted to face Kit's mother. One needed all of one's wits when facing the clever and daunting Mrs. Kittredge.

Victoria waited until the driver came round to open her door and took a deep breath. The house was far more ostentatious than her uncle's stately London home. The Kittredges were new money, and like many of the new rich, they tended to throw their money around in all the wrong places. The house took up almost an entire block and included a carriage house, which now housed the Kittredge motorcars, and a stable in the back.

The butler led her to the drawing room, and Victoria's heart sank when she saw the guests seated proper and upright in their seats. Her eyes swept to Kit, and her heart sank even lower at the sour expression marring his handsome face. Mrs. Kittredge was nowhere to be seen.

Kit stood, a look of relief crossing his features. "Victoria, how wonderful to see you. I'm sure you know Mrs. Gertrude Asquith, Lady Elizabeth Reinhardt, Lady Eloise Cash, and Mrs. Genevieve Balfour."

Victoria nodded with a pleasant smile on her face, her eyes darting to Kit. "How do you do? It's so very hot outside, isn't it?"

She addressed this last part to the room in general, but Kit jumped on it as if he had been waiting for something to do.

"Yes, it is. Would you like some lemonade?"

"That would be very nice, thank you." She looked at his vacated spot on the sofa. She did want his support if she was going to be stuck having tea with these society women who had no doubt heard of her incarceration, but she didn't want to give him any ideas. However, the only other available seat was between Mrs. Asquith and Lady Cash, and she just couldn't make herself do it.

She took the spot on the sofa and gave a vague society smile to the women around her. She suppressed a little shiver as they stared at her with varying degrees of curiosity and general disapproval, no doubt because she had come into their august presence wearing a simple serge walking skirt and a short-sleeved blouse of white lace. Too late she remembered the matching jacket she'd taken off in the heat of the motorcar.

"How are your sister's wedding plans coming along, my dear?" Mrs. Asquith asked. She wore a fancy visiting dress of tobacco-colored satin and a kimono-sleeved bodice, but most startling to Victoria was her straw hat, upon which an entire brown bird was impaled at the front of the crown. Surely that wasn't a real bird?

Victoria forced her eyes away from the pitiful figure. "It's going wonderfully well. Though they did decide to move the date out a bit further."

Lady Cash clucked critically. "Isn't this the second time the wedding has been delayed?"

The women all leaned forward ever so slightly in unison, as if they were about to hear some previously undisclosed gossip. Victoria pressed farther back in the sofa.

"Yes. Sebastian's older sister is in her confinement and he very much wishes her to be at the ceremony."

Lady Cash looked disappointed, while the others glanced at one another as if wondering if Victoria should be chastised for mentioning the word *confinement.*

"Here you are." Kit handed her a glass of lemonade.

She took it thankfully and eyed the seat next to her. *Too bad,* the look said. *If I have to put up with this, so do you.* Kit caught her meaning and sat with the aggrieved air of someone standing at the mark. Where was Mrs. Kittredge? Why had Victoria been asked to this happy little tea party anyway?

"Are you in London with your aunt?" Lady Balfour asked.

Victoria's spirits were revived by the cold drink and Kit's proximity, and she instinctively adopted the same breezy tone she used with Aunt Charlotte. "No. I'm here by myself. I'm flat shopping, actually."

Lady Balfour arched her eyebrows. "Whatever for?"

"Oh, I'm moving to London to take a job. Or

volunteer, to be more precise. I am going to work at the Rodgers Settlement House."

Lady Reinhardt, who had remained silent until now, audibly gasped, and even Mrs. Asquith's dead bird seemed to look at Victoria reproachfully.

Next to her Kit stifled a laugh, and Victoria felt the devil rise up in her.

"Well, I never heard of such a thing!" Lady Cash said.

"Oh, yes." Victoria nodded. "I'm going to be a lady bachelor. My nurse from prison will be living with me."

The silence dropped into the room like a bomb. The women glanced at one another, unsure as to what to do or say next. Victoria was, after all, the niece of their friend the formidable Lady Charlotte, and the daughter of a knight.

"Victoria, are you shocking my guests?"

Every head in the room turned toward Mrs. Kittredge's low, sultry voice. It was early afternoon and Mrs. Kittredge wore a peacock-blue tea outfit with insets of lace as if it were state dress. As always, the style was slightly oriental, with kimono sleeves and a low bodice. She wore her dark hair back with a wicked straight fringe across her forehead that accented her dark-almond eyes. The expression on her face showed amusement, but her eyes held a warning that Victoria caught immediately. She would allow Victoria to go only so far as she found it entertaining, but anything that would threaten her own status was out of the question.

Victoria understood. Mrs. Kittredge had taken her husband's fortune and turned it into a stepping-stone into society, and her position was precarious. As unorthodox as she was, she still played by the rules, and now that her husband was dead, and the aristocrats no longer relied on his business to make money, her position was more precarious than ever.

Victoria kissed Mrs. Kittredge on the cheek, as did Kit.

"I'm so sorry I'm late. I had an unavoidable delay. Thank you all so much for coming. Where is that unfortunate butler with the tea?"

As if in answer, the butler appeared in the door with a tinkling tea cart.

"Victoria, would you do us the honor of pouring tea, darling? Gertrude, wherever did you get your cunning hat? I've never seen anything like it."

Victoria poured tea as graciously as she could muster while Kit fidgeted next to her. He hated this sort of thing and avoided it like the plague. Again she wondered what they were doing here.

She handed him a cup. "You owe me one," she whispered.

He gave her a cheeky grin. "So, have you found a flat?"

The other women went quiet, listening. "Yes, actually, in Chelsea."

"Isn't Chelsea full of unemployed actors and opium dens?" Lady Balfour sniffed.

Victoria nodded eagerly. "Oh, I hope so! How exciting! Did you know that Percy Bysshe Shelley used opium?" She recited:

> *Silver key of the fountain of tears,*
> *Where the spirit drinks till the brain is wild;*
> *Softest grave of a thousand fears,*
> *Where their mother, Care, like a drowsy child,*
> *Is laid asleep in flowers.*

"Bravo!" Kit burst out, clapping. Victoria nodded.

Mrs. Kittredge blinked. "Just so." She cleared her throat, then, looking pointedly at Victoria, said, "So when are you and Kit going to announce the engagement?"

Victoria froze, her tea raised halfway to her lips. "Mother!"

Kit's voice was indignant, but a shot of anger ricocheted through Victoria's chest nonetheless. He had to have set her up for this. How else would his mother have been led to believe that an engagement was imminent? How *dare* he lead his mother to believe they were to be married?

His mother shrugged elegantly while her guests watched wide-eyed. "It's a legitimate question.

You two have spent every available moment together for months."

Victoria was reeling. Suddenly her former perception of Mrs. Kittredge shattered. The woman clearly didn't care one whit about her reputation if she was willing to start a family row in front of these gossips.

"Oh, we're never getting married," Victoria managed to spit out, finally bringing her tea to her lips. It tasted like tar and betrayal. "We're just jolly good friends. I don't know that I believe in matrimony." She took a long sip. "And if I were to marry, it certainly would not be to Kit."

She set her tea down and gave a hollow laugh. She fixed Kit with a stare. "I'm sure he feels the same way. Why, we're practically brother and sister. More tea anyone? . . . No? Very well. I apologize for my appalling manners, but I'm afraid I must be going. I have to go see my solicitor about signing the papers on my lady-bachelor flat."

She stood, and next to her Kit popped up like a jack-in-the-box.

"I'll see you out," he said, tripping over the carpet in his haste to escape.

After bidding farewell to the women and wondering how long it would take the story to reach her aunt, Victoria followed Kit. Once they were away from the sitting room, she doubled up her small fist and punched him in the arm. Hard.

"Ow!" Kit clutched his arm. "What in the devil was that for?"

"That was for setting me up!"

"I don't know what you're talking about!"

She went to hit him again, but he caught her hand midair. He held her easily as she struggled.

"You told your mother you wanted to *marry me?* After I've told you repeatedly that I don't want to marry? Did you tell her to corner me in front of those women to humiliate me? Or worse, to apply pressure? What kind of friend are you? What kind of *man* are you?"

"Of course I told my mother I wanted to marry you. That's certainly no secret, though why I would want to spend the rest of my life with a lunatic is suddenly beyond me," he spat back, unwilling to back down.

Stung, she jerked her arm away. She would absolutely not give someone control over her life or abdicate all of her freedom to appease social custom. Especially not just as she was about to escape her uncle's authority. "It doesn't matter if you want to marry me or not because I've already told you, very definitively, *no!*"

Kit's jaw tightened and her stomach clenched at the pain she glimpsed on his face. She couldn't help but soften, suddenly longing to reach her hand out and touch his face just to make the look go away.

"You have made that abundantly clear. I just

happen to think you are going to change your mind."

She gasped, all sympathy forgotten. "You, sir, are the one who is deranged. Of all the egotistical blather!" Her hand itched to slap the smug look off his face, but instead she turned on her heel and stalked away.

"Does this mean we're not going to see the Russian ballet tomorrow night?"

Outraged, she whirled around, only to find him leaning against the wall with his arms crossed. His blue eyes were annoyingly amused. He was such an insufferable tease! He recited:

> *What's friendship? The hangover's faction,*
> *The gratis talk of outrage,*
> *Exchange by vanity, inaction,*
> *Or bitter shame of patronage.*

Alexander Pushkin! How dare he use her own trick against her, quoting the celebrated words of another to add punch to his own argument. She turned and stalked out the door.

"I'll have the motorcar pick you up at seven," he called.

"Don't bother. I have my own!"

Of all the conceited . . . she wouldn't go, of course. She wouldn't. But she already felt herself weaken as the driver opened the door for her. Of course she would go. He had box seats and she did so love the Russian ballet.

CHAPTER FOUR

Rowena kept her eyes closed against the morning sun. She lay on a chaise lounge on the vast Summerset lawn, sipping an iced tea and reflecting on the many things she had yet to do to prepare for the wedding.

After her and Sebastian's interlude, the wall of lethargy she had built up around herself had come tumbling down. Shaken out of her previous trance, she felt ready to begin the next chapter of her life. Maybe her aunt was right. Maybe the only true freedom a smart woman had was through a good marriage, and for all intents and purposes, her marriage to Sebastian had every possibility of being brilliant, if not necessarily passionate.

So, for the first time since the engagement, she actually looked forward to her wedding, if only as a means to an end. Being the mistress of Eddelson Hall, though it was not as grand as Summerset, would be a welcome distraction, and best of all, Sebastian's wedding gift to her was a hangar that would hold her Vickers aeroplane. Thoughts of Jonathon grew less and less frequent, and they were no longer accompanied by a stabbing pain; instead, she felt only a sense of regret and loss when he entered her mind.

It was indeed past time to get on with her life.

Aunt Charlotte, languid and unusually quiet, flicking through a periodical, lay next to Rowena, while Elaine lay on her other side. Victoria and Eleanor were off furnishing their London flat, and as happy as Vic sounded, Rowena knew her sister wouldn't be back until a week before the wedding, which was now only six weeks away.

A shadow fell over Rowena and she glanced upward from under the protective brim of her straw cartwheel hat, purposefully designed to keep the sun from touching her pale skin. It wouldn't do to get tanned or coarse before the wedding, as Aunt Charlotte was always telling her.

"Colin!" Elaine cried, leaping from her chair. Her brother pulled her up in a hug. "What are you doing here? I thought . . ." She stopped mid-sentence and glanced nervously at her mother.

Rowena, too, glanced at her aunt, wondering what she would say. It had been over a week since Colin had finally broken the news to his parents about joining the army, and Aunt Charlotte had dramatically ordered him off the property.

"I sent for him," Aunt Charlotte said calmly.

"I knew you couldn't live without me." Colin grinned. Only he could tease his mother like this.

"You flatter yourself. Your father talked me into having you here. Apparently I behaved too rashly in his mind."

"Admit it, Mother. You would miss me."

His mother gave an indelicate snort. "Actually, I begged your father to use his connections to save you from your folly, but he has decided that the army may be exactly what you need. And while it's clear that you need some more discipline in your life, there are undoubtedly other ways more suited to your title and less fraught with peril." She let out an exaggerated sigh. "What is it with men and their obsession with playing soldier?" She directed this toward Rowena and Elaine, but they both knew better than to answer. She pointed an elegant finger at Colin. "You are going to regret this, young man, mark my words."

"Yes, Mother." Colin sighed.

"Do you want to join us?" Elaine asked, her voice anxious. "We can have the servant bring you a lounger."

Colin shook his head. "No. I want to talk to Father. I got my orders and I know that he, at least, will be interested in my assignment." He cast his mother a sidelong look, which she ignored.

"I'm very interested," Rowena said.

Colin seemed proud of himself and preened as if his drab, olive-green calvary uniform were evening formals. "You are now looking at a member of the 1st King's Dragoon Guards and I will be stationed in Lucknow, India."

Another snort from his mother told Rowena her aunt was less than impressed with her son's assignment.

"That's wonderful!" Rowena exclaimed, even though she wasn't sure if this really was good news. She just thought that someone should make up for his mother's disapproval.

"Then we could come visit you!" Elaine said, clapping.

Aunt Charlotte stood. "Maybe you would actually be able to find a husband in Lucknow, darling. I'm sure they aren't too picky out there in the middle of nowhere."

With that, Aunt Charlotte turned on her heel and sauntered off as if she hadn't just sent a poisoned arrow into her daughter's chest.

Elaine's eyes filled with angry tears.

"Don't be upset, Lainey," Colin said, slipping an arm about his sister's shoulders. "She's angry with me and taking it out on you."

Elaine gave a bitter laugh. "It wouldn't have mattered. I've never been able to please her. How could I? I'm not a boy."

Rowena shifted uncomfortably. "I'm sure she loves you. She just has a hard time showing affection."

"And yet she seems to have no problem showing it to Colin. Well, most of the time. She's just angry with him right now." Elaine shrugged. "I shouldn't be surprised by what she says, but sometimes I still am. Silly me. But enough of that. I'm not going to ruin my brother's visit crying over something I can't change."

She linked her arm through her brother's and held out her other arm to Rowena. "Let's go find something alcoholic to celebrate my brother, who is surely the handsomest second lieutenant in the First Dragon or Dragoon or whatever it is."

Rowena stood and joined her cousins. "Are you going to be here for the wedding?" she asked. "If not, we'll have to find someone to take your place, and I'm not sure Annalisa Watkins will like that."

They walked for a moment across the wide expanse of Summerset's manicured lawn toward the conservatory door. "Oh, I think they are going to make sure I am home for the wedding. Both mine and yours."

Elaine stopped short and hit her brother in the arm. "You wicked! Who?"

Colin pulled away and laughed. "Haven't you guessed? Annalisa, of course!"

Rowena's eyes widened. "How did that come about? What a sly boot she's been! She hasn't said a word."

Elaine squealed. "I adore Annalisa. At least it's not Daphne," she said referencing another member of the Clever Coterie.

Colin snorted. "Daphne? Hardly. One doesn't marry girls like Daphne. Besides, Mother would make mincemeat of her."

"When are you planning on telling Mother and Father?" Elaine asked.

"I already told Father. That's one of the reasons

I'm back here. He thinks my upcoming nuptials will appease Mother."

"I don't think anything will appease Mother."

Elaine's voice was dry, but Rowena could detect the hurt underneath. She wondered briefly what her relationship with her own mother would have been like. Her memories of her mother were hazy at best, as she had died shortly after Victoria was born, but she did know her father, and any woman he chose would have to be loving and special indeed. Her heart ached for her cousin and rather dimmed the happiness she felt for Colin. "When are you getting married?" she asked.

"That's what I wanted to talk to you about. Annalisa and I don't care to have a big wedding, but you know Mother, she is going to insist—but we don't want to wait. After some preliminary training here, I'll be sent off to India, and we would like to be married before then so she can follow me as soon as our affairs are in order." He stopped walking and looked at Rowena, his blue eyes pleading. "We were wondering if we could combine our nuptials with yours and Sebastian's?"

Elaine clasped her hand over her mouth in excitement, and Rowena laughed at the expression on her face.

"That would be brilliant!" Rowena told him. "It would be such fun to be standing up there with you and Annalisa. I must speak with Sebastian, of course, but I can't see that he would have a problem with it."

Colin reached out and squeezed her hand. "Thank you, Rowena! Timing-wise, it works out perfectly. And best of all, the wedding will be grand enough that Mother won't feel cheated."

Elaine did a little jig between them. "No, best of all, it takes the pressure off of me for a bit. Ha!"

She linked arms with Rowena on one side and her brother on the other. "Come, let's telephone Annalisa and give her the good news so she can make the trip out and we can start planning."

They were nearing the conservatory when they heard a cry and the crash of china against its brick floor where afternoon tea was being set.

"There goes another maid," Elaine murmured. "Mother hates it when they break her china."

But then a keening noise filled the air, and Rowena's stomach knotted. The three picked up their pace and hurried through the wide-open doors of the conservatory, then, as if in accord, they all stopped in shock, staring at the tableau before them.

Rowena could hardly reconcile what she was seeing. Her cold, manipulative, austere aunt Charlotte was doubled over in her husband's arms while an unearthly moaning came from her open mouth.

Charlotte spotted them in the doorway and put up one hand in a claw. "You stupid boy!" she screamed at her son. "You stupid, stupid boy!"

Hortense, Aunt Charlotte's lady's maid, rushed into the room and put her arms about her mistress.

"Take her upstairs," Uncle Conrad ordered. "I will be up shortly to check on her. Give her some laudanum, if necessary."

"It won't help, it won't help," Lady Summerset sobbed as she was led out of the conservatory.

A wide-eyed maid appeared out of nowhere to clean up the mess covering the red tiles.

Rowena could feel Elaine trembling next to her, and Colin was as white as a sheet. Lady Summerset was never out of control. Never.

"Was that about my wedding?" Colin asked, his voice tight.

Uncle Conrad shook his head, and Rowena noticed that sweat had beaded on his forehead. "No. I had just delivered some news. I didn't know how hard she would take it. I had no way of knowing."

His voice broke and Elaine rushed to his side. "What is it, Father?" she cried.

For the first time Rowena spotted the crumpled paper in his hand. She stared at it, knowing that whatever it contained had caused her aunt's undoing and her uncle's grim countenance.

Her uncle held his fist up and stared at the paper. "Britain just declared war on Germany."

Rowena froze and Elaine gasped. Colin remained motionless.

Even the maid, on her knees before them, stopped cleaning the broken bits of china.

Elaine finally found her voice. "Why on earth would we do that?"

"Haven't you seen the newspapers, Lainey? Austria declared war on Serbia. Germany invaded Belgium. It's a tangled knot of alliances." Colin turned to his father. "I didn't think Germany would invade Belgium."

Rowena looked from her cousin to her uncle, horror rising in the pit of her stomach. "I thought Belgium was neutral."

Her uncle nodded, his eyes bleak. "And like a house built of cards, all the countries fall."

Elaine turned to her brother, shock and confusion marking her pretty face. "What does this mean for you? Will you not be going to India now? I don't understand . . ."

Colin turned to his father. "I should get back to London. I don't know what exactly the army is going to do with me now. They will be mobilizing and may not want me to ship out to India if they are bringing the 1st King's Dragoon home."

Elaine whimpered and Rowena took her hand.

Uncle Conrad nodded, though his mind seemed far away. "Don't forget to say good-bye to your mother. She's quite upset, you know," he added accusingly, as if they hadn't just witnessed his wife's breakdown. "But it's because she loves you, and she's worried for your safety. War isn't child's play, my boy."

Colin nodded and, after a squeeze to his sister's shoulder, left the room. With a nod to Elaine and Rowena, his father followed him.

Rowena and Elaine stood frozen, still holding hands.

The world had gone mad, Prudence was sure of it. Overnight, it seemed, London had given birth to thousands of soldiers. Prudence tried to shut the sounds and sights of war out of her head, but newspaper boys, screaming headlines in their high-pitched voices, trumpeted the latest combat news on every corner.

Apparently war sold newspapers.

She picked up a pound of tea, wincing at the price. During the first couple of weeks following Britain's declaration of war, people had panicked and bought everything they could get their hands on, causing shortages and skyrocketing prices. Even though things had settled down a bit, prices remained inflated, and Prudence worried that they would have to dip too heavily into her savings just to survive. That money was needed to pay Andrew's tuition to veterinary school, but even that wasn't her biggest concern. Her worry was that Andrew would enlist.

The news from the Battle of Mons was heartbreaking, and she knew the thought of the

Royal Army's retreating before German aggression did not sit well with her husband. Every night she feared he would come home and tell her he had volunteered. He wasn't the type of man who would sit idly by while his countrymen sacrificed themselves for their King.

What would happen to their dreams then?

Her last stop was the greengrocer under their flat. She picked up an onion, several pounds of potatoes, a firm head of cabbage, and a bunch of carrots and added them to her basket, along with the tea and the small slab of brisket she had splurged on. Her cooking was still hit-or-miss, but her friend Muriel had taught her to make boiled dinner, and even Prudence was hard-pressed to spoil that.

She paused at the bottom of her stairs, feeling strangely dizzy. Why did the heat of Camden Town seem so much hotter than the heat in Mayfair? It hadn't settled well on her and she was frequently out of sorts, experiencing headaches and dizzy spells more and more frequently. Andrew had told her to rest today, but who would do the shopping and cooking if she didn't? She refrained from mentioning that to him, of course, because it only emphasized his failure to provide her with a maid to help.

Carefully, she hefted her marketing basket on one hip and made her way up the stairs. When she opened the door, she stopped short upon finding

Andrew sitting at their makeshift kitchen table. Her stomach plummeted when she saw the firm-jawed resolve of his face coupled with the pleading in his eyes.

The loopy, dizzy feeling returned, but she fought against it. Leaning against the door, she shut her eyes for a brief moment before bracing herself for his news. "You're home early."

"Yes." He got up from the chair and relieved her of her basket. He set it on the table and began putting things away, methodically, the way he did everything. She remained where she was by the door.

The sounds of traffic outside and the low hum of the fan motor buzzed about her ears, but she focused on Andrew. She knew what he was going to say, and suddenly she wanted more than anything to put it off for as long as possible.

Once the dizziness passed, she moved slowly into the room, shutting the door behind her. She helped him put the rest of the groceries away. "I thought we would have boiled dinner tonight. You like boiled dinner."

"Yes, I do. Prudence . . ." His voice was low and entreating.

"Could you fill the pot full of water and set it on the cooker?" she asked, turning away.

Without waiting for an answer, she slipped into the water closet and ran some water into the tiny basin. She was going to cry and didn't want him to know, because he was going to leave her and go off to war and she couldn't do anything about it. He was set to enter the Royal Veterinary College in two weeks, but that didn't matter. Everything they had worked so hard for since their impromptu wedding last winter didn't matter.

Tears ran down her face. She loved him and he was leaving her. Her mother had left her, Sir Philip had left her, Rowena had left her, and Victoria was embarking on an exciting new life that had nothing to do with her. One reason she had married Andrew was because she had known he would never leave her. Never.

And now he was leaving.

She splashed cool water on her face and dried her eyes. Taking down her hair, she brushed it out, before coiling it back up into a simple chignon. After a deep breath, she walked out of the bathroom to face the inevitable.

He stood in the center of the room, his arms hanging loosely by his sides. He looked more unsure than she had ever seen him, and even though her heart throbbed, she knew she couldn't let him see her pain. She couldn't let him know. All over Britain, women were saying good-bye to their men. She didn't want him worrying about her as he marched off to war.

"Prudence . . ."

She went to him then and took his hands in hers.

They were rough, his hands, but so strong and so gentle when he touched her. Bending her head, she kissed the calluses on his palms.

He slipped his arms around her and she took a deep, shuddering breath. "I know, my darling, I know," she said.

"It's the right thing to do, Pru."

A slow burning ignited in her chest. *The right thing for whom?* Not for her and not for him, surely. For the Crown? For the realm? She tamped the anger down. Arguing wouldn't stop him from going any more than tears would. She knew with knowledge as old as time that nothing would sway him from his purpose.

"When?" she asked, her voice muffled against his chest.

"I'm not sure. I just signed up today. There's a bit of confusion right now because of all the volunteers, but I should be sent to Salisbury for training."

Prudence nodded, unable to articulate anything around the lump growing in her throat. Andrew tilted her chin up until she was looking into his eyes. In her flight from Summerset and the truth she'd discovered about her heritage, Andrew had been the rock that she'd clung to. She clung to him now, wishing she didn't ever have to let him go.

"Thank you," he said.

"For what?"

He didn't answer. He bent his head to put his lips to hers, and with a grief-stricken desperation she kissed him back, soaking in every bit of her husband her heart could hold.

CHAPTER FIVE

Victoria flung her bag on the small table just inside the door the moment she walked into her flat. Not even after dancing until dawn at some society function had her feet hurt so brutally. "Susie! Please, if you have a heart, bring me a cup of tea and a tub of water for my feet."

Susie, who had been a scullery maid before filling in as an emergency lady's maid, had been only too happy to leave Summerset and Lady Charlotte behind to become Victoria and Eleanor's housekeeper, where she dined alongside the girls, slept in a warm, clean bed, and enjoyed an entire day off once a week. Even though London still frightened her, her daily life had improved and she considered Victoria a saint.

"You shouldn't have stayed so late, miss," Susie called from the kitchen. Victoria could hear the running of water and knew she would soon have her aching feet soaking in a steaming tub of water sprinkled with lavender and bath salts.

"I stayed as long as I had to," she called back, peeling off her uniform cape and entering her spacious sitting room. She and Eleanor had been living in the flat for several weeks, and a transformation had already taken place. They had done most of the cleaning themselves until Victoria had sent for Susie to help with the more difficult tasks of painting the walls and repairing the plaster. The flat contained an eclectic mix of fine furnishings from Victoria's former home in Mayfair and more worn pieces from Eleanor's home. The back of their blue-and-gold Chippendale sofa was covered with a worn quilt made by Eleanor's grandmother, and Victoria found the jumble homey and charming.

"They are working you too hard," Eleanor mused from where she reclined on a lounge in front of the windows.

Victoria startled. "I didn't know you were home. And don't talk to me about working too much. You didn't get home until two this morning and left before I awoke."

Eleanor shrugged. "I trained VADs like you all day. The more volunteers we have, the less I have to work."

Victoria snorted, collapsing into a red wingback chair. "As if you would work any less." Eleanor had taken a position with the Red Cross as a training nurse and now educated young women like Victoria in basic first aid and nursing. Wounded soldiers were already arriving from the front by the thousands, and makeshift hospitals were being assembled in community centers and private houses. Soon there would be a nursing shortage unless volunteers were trained and quickly.

"I gave up the job at the prison," Eleanor protested.

"Only when you had to."

"What about you? You train all day, volunteer to write letters for soldiers, and go out all night with Kit. As your nurse, I must protest."

Victoria grinned at the woman who had become as close to her as her own sister. "I'm perfectly fine now, as long as I don't run or catch cold, and you know it, too."

Susie came into the room carrying a tray with a teapot and miniature tea sandwiches. "And I suppose you won't catch cold working with all those sick men?"

Victoria took the cup Susie held out to her, then helped herself to a plate of sandwiches. "Oh, thank you, you blessed creature. And they're wounded, not sick, so don't bother fussing. Prudence, Rowena, Elaine, and Eleanor have already tried to talk me out of volunteering—all to no avail. The settlement house where I was going to volunteer, if you remember, has been turned into a recovery home for soldiers, so I had to change my plans. One does what one must." Victoria waved her cup, almost spilling her tea.

Susie harrumphed and left the room, and Eleanor gave Victoria a weary smile.

The doorbell rang and Eleanor started to rise before Victoria waved her back down. "Susie will get it. You look fagged out."

"I am," Eleanor admitted, settling back onto the chaise. "I never thought I would live to see the day where I had a housekeeper to answer the door. Have I told you how much I love living here?"

"Only a dozen times a week."

"I can't possibly say it enough."

"Say what enough?" Prudence asked, coming into the room.

"Pru!" Victoria stretched up her arms to give her friend a hug. "I would get up to greet you, but I can't feel my feet. Susie! Bring some more tea!"

"As if you have to tell me how to do my job?" Susie yelled from down the hallway.

"Such impertinence!" Victoria exclaimed with a grin. "What brings you to Chelsea? Not that you need a reason. I'm always so happy to see you!"

One of the best things about living in London again was that she got to see Prudence on occasion. Now that Andrew was in training in Salisbury, Prudence had become a frequent visitor to the flat Kit fondly called the Hen-Pen.

Victoria looked at Prudence sharply. Shadows marked her friend's eyes and she looked thin and tense despite that her cheeks looked rounder.

"Other than just seeing your sweet self?" Prudence asked after greeting Eleanor. "I've come to ask a favor, actually."

Susie brought in another cup for Prudence and then helped Victoria remove her shoes.

"What sort of favor?" Victoria asked, intrigued. Prudence rarely asked for favors, even while they were growing up together.

Prudence sat on the velvet sofa and set her cup carefully on the low table in front of her. "You told me that Colin is in the 1st King's Dragoon, right? When will he be joining his regiment?"

Susie brought in a steaming tub of hot water, and Victoria gingerly put her feet into it before answering, "I'm not sure. They are on their way back and then will no doubt be heading to France or to Africa or some hellish place like that. Why?"

Prudence stared into her tea as if she were reading the future. Victoria leaned forward, her shoulders tensing. Whatever Prudence wanted, it was important.

When Prudence finally looked up, her green eyes were pleading, and Victoria caught her breath. Prudence looked so much like Rowena, Victoria couldn't believe they had grown up oblivious to the family resemblance.

"I don't want Andrew to go to the front. I know, I'm being selfish, but I want him to come home alive. I was going to ask you if you could talk to Colin, see if he can't do something. As gentry, he may be able to have Andrew assigned to the remount depot, where he can work with the horses. Andrew would like that, and he wouldn't be fighting."

The fear Prudence felt for her husband etched her pretty features with misery. When she closed her eyes and drew in a deep breath, Victoria's heart swelled in sympathy. "Of course, I can ask him. I don't know how much pull Colin has, but I will talk to him as soon as possible."

Prudence opened her eyes and gave Victoria a tired smile. "Thank you," she said simply.

"Of course! I would do anything for you, you know that. Now do you want some biscuits? Susie? Do we have any of those chocolate butter ones I like so much?"

Susie went to fetch the biscuits while Victoria turned back to Prudence, careful to keep her expression cheerful. "Have you seen Katie lately?" she asked, to change the subject. Prudence looked relieved, and they gossiped about mutual friends until Susie came back in with a colorful tin of biscuits.

Prudence started to choose one and then paled. Pushing the tin away, she clapped a hand to her mouth and rushed from the room. Victoria blinked. She would have followed her, but her feet were still soaking.

"I'm going after her. She may need a cold cloth." Susie left the room, her thin face drawn up with worry.

Victoria turned to Eleanor. "What's wrong with her? Go after her. You're the nurse."

Eleanor shook her head. "It'll take nine months to fix what's wrong with her." She looked smug.

"Nine months? Whatever do you mean? What?" Then Victoria's jaw dropped. "Oh!"

"Probably more like seven months, actually," Eleanor continued.

Victoria jumped up, sloshing water over the side of the tub. Not bothering to dry her feet on the towel Susie had left, she raced across the room, sliding once her feet hit the bare floor. Righting herself, she hurried down the hall to the water closet.

Susie stood in front of the door holding a rag in her hand.

Victoria ignored her as well as the retching noise she heard coming from the WC. She knocked on the door. "Am I going to be an auntie, Prudence? Am I?"

Prudence retched in response and then Victoria heard a weak "Maybe . . ."

"Hurrah!"

Victoria grabbed Susie around the waist and did an impromptu polka down the hallway. A few minutes later Prudence emerged, pale and tired. Susie handed her the cloth while Victoria slipped an arm around her waist and helped her to the sitting room.

"How long have you known and why didn't you

tell me straightaway?" Victoria said. "If you weren't so wretched looking, I'd be mad at you for not telling me sooner!"

"One hardly goes about announcing such things," Prudence said, a blush highlighting her cheeks. "Plus, I'd only begun to suspect since I began getting sick every single morning, with no other explanation."

"Oh, pooh!" Victoria said. "You always were the most conventional one of us all."

"How far along are you?" Eleanor asked, after they had settled Prudence on the sofa.

"I'm not sure, but I am thinking the baby will be born in late April or early May."

Susie brought Prudence a cup of tea and cleaned up the water mess Victoria had made. Victoria sat down and beamed. "Just think! A baby!" A sudden thought struck her. "Does Andrew know?"

Prudence shook her head. "No. And I'm not going to tell him either. At least not while he's training. He would just worry and there's nothing he can do about it. The last thing I want is my husband distracted while engaging in rigorous physical trials—"

"That's why you don't want him going to the front," Victoria said, reality dawning on her.

Prudence bit her lip. "I just couldn't stand for anything to happen to him. I mean, I couldn't have stood it before, but now, with the baby . . ."

"Oh, my dear." Victoria moved to Prudence and put her arms around her. For the first time, Victoria felt as if she were comforting Prudence rather than the other way around. "Colin will be able to help. We will keep him safe and sound so he can change nappies."

Prudence giggled just as Victoria had hoped she would. "Imagine a man changing nappies!"

A knock sounded on the door and Victoria heard Susie answering it. Victoria got to her feet just as Kit breezed into the room. They had been excessively careful of one another since the fiasco at his mother's tea. Neither of them had mentioned the incident, but they hadn't completely fallen back into their old teasing relationship.

"I'm going to be an aunt!" she blurted the moment he filled the doorway.

His eyes widened before she realized what he was thinking.

"Oh, no!" She laughed. "Not Rowena and Sebastian! Prudence!"

"Oh." Relief crossed Kit's face. "That's good, considering their wedding has been postponed again." He inclined his head toward Prudence. "Congratulations."

"Thank you." Prudence stood and bade everyone farewell, and to Victoria's consternation within minutes everyone had left her and Kit alone together.

They needn't have bothered, she thought resentfully. Why did everyone insist on pairing her with Kit?

Kit poured tea for both of them from the pot Susie had left and took the seat Prudence had just vacated. He crossed his long legs, and Victoria found herself annoyed at how handsome he looked in his olive-colored uniform.

"I find it difficult to believe that the fates decided to make you an auntie." He sounded like his old mocking self and Victoria responded in kind.

"Don't you think I'll make a good auntie?" she demanded. "Can't you picture me bouncing the babe on my knee, reciting poetry and fairy tales?"

He tilted his head. "Perhaps you would be a good auntie . . . as long as the Good Lord doesn't make you a mother."

"Ha! We finally agree on something. Mother-hood is one adventure I will pass on, thank you very much."

"As will I. Fatherhood, that is," he clarified at her amused look. "You know what I meant."

She toasted him with her teacup. "Aren't you supposed to be off fighting Germans or Austrians or something like that?"

"Can't wait to get rid of me? Actually, I've come on an errand of the utmost importance. Colin's leaving the day after tomorrow. I've been sent to inform you that he and Annalisa are getting married in the morning."

Victoria clapped her hand over her mouth. "Tomorrow? What does Aunt Charlotte say?"

Kit shrugged. "What can she say? War changes things, and he and Annalisa don't want to wait. After Sebastian was called up so quickly and the wedding was postponed yet again, they weren't left with much of a choice. Sebastian has no idea when he will get leave and Colin doesn't want to take the chance that the same thing will happen to him and Annalisa. Your aunt, Rowena, and your uncle are coming up on the train just before the ceremony, and then we will be having a wedding breakfast right after."

A sense of sadness settled over Victoria like a fine powder. "All of our friends are leaving. Sebastian has been gone for several weeks already. Colin is leaving. Even Edward and the rest of the boys are gone. Soon the Clever Coterie will be completely bereft of all its masculine members."

"The war can't last that long," Kit said, his voice hearty.

"You don't believe that, do you?"

He sighed and shook his head.

"I don't either. I read the newspapers and I can read between the lines, as well. I think the whole world has gone mad." She quoted Robert Southey, her voice pained:

When innocent blood,
From the four corners of the world cries
  out
For justice upon one accursed head.

"Ah, but whose accursed head shall we heap the justice on?" Kit asked.

She shrugged. "Any of them. All of the leaders. Old men over their cognac and cigars planning war like a chess game while all our friends are sent to face death in foreign countries."

There was a moment's silence. "Victoria, I'm leaving for France next week."

Her breath caught and her entire being went still. The light coming through the windows had dimmed as they spoke, but she could still see the pensive expression on the intelligent planes of Kit's face. Something caught in her heart and she wanted to go to him and offer comfort, much as she had Prudence earlier.

"Kit," she said softly. He gazed at her with such yearning on her face she almost cried out.

Susie came in and lit several small gas lamps. "Sorry for interrupting. You don't want to be sitting here in the dark."

And the moment was broken.

"Would you like to stay for supper?" Victoria asked. Even to her own ears the invitation sounded false. She didn't know why she suddenly felt uncomfortable.

He must have heard her insincerity because he stood. "No. I'm meeting some friends at the club. I should be going, actually."

She stood and he stared puzzled at her still-bare feet. He raised his eyebrows.

She blushed. "We're very informal here."

"God bless informal Hen-Pens. See you in the morning?"

"Yes, where?"

"We're meeting at your uncle's house at nine and then going over to the church together."

Their farewell was oddly formal, and she was glad to see him leave. As much as he'd been needling her recently, she couldn't help but feel that she already missed him, and he wasn't even gone yet.

God only knew how she would feel after he actually left.

CHAPTER SIX

Rowena stood at the altar next to Annalisa, watching her cousin and her friend get married and wondering when she and Sebastian would finally be wed. Now that she had made up her mind to get on with her life, fate had conspired to keep her stagnant.

Annalisa's brown eyes were soft with love every time she looked at her husband-to-be, and

Colin couldn't stop staring at her. Rowena's heart twinged with longing and regret. This was how it was supposed to be. They were blissfully happy at the prospect of a lifetime with one another.

After the ceremony, the family, including Annalisa's parents and younger sister, all attended an elegant wedding breakfast at the Coburg. The floor-to-ceiling, beveled mirrors, ornate columns, crisp white linens, and delicate gold-and-white Spode china, all set a festive tone to the wedding party. Platters of scones, kippers, fresh fruit, deviled kidneys, and sausages were heaped on a table beautifully decorated with orange blossoms, ferns, and lilies. Aunt Charlotte and Annalisa's mother had accomplished a great deal in little time. It seemed incredible how quickly things had changed, and how drastically. The wedding Rowena and Sebastian were meant to have had taken months of planning already, whereas this spur-of-the-moment ceremony was sweet in its simplicity and in the obvious love the bride and the groom felt for each other.

Victoria talked animatedly to Annalisa's mother, Aunt Charlotte, and everyone besides Kit, who was rather silent, especially for Kit. Rowena wondered what was going on, but knew better than to ask her little sister, who had always been rather cagey on the subject of Kit.

As Rowena chatted with the others in this

stunning and extravagant restaurant and toasted the couple's happiness, a lonely hollowness carved itself out in her chest. She desperately wished Sebastian were with her. Sebastian had been a steadfast friend, and over the past months as she'd healed from Jonathon's departure, they had forged a deep friendship during the planning of their wedding. She missed his warm presence and quiet sense of humor. Funny how dependent on him she'd become.

After the newly wedded couple finally departed, Victoria urged Rowena to join her at her flat. Though Rowena knew her sister was eager to show her what she had done with her new home, she declined, promising to visit soon. Somehow, the thought of going to see Victoria's new life as an independent young woman depressed her. While Victoria trained to be a volunteer aide, valiantly helping others while also tending to herself, Rowena still languished with family and waited idly for her fiancé to come home. How stale and predictable. Her father hadn't raised her for this.

She wished her aeroplane could be stored closer to Summerset. Suddenly she thought of the hangar Sebastian had started building for her. Was it finished yet? Why shouldn't she go see it? Wasn't she to be mistress of Eddelson Hall? Sebastian's mother had always been warm and welcoming. Excitement rose in her chest. She would make arrangements to go for a visit right away to check on the progress.

Within a week she was standing in Eddelson's grand foyer as Sebastian's mother, Lady Billingsly, chatted next to her.

"I am so glad you came, my dear. I admit to being quite lonely now that Sebastian's gone and wanted to run an idea past you over tea. I had Cook make a sponge cake for your arrival. I don't bother with treats unless I'm expecting company. Sebastian was the sweet tooth, you know."

Rowena didn't know, but felt that was one of the things she should know about her intended. A whisper of guilt ran through her. Had she always been so self-involved?

After tea, she told her future mother-in-law that she wanted to go see the progress on her hangar.

"I'm afraid you will find very little. Most of the young men have run off to join the army, and we need those who remained to look after the grounds. They work on it sporadically, of course, but I'm sure that once the war is over, it will be completed."

As the gardener drove her out to the hangar location, her heart sank. They wanted it to be far from the stables and the horse pastures so the sound of the plane wouldn't spook the animals. Sebastian had chosen the spot well: the hangar was backed up against a hill with a long field in front of it for taking off. The hangar would be large enough to hold her plane wing to wing with room enough to include racks on one side for equipment and parts. Her heart swelled with tender gratitude at his thoughtfulness. But though the foundation had been finished, the frame stood unfinished like a skeleton against the green of the trees. Any hope that she could get her aeroplane here anytime soon vanished.

She stayed with the Billingslys for several days and found herself liking life at Eddelson Hall more and more. The manor house reminded her far more of the home she'd grown up in than did Summerset. The rooms were bright and airy and designed for comfort rather than show. It wasn't as old as Summerset and she could tell the inhabitants enjoyed their creature comforts as Sebastian had already installed central heating, plumbing, and electricity throughout the entire home, including the servants' quarters.

Sebastian's mother, rather a dragon lady like Rowena's aunt Charlotte, began to grow on her, too, and she realized she could be happy in this house and in this family. Especially with access to her aeroplane guaranteed.

On impulse, she had the driver take her to the barn where Mr. Dirkes kept his aeroplanes before returning her to Summerset. The place was deserted of course, and the barn doors were locked up tight. She'd heard Mr. Dirkes had received a big government contract for aeroplane parts and would be extremely busy. Luckily, she knew where the extra key for the workers was hidden, and leaving her driver and car in front, she entered the small back door of the barn.

Only two aeroplanes were housed in the cavernous barn now. A bittersweet regret filled her as she recognized the Flying Alice she had first gone up in. Closing her eyes, she once again saw the cloud crystals becoming brighter and brighter and the awe-inspiring moment when they had broken through the cloud cover to the blinding-blue sky on the other side. She ran her fingers over the dusty wings of the Flying Alice, remembering the profound enchantment that flying had cast over her. At the time, she had thought it was Jon that made her feel so unfettered and blissful, but she couldn't help but wonder how much of her love for him had been mixed up with her love of flying.

She breathed the scent of oil, gasoline, and straw and was transported back to the time she had flown solo for the first time. She'd been impulsive and rash, making a split-second decision to follow Jon into the air after discovering that he was angry with her. Though the impulse had been reckless, her flight hadn't been: she'd flown it perfectly. But no matter. Jon had ultimately walked away from her and never come back.

Her chest tightened and she walked quickly out of the barn and locked the door behind her, breathing heavily. Why had she come back here? Why had she risked certain pain?

Because she missed her aeroplane. Suddenly she decided that the risk of meeting Jon here would be worth it if she could have access to her Vickers. Besides, it didn't look as if anyone was coming out here too often. Mr. Dirkes's factory was in Kent, and if they were overrun with orders, they probably wouldn't be testing new aeroplanes much. As soon as she arrived home, she would telephone Mr. Dirkes. He would give her permission, she knew he would. He had been one of her biggest supporters when she'd wanted to learn to fly.

Excited, she rounded the corner to the motorcar and stopped short when she saw a young girl on a large, handsome horse riding toward her.

The girl reined in her horse and stared. Rowena's heart raced when she recognized her. The girl seemed to realize who Rowena was at that same moment and swiftly steered her horse away.

"Cristobel," Rowena called softly.

The girl reined in her animal but didn't turn around. She sat on her mount, her back ramrod straight, with her long, dark hair streaming down her back from under her riding hat.

Rowena walked around and faced her. The girl's features revealed a mixture of longing and anger. Jonathon's little sister didn't much look like him.

Her hair and eyes were dark, unlike Jon's, whose blue eyes looked like the sky he flew in and whose strawberry-blond hair belied their Scottish heritage. But the stubborn expression the girl wore showed the family resemblance.

"Many times in the past few months I have wondered how you were," Rowena said. "I hope you and your mother are well."

She hated the formal sound of her voice, but the girl's sudden appearance had rattled her. Between the visit to the barn and the sudden appearance of Jon's sister, she hadn't felt his absence from her life this keenly in months.

"We're fine," the girl said tightly. "Not that you would care."

The tragedy of her father's suicide and the loss of the family's fortune at the hands of the Buxtons had isolated the girl from society. Rowena knew Cristobel had thought of her as a friend and no doubt felt doubly betrayed at Rowena's sudden disappearance from their lives.

"That's not fair," Rowena said. "Jon was no longer interested in a relationship with me, and I couldn't maintain a friendship with you after he made it clear that I was no longer welcome."

"Jon? Oh, pooh on Jon. He's only been home twice all summer and he was a bear both times. There was no reason for you not to visit. Or I could have visited you. You promised to take me on a hunt."

Cristobel's dark eyes accused her, and Rowena felt a pang of guilt. She *had* promised. "What would George have said to that?"

The girl shook her head. "Oh, pooh on George, too. Besides, he isn't home either. He joined the army like Jonathon."

Rowena's stomach tightened. "Jonathon joined the army? I didn't think he would. The production of aeroplanes has been stepped up."

"He joined the Royal Flying Corps." Cristobel shifted in the saddle, her dark brows knitting together. "I shouldn't be telling you this."

"It's all right. I'm glad you did. I'd wondered . . ."

Rowena stared up at Cristobel, whose features had matured since she had seen her last. She'd once thought this engaging young girl was going to become her sister and had opened up her heart to her. She barely knew Sebastian's sister, who lived in Coventry and was busy bringing up her own children. Her heart ached with loss. So many regrets.

"Maybe we can go riding together sometime," Rowena finally said. It was an empty-sounding promise, the kind of thing one said socially, but didn't mean. From the look on Cristobel's face, she knew it. "No, really," Rowena insisted, even though she knew she shouldn't. A friendship with Cristobel would undoubtedly ruffle feathers in both families, but she couldn't disappoint this girl again.

Cristobel nodded cautiously. "Tomorrow? I ride this way every day about this time."

Rowena nodded. "I'll be here," she promised, even though it made her vaguely uncomfortable. She had a feeling Cristobel probably wouldn't be telling her mother about their meeting.

Cristobel, trying not to look delighted, waved a casual hand and nudged her horse into a dignified trot. The line of her back and neck was straight as she posted away.

Rowena climbed into the back of the motor-car and tried to ignore the goose bumps that shivered across her skin. Seeing Cristobel, maintaining their friendship, was that a way to hold on to Jon even as she moved forward with Sebastian? She felt as though she was playing a dangerous game in which there would be no winners.

Prudence read the note from Victoria over and over, trying not to feel too hopeful.

Dearest Pru,

Just a quick note to tell you I haven't forgotten about what you asked. Please don't worry, I believe it has already been taken care of and the father of my darling niece or nephew won't be going off to fight. I'm not sure where he will be stationed, no one can control that, but he will be in the remount depot so never fear, all will be well.

Dreadfully busy, but will come to see you soon.

Much love in exhaustion,
Vic

PS. Found the most cunning little bassinet and matching coverlet. It will be delivered soon.
V.

The bassinet had been delivered shortly after the note had arrived, and Victoria had been right—surely it was the loveliest bassinet that had ever been made. The ornately carved mahogany shone darkly, and the knobs at the bottom were whittled into the shapes of pineapples. The top of the cradle was a box that would hold nappies, pins, talcum, and whatever else the baby might need. It was a beautiful thing, and Prudence had the deliverymen take it into her and Andrew's bedroom. It looked rather incongruous there, such a fine piece of furniture among their worn odds and ends. She wondered what Andrew would think when he saw it. Would he be happy that Victoria had been so generous or scornful that Prudence's highborn past was still intruding on their much simpler life?

When she'd first discovered she was pregnant,

she had been by turns fearful and excited. Fearful because her husband was going off to war, and excited because maybe a baby would give her lonely days some sort of purpose.

A muffled knock on the door sounded and Prudence frowned, wondering if Victoria had bought something else. She had a feeling Victoria might be a problem; her enthusiasm often overtook her common sense.

Smiling, she opened the door, shocked to find her husband standing on the other side, holding a large duffel bag in one arm and a bag of groceries in the other.

She wanted to hurl herself at him, but refrained, fearing to upset his precarious load. "What? How?"

She stepped away from the door and he deposited his burden on their table and then turned to her, his arms outstretched. She ran to him and he swept her up and whirled her about.

After setting her back on her feet, he bent and kissed her mouth before drawing back and taking a deep breath. "Lord, I missed you. I was lucky enough to get a two-day leave. My commanding officer told me I was a blessed son of a bitch and to get out before he changed his mind. I didn't stick around to find out if he was kidding me or not."

She clung to him, her heart so overjoyed and full she could hardly speak.

Now, in light of Victoria's news, she could finally tell him about the baby. It had been the most difficult thing she'd ever done to keep it from him.

But that thought went out of her head the moment his mouth crushed against hers again and he picked her up in his arms.

"I've missed you," he said, a blush staining his cheeks as he walked her into the bedroom.

She laughed. Only her shy husband would still turn red over the thought of their lovemaking.

"Are you laughing at me?" He tossed her onto the bed and removed his shirt.

"What about the groceries?" she said, still laughing.

"They can wait." He joined her on the bed, and soon she was incapable of thinking of anything except the love that flowed between them.

Sometime later they lay in one another's arms and she pulled the quilt over the top of them. The October afternoon wasn't cold, but it wasn't warm either, and she grew chilled as the heat from their passion cooled. She briefly wondered if he had even noticed that she was growing plumper.

She turned over and looked at him. His eyes were closed and she stared at his face as if to memorize it. The bump in his nose, the stubble shadowing his chin. She reached up and ran her fingers down the line of his jaw.

His arm tightened around her at his touch. His

eyes flickered open. "My commander is right."

"What's that?" She nestled her head back in the crook of his arm.

"I am one lucky son of a bitch. I had originally been slated to head to France with the rest of the foot soldiers, but I was switched to the remount depot in the 1st King's Dragoon at the last moment."

She cleared her throat. "That's good, though, right?"

"Granted, I would much rather work with horses than fight. I may still get sent to France or Africa, but I won't be fighting. I just wonder how many of the young men I trained with will be sent to the front." He paused. "And I wonder why I was selected for remount when no one else was."

Prudence shifted in his arms, thinking of the note from Victoria still in the pocket of her cardigan. She knew Andrew struggled with living off her money; how would he feel if he knew that she had pulled strings to get him out of fighting for his country, especially considering that he felt strongly enough for the cause to enlist? "Perhaps someone heard that you were enrolled in veterinary school? I'm sure it is on your record somewhere that you grew up on a farm. It's not so surprising."

"Maybe, but half of the men in my squad were brought up on a farm, so that can't be it." He suddenly frowned. "What's that?"

Her stomach tightened. For a moment she thought he had seen the note, but that was silly. "What's what?"

He pointed across the room. "That." He raised himself up on his elbows, frowned, and then sat up.

She followed his finger and realized what he was pointing at.

The bassinet.

"What do you think it is?" she asked carefully.

"Well, it looks like . . ." Understanding crossed his face and he turned to her, incredulous. "Are you? Are we?"

She blushed and lowered her eyes. "Yes, as a matter of fact . . ."

He jumped off the bed. "Why didn't you tell me? What if we hurt it?" He stared at her stomach, horrified.

She began to laugh uncontrollably, her joy immeasurable. Everything that had come before, her sorrow over losing Sir Philip, her pain over Rowena's betrayal, her confusion and heartache over Sebastian, all of that was worth it if it led to this moment of near-perfect happiness.

But she was brought down to earth when she remembered that she was still hiding something from him.

The corners of his mouth began to twitch upward until finally he broke into a sheepish grin. "I suppose you think me pretty amusing, but how would I know? I've never been pregnant before." His hazel eyes grew serious. "Oh, my love, what a time for us to start a new life, eh?"

She sat up and held out her arms. "I think it's the best time. How should we meet the death and destruction of war except with the hope and faith of new life?" She smiled. "And, no, we won't hurt the baby. Now come back to me. I'm getting chilly!"

They nuzzled under the covers until Prudence felt drowsiness overcoming her. She struggled to make herself get up and put the groceries away, but the lure of sleeping in her husband's arms was too tempting, and she fell asleep hoping nothing was in the bag that might spoil.

As she slept, images of blinding gunfire and the echoes of guttural screams flitted through her mind. She awoke with a start, her heart pulsing rapidly. Frozen with tension, she listened intently, but of course the flat was dark and silent. The only sound she heard was her husband's light breathing next to her.

Quietly, Prudence slipped out of bed and put on her robe. She shut the bedroom door softly behind her and turned on the small lamp above the kitchen table. Putting the groceries away, she found a small package of coffee beans in the bag. Holding her grinder between her knees, she ground the beans, a grim satisfaction filling her as the scent of coffee permeated the air. She had come a long way, she thought. Starting as a woman who didn't know how to cook, clean, or do laundry, she had learned to do all three—with varying degrees of success. Unfortunately, familiarity with such chores hadn't increased her fondness for them, but she *had* learned to appreciate them. She'd come to realize that knowing how to grind coffee and make supper was far preferable to doing without.

Andrew had also picked up a loaf of fresh bread, a round of Stilton, several perfectly ripened apples, and a bottle of ale. Apparently, he thought she wouldn't have much food in the house with his absence. She did prefer grabbing something from a street vendor or eating with her friend Katie rather than cooking. It seemed like an awful lot of trouble to go through just for herself. She looked at her stomach with a mixture of joy and trepidation. She guessed it wasn't really for one any longer, was it?

She sliced up some bread and apples. The cheese was soft and warm and would be good spread on the bread. She hoped Andrew wouldn't expect anything more.

"I can't tell you how wonderful it is to be standing here, with you in our own little home."

She turned with a smile to where Andrew leaned against the door. He had put his trousers back on, but his torso was bare, giving her a good view of the chest etched from years of labor. Most footmen were not so well built, but his early years on the farm had given him a strength most of them lacked and she gloried in it.

"We may not have had the most regular start to our marriage, but we have made something pretty wonderful out of it, haven't we?"

"We have. Come and sit. The coffee is almost done. Are you hungry?"

His eyes glowed. "Starved."

Prudence blushed, knowing he wasn't just talking about his stomach. "When do you have to go back?"

He sighed and sat, slipping an arm about her backside as she put a plate in front of him. "I have to leave in the morning."

"So soon?" she cried. "That wasn't nearly enough time. I thought you had two days!"

"I do, but it will take most of the day to get back to Plymouth. But let's not talk about that. Let's talk about only good things. Let's talk about the baby."

Prudence poured them both a cup of fragrant coffee. "What about the baby? I haven't met him yet so I don't know him."

Andrew's eyes widened. "A boy? Are you sure?"

"You're so easy to tease. As if I would know!"

He rose from his chair. "It gets chilly fast once the sun sets. Do you want me to put some coal in the stove?"

"If you're cold. I don't have that much left, though. This is the first cold snap of the year."

"I'll just put on a shirt."

She smiled. "That would probably help."

He went into their room. "It looks like a hurricane blew your clothes off in here." He laughed.

She snorted. "I think one did." She refilled their coffee cups and put the pot back on the stove. "Would you like me to get the Sunday paper? It's a few days old and the news isn't much fun, but we could read something besides war news."

The hair on the back of her neck prickled at the sudden silence from the bedroom. *No. Oh, please, no.* She whirled toward the bedroom, only to find Andrew already standing in the doorway, holding a piece of paper.

Victoria's note.

"What is this?"

She stood frozen, her heart beating in her ears. She searched his face, desperately looking for any signs of how he was feeling, but his features were inscrutable.

She couldn't deny what she had done, so she took the offensive. "I asked Victoria to see if she could have Colin move you to a safer job. Remount duty is more suited to your abilities, anyway."

"Actually, I discovered in training that I'm a

crack shot. And that is hardly the point. When were you going to tell me about this?"

She swallowed against the lump swelling in her throat.

"You weren't going to, were you?"

Prudence stared at the worn red-and-beige mat on the floor. She shook her head ever so slightly. She felt as if she were a naughty schoolgirl who had been caught out.

"So you used your abovestairs, posh friends to keep your poor farmer-turned-coachman husband out of harm's way?"

"What would you have me do?" she cried. "Watch you march away to battle while I'm left to care for a baby all by myself?"

His jaw clenched several times before he took a deep breath and answered, "Yes, as a matter of fact that is exactly what I expect of you. That is what women all over England, nay, all over the world, have to do. Why should you be any different? Why should I be exempt from fighting while my countrymen have to do battle in the muck and the mire? Did you expect me to hide behind your skirts?"

She moved toward him, her hands clenched. "No. I expect you to live. I expect you to come back to me alive and in one piece! Someone has to care for the horses, why shouldn't it be you?"

"And why should it be? Because you decided to play God?"

She had never seen him so angry and disappointed. Her heart sank and the babe within chose that moment to make its presence felt for the first time. It shivered inside her like a butterfly testing its wings. She wanted to cry out and tell Andrew, but the disgust on his face stopped her. Her anger, confusion, and fear rose to the surface, and she lashed out in frustration, sweeping the cup nearest her onto the floor. It shattered, shooting shards of glass everywhere.

She stared at the pieces, shocked at her own temper. Andrew turned and went back into the bedroom without a word.

Carefully, she picked up the pieces of pottery and mopped up the mess. Tears streamed down her face. She was just finishing up when Andrew came back out, fully clothed.

"Where are you going?" she cried, fear and regret hollowing out her chest.

"Out," he said shortly. "We're too upset right now to discuss this further. I'll be back later for my things."

Part of her wanted to cry out and stop him from going, but the other part wanted to insist that everything was his fault in the first place. *He* had decided he needed to join the army. To leave her and their baby. She was only trying to help him, to *save* him. Who cared about his absurd pride if his life was kept safe?

She waited until he was out the door before

running into their bedroom and throwing herself onto the bed that had so recently been the site of their lovemaking.

She wept, ugly sobs that she hated herself for, but she couldn't help it. Only one year ago, she had been living in a fine home, with a family who loved her and servants to care for her. Life had been leisurely and lovely, with music, books, social gatherings, outings to museums, and constant companionship. Now she was lonely and afraid, and the one person who kept her safe had chosen to leave her. No matter how hard she tried to understand, it was beyond her realm of acceptance.

She must have slept because she awoke sometime later, hearing the closing of the front door. She froze, her heart clenching. Had he left without even saying good-bye?

Then she heard him moving about quietly, gathering his things, as she lay racked by indecision. Should she get up and tell him she was sorry? Beg him to forgive her? But for what? For doing whatever she could to keep the father of her baby alive? For that she needed to apologize?

She shut her eyes when he came into the bedroom and held her breath as he stood over where she lay curled up on their bed. Then she felt his hand on her shoulder and he drew close. He pressed his lips briefly to her cheek and she crumpled. Grabbing his hand with hers, she pressed it to her lips. She couldn't let that row be their last interaction before his departure.

His other hand ran over her hair, just once, and then he pulled away, gently but insistently. He was leaving and she could do nothing in the world but let him go.

CHAPTER SEVEN

Rowena stood, arms folded, just inside the barn, watching the men from the village checking out the aeroplane. She had already gone over it, but apparently they didn't think she was capable of inspecting it herself. Fine.

Granted, when they had agreed to ready the plane for its flight to Kent, they had no idea the pilot would be a woman, but that didn't give them a right to treat her with disrespect. She suspected that the only reason they hadn't refused was that one of the men recognized her from when she used to come with Jonathon.

Rowena carried a small overnight bag with her and was dressed in the pair of soft cotton trousers she'd had a local seamstress make up after Aunt Charlotte's lady's maid had refused. She wore a warm woolen jacket and had tied her hair back and tucked it down the back of the jacket. Her helmet and goggles were already on her head. Her clothes were logical and practical, and Rowena wasn't about to let a bunch of ignorant townsmen make her feel uncomfortable.

When she had telephoned Mr. Dirkes the previous week to find out if she could store her Vickers here, he'd mentioned that he'd been struggling to find competent pilots to ferry his planes around since the outbreak of war. He wanted to bring the aeroplanes currently housed in the barn to his factory so they could be used in the war effort.

Rowena hadn't even let him finish before she offered to help. Mr. Dirkes had given a perfunctory protest, but, at her insistence, had agreed with relief. He knew she was fully capable of flying.

When the men finished the inspection, they pushed the aeroplane out onto the field. Rowena's mouth had gone dry and her palms were slick with sweat. Nerves always struck before her solo flights. During the early weeks of summer she had stayed in Surrey and had taken her Vickers out almost every day. She had earned her pilot's license in a little over a month, joining a small, select group of women pilots in Britain. Her triumph was only partially marred by her not being able to share it with Jon.

The day shone clear and crisp and she was glad she'd worn a scarf. The wind was light out of the northeast, though she knew it would no doubt pick up the closer she got to the coast.

When she got to the Flying Alice, she realized

she'd forgotten the small wooden toolbox she used to climb up in the aeroplane. The smirk on one of the men's faces told her he had noticed her error.

Impatiently, she motioned to the other man to lift her up. He did, his hands lingering on her back end. Her face burned and she resisted the urge to smack him. How dare he? The look on his face showed both his trepidation at manhandling a noblewoman and delight that he had put a trouser-wearing hussy in her place. He glanced at the other man for approval and he guffawed.

Rowena held her hand out for her small case, and once she had it, she leaned forward. The man stepped forward to hear her, still leering.

"How dare you, you little pissant of a man. My uncle will make mincemeat of you."

He stepped back and shrugged, though she could tell she had shaken him. "I can't imagine the lord of the manor is too thrilled with his niece wandering around dressed like a tart."

Her face burned and she suspected it was true. "Start the propeller," she snapped.

He gave her an insolent salute and went around to the front of the aeroplane.

It took him several attempts to start the propeller, and Rowena took deep breaths to calm herself. She didn't need to be distracted as she flew. She'd never crashed, but knew it was a very real possibility every time she flew.

She pulled down her goggles and scanned the gauges in front of her. Like those in her Vickers, they were fairly basic. Oil-pressure gauge, speedometer, and fuel pressure. The red tick marks on the speedometer indicated maximum speed and the speed at which the aeroplane would stall. As she performed these mundane but important tasks, her pulse sped up. It had been too long, far too long, since she had been in the air. Her envy at Victoria's purpose-filled life faded as she readied herself and her aeroplane for flight.

She worked the rudder pedals and rode out the bone-jarring trek across the field as she picked up speed. She pulled back on the yoke, her heart lifting along with the nose of her aeroplane.

Then she was flying.

Once the aeroplane was in the air her nervousness ebbed, and she kept one eye on the speedometer while enjoying the never-ending thrill of watching the earth fade behind her. The wings flexed and the plane pulled to the right as a gust of wind hit, but Rowena held steady and climbed a bit higher. Once she reached the speed and the altitude she wanted, she straightened the nose out and turned until the compass needle read southeast.

As always, the sensation of being above all of her problems filled her with a sense of well-being that she had never felt while her feet were on the ground. The sky was bluer, the air crisper, and the sun brighter. Up here she was in control of her own destiny. Yes, she depended on the machinery to perform, and the weather to behave, but she had only herself to rely on, and somehow she trusted herself to rise to any occasion. Whereas on the earth, indecision held her captive and she doubted her choices to the point where she often couldn't act at all. It had become worse after she had made the rash decision last fall to beg her uncle to allow Prudence to join them at Summerset. That decision had been catastrophic, had placed Prudence in a horrible situation, and had led to the end of a relationship Rowena had valued above almost all others.

Then, even knowing that she and Jonathon faced almost insurmountable obstacles to their relationship, she had allowed herself to be seduced, only to be brokenhearted when he had, unsurprisingly, walked away from her.

No wonder she was insecure about her decisions.

But here, up here alone in the sky, she was as confident as a sea eagle soaring among the cliffs. In the air she was powerful. Brave. Dauntless.

She took a deep breath and let this rare feeling of assuredness wash over her. It would be at least two hours before she arrived in Kent, and then she had to look for Mr. Dirkes's factory and landing field.

At least she wouldn't have to worry about

running into Jonathon there. She'd learned from Cristobel on their ride that he was in Larkhill with the Third Squadron, RFC. She tried not to think about the rumors that the Second and Third Squadrons were primarily photographic squadrons, going deep into enemy territory to take pictures.

She'd been out riding with Cristobel twice since she had met her at the barn. Rowena didn't know if she was meeting her because she missed Cristobel's dizzy, heedless outlook on life or if she was waiting for the few tidbits about Jon the girl occasionally let slip. Rowena felt just enough guilt about that to be overly kind to the girl, even offering to send the Summerset farrier out when they discovered Grenadine had a loose shoe.

On the telephone she had casually asked Mr. Dirkes about Jonathon's assignments, but he had denied having any knowledge of what the aircraft squadrons were doing. She wondered how dangerous it might be.

Beneath her, seagulls cavorted and she was reminded how near the coast she was. She had never flown over the water, but knew it was trickier with odd air currents and confusing cloud formations. She had always wanted to try it, but her instructor at the Brooklands Aero Club had warned her against it. But then, he wasn't too thrilled about taking on a female student. Only the amount of money her uncle had offered had persuaded him.

As always when Rowena was in the air, the time passed swiftly, and her coordinates told her she was close to Kent. She rolled up her flight log and stuck it next to her before descending to get a closer look below her. Spotting the airfield almost immediately, she flew toward it. She glanced at the gold wristwatch her aunt had bought her for her birthday. Right on time. Mr. Dirkes would be expecting her.

Takeoff and landing were the most dangerous stages of a flight, and Rowena's concentration sharpened. All her senses increased during these times, and she felt vibrantly alive. A northern wind had sprung up, and she fought to keep her aeroplane on the right trajectory. She was relieved when her wheels hit the ground with a teeth-rattling jolt. Turning the nose of her aeroplane toward the enormous metal hangar, she spotted Mr. Dirkes's large form hurrying toward her before the aeroplane even stopped.

She handed down her bag and then climbed out of the cockpit. He tossed the bag to a worker who had come with him and then reached up to help her down.

"You're a sight for sore eyes, lass." He squeezed her breathless before placing her carefully on her feet. His eyes widened with astonishment. "Look at you! I could barely tell you from a pilot!"

"I am a pilot," she said tartly before taking her bag.

"I meant no offense, my dear. Your clothing makes sense. Just took me aback."

She took off her goggles and helmet. She had tied her hair back and tucked it down the back of her jacket. But it had come loose and now flew about in the same wind she had fought on her landing.

The workers took the plane off for inspection while Mr. Dirkes led her toward the hangar. He towered over her and looked deceptively clumsy, but she knew from experience how quick and nimble he actually was.

"I'm so glad you're here," he said with the accent that belied his Scottish heritage. "Thanks for bringing the aeroplane. I didn't know how I was going to get it here, and we need all the birds we can get right now. I am at full production but I can still only put out so many per month. The lads are crashing them as quickly as I can make them."

They walked into the cavernous space and he showed her the water closet where she could freshen up.

She ignored the dirt on the floor and the black grease on the porcelain sink and changed into the dark wool walking skirt she had brought for the occasion. Taking combs out of her pocket, she twisted her hair up into a knot. Though she was protected here by Mr. Dirkes's presence, she knew that her trousers would just make the factory workers uneasy.

Mr. Dirkes smiled when she exited the WC. "That was a quick change. You don't even look like the same girl. Come along and I will give you a quick tour of the factory before we go for tea."

The hangar held rows of aeroplanes in varying degrees of completion, and Rowena was shocked to see several women working alongside the men.

Mr. Dirkes noticed her curiosity and gave her a smile. "Adapt or die, young Rowena. We need as many men as we can get on the front and more to ferry aeroplanes to our bases around Britain. We've already lost so many men, I feel as if it is my patriotic duty to hire war widows whenever I can."

She smiled up at him. "You're a good man, Douglas Dirkes."

After they had toured the facilities he drove her to the Rusty Arms, a small inn on the outskirts of town, for tea. The dining room was small and shabby, but the scents coming from the kitchen made her mouth water.

"So have you heard from our boy yet?" The look he gave her was keen, and she suspected that he was aware of exactly what had happened between Jonathon and her. Not only did he and Jon work together, but Mr. Dirkes was an old friend of Jon's mother.

She looked down at the stained white tablecloth. "No. We haven't spoken in months." She glanced up at him accusingly. "And you know it, too."

He heaved a sigh and poured himself more tea from the cracked pot the waitress had set down in front of them. "I was hoping the lad had come to his senses. I don't know what happened between the two of you, but I do know that when you find yourself in a pair as compatible as the two of you were, you don't squander it."

"Apparently you do. But that is all water under the bridge. You know very well I'm to be married to Lord Billingsly."

"Yes, your uncle told me."

"I don't know how you and my uncle ended up being such good friends," she said, deftly changing the subject.

Mr. Dirkes grinned. "He invested in my company. A smart man, despite his pomposity. He saw the writing on the wall."

She arched her brows. "How is business going anyway? You said you can't keep up with demand?"

Mr. Dirkes shook his head, suddenly serious. "Training pilots is taking up a huge number of planes. We lose too many planes and young men that way. The statistics are frightening. We're making new scientific and mechanical inroads all the time, but it's just taking too long, and changes in design are hard to implement, especially now that the need for aeroplanes is so high."

"What statistics are you talking about?" she asked, genuinely fascinated.

"We simply do not have enough qualified pilots to train, ferry the aeroplanes to the various bases, and do reconnaissance. Too many of our pilots are undertrained, and they're dead within weeks of signing on. And it's not the enemy, but their lack of training that is doing it."

Rowena's chest hollowed at the harshness of his usually merry voice.

She remembered how many men she'd met while working to obtain her pilot's license who shared her passion for flight. She wondered how many had already had their lives cut short before they really got a chance to explore the skies.

"What can be done?" she asked.

Mr. Dirkes sighed as the serving woman brought a plate of sandwiches. "Not a whole lot, I'm afraid. What they need to do is combine the RFC and the Royal Naval Air Service under one department, as there is too much confusion over who is supposed to be performing which missions. There's simply too much overlap."

"Don't they have an established training manual that can be used by everyone?"

He shook his head, and she noted the newly hatched gray hairs threaded through his hair. "All of that takes time and a single-minded goal. We're not there yet. Hell, some of the powers that be still aren't convinced of the value of aeroplanes for use during wartime. Excuse my language, Miss Rowena. I forget I'm talking to a lady sometimes."

She gave him a sad half smile. "Sometimes the situation warrants strong words, Mr. Dirkes."

"That it most certainly does. And right now I'm frustrated that I can't move the birds to where they're needed faster. You saw all those aeroplanes, right? I have several that need to be taken to Plymouth and two more to be taken to Hampshire, but the government has my pilots doing other things and they won't be back for several weeks. In the meantime, I'm left with a logjam in production."

She sat up, excitement kicking her pulse up a notch. "So let me do it. I can do it. You know I can."

He shook his head. "That's not the point. Of course you can do it. But *should* you? That's a whole other ball of wax. Now eat your sammies, lass."

He calmly took a bite of his cucumber sandwich while she fumed. "Give me one good reason why I shouldn't."

He snorted. "I can give you several." He ticked the reasons off with his fingers. "One, your uncle wouldn't like it. Two, we're in a war and it could be dangerous. *Will* be dangerous. Three, you would be ferrying the aeroplanes to naval and air bases where there are any number of army officers who would not appreciate a young woman flying their aeroplanes. Four, we would be dependent on these same officers to bring you back to Kent, and you would be left alone with them for hours. Unchaperoned."

"Are you saying that officers in the King's army would not act like gentlemen?" she pushed.

"I'm saying that seeing you fly a plane like a man, dressed in trousers and leather like a man, might lead them to behave in ways that are not gentlemanly."

She ground her teeth, thinking of how the two men at the barn had treated her just that morning. But there had to be a way around it. She didn't answer, but ate in silence for several minutes, thinking hard. She noted that he watched her closely, knowing she would refute his words. Why could young men go off to war and make a real difference and the only avenues open to her were nursing or volunteering to write letters or read to wounded soldiers? She knew that if the war went on for too long, women would be participating more from sheer necessity, but it hardly seemed fair that Victoria could be helping the war effort because she had a knack and a heart for nursing, while women like Rowena were overlooked and underutilized.

Finally, she pushed away her food and put both hands on the table. "Why couldn't I be a support volunteer for the RFC? If I wore some sort of uniform, that would lessen the confusion."

He shrugged. "I'm not sure if you could. I've never heard of a woman in the RFC, and I'm fairly sure it's never been done." He stroked his chin thoughtfully. "But the uniform is a good idea. Or at least an outfit that wouldn't garner as much attention as trousers."

"We could arrange for me to arrive in the evenings when there are fewer officers about."

"But then you would have to either stay the night or drive home with a young man in the dark, which neither your uncle nor I would approve of."

She felt a spurt of anger. "Why do you keep bringing up my uncle? I am twenty-three years old, for heaven's sake."

Mr. Dirkes shook his head. "Things haven't changed *that* much, Miss Rowena, and you know it. Don't be naïve."

"I'm not being naïve. You have always said adapt or die, and quite frankly, this is the time to adapt. We're at war and people *are* dying. To make our troops wait for the training aeroplanes they need because you don't want a fully qualified woman to pilot them is not just silly, it's criminal!"

He paused, then slowly nodded. "Well put, my dear." He sipped his tea thoughtfully. "And it looks like that is exactly what I will tell the squadron commanders when I inform them that you are to bring their aeroplanes."

Triumph shot through her and she tried to keep the elation off her face.

"But know that I'll threaten them with death if

you are in any way, shape, or form molested or mistreated while in their care. I do have one condition, though."

"What's that?"

"*You* have to be the one to tell your uncle."

Relief colored her laughter. "Done and done. And you will not regret this, Mr. Dirkes."

She extended her hand and he looked at it for a moment before raising an eyebrow.

"Come on," she urged. "Aren't you going to shake the hand of the first woman pilot you have in your employ?"

"My employ?" He sounded amused.

She grinned at him from over her teacup. "Of course. You have just given me my very first paying job."

He laughed. "I think I've been royally had."

"Yes, Mr. Dirkes," she told him gleefully, "you have."

CHAPTER EIGHT

Victoria hurried to the makeshift hospital, dressed in her Volunteer Aid Detachment uniform. Susie had carefully ironed her blue chambray dress and bleached the starched apron until it was stiff and sparkling white. The head-dress, equally starched and bleached, scratched her forehead, but it also set her apart, and the soldiers, taking air in the garden through which she hurried, gave her appreciative nods.

Victoria beamed back at them, not noticing the missing limbs or the bandages. These men were the lucky ones, and many worked hard to be allowed out in the garden on such a fine late-October day. Others, too many others, would not be so lucky.

That was the most difficult part of her new job: holding the hands of those who were never going to go home or see their loved ones. Thankfully, in this home, a fine mansion just off Berkeley, most of the soldiers came to convalesce and few actually passed away here. Only those who contracted some sort of infection. Too many had had their surgeries performed hurriedly in the field hospitals or dressing stations close to the front and arrived fighting off the complications due to such impromptu work. But in spite of the sadness, she loved her work. The soldiers were appreciative of her efforts, and the doctors occasionally consulted with her for her knowledge of herbs and tinctures. A few even credited her with their relatively low infection rate.

Some of the nurses, jealous of the attention she received from both the doctors and the patients as much as for her herbal knowledge, were less thrilled, but Victoria didn't care. For the first time in a long time, she was useful and satisfied. Her work was important.

Her father would be proud.

So she went to work every morning and stayed long into the night, far after she should have gone home. She ignored the swelling of her feet, the ache of her legs, and the asthma attacks that occurred with increasing frequency now that she was back in London.

Eleanor had been fussing at her for weeks, but she ignored her, too. She had a few days off starting tomorrow. Nanny Iris was visiting from Summerset and, Victoria knew, would be bringing more herbs and planned on teaching her more about poultices. Victoria would have plenty of time to rest during her friend's visit.

Victoria entered through the servants' door and nodded at the cook. The casualties had overrun London hospitals after mere weeks of war, and it was becoming quite the thing for rich families to donate their mansions to the cause while they lived in their country homes. Victoria worked in such a converted mansion. Even though the family had moved to their country house after offering their home, much of the kitchen staff had been retained. Only now, instead of cooking fancy food for parties of two hundred, they cooked plain fare for an endless stream of soldiers.

She went into the study, which had been transformed into a makeshift office for the doctors and nurses. Nurse Baxter sat at one of the desks writing in her log and took several minutes to acknowledge Victoria's presence, even though she had to know Victoria was there.

"Good morning, Miss Buxton. I hope you are feeling better this morning."

Victoria kept her nebulizer in the nurses' office and had needed to use it before heading home the previous night. Apparently, word had gotten to the head day-shift nurse. "Good morning, Nurse Baxter. I'm perfectly well physically, though my spirit is a bit disheveled."

The older woman looked up sharply. "And why would that be, Miss Buxton?"

"I have several days off and shall miss the boys when I am gone."

Nurse Baxter's features were angular and pointed, but not unkind. Eleanor had taken classes from her when studying nursing and adored her, though Victoria couldn't figure out why.

"You must occasionally take time off to avoid becoming overtired, Miss Buxton. While I have no doubt the army appreciates your dedication, it will do no one any good for you to become ill."

The older woman's firm rebuke stung, and Victoria lowered her eyes. "Yes, Nurse Baxter. I understand."

"Excellent." She handed Victoria an assignment sheet and a list of names. "These men will be under your care today."

Victoria scanned the sheet for the name of the nurse in charge. Like the soldiers, she had nurses she liked better than others. "Who am I to be working under?" she asked, not seeing anyone.

"You will be in charge of the library yourself, though Nurse Farner will be checking in on you frequently." Nurse Baxter bent her head to her work again as if she hadn't uttered anything out of the ordinary.

"By myself?" Victoria squeaked out. Volunteer aides were never left in charge of wards by themselves. Granted, the library only held twenty men who were in good health compared to many others, but still, she'd never been in charge on her own before.

"Yes, of course. We're shorthanded and Dr. Blake and I decided you were fully capable of caring for them on your own. Most of the men there are close to being discharged. Unless, of course, you don't think you can handle it?" Nurse Baxter looked over her wire-rimmed glasses at Victoria.

"No, I am sure I can do it."

"Good. Don't disappoint us, Miss Buxton."

"No, ma'am."

Victoria forced herself to walk sedately out of the room and down the hall, though she couldn't help but bound up the stairs two at a time, which turned out to be a mistake as she had to cling to the banister at the top to catch her breath.

Her hard work and dedication hadn't gone unnoticed; they trusted her enough to leave her on her own. Victoria could hardly believe it. She waited until her breathing stabilized, then went to the cupboard where the clean towels and linens were kept. Four men were bathed a day, allowing for everyone to have a bath once a week, except for those who had sponge baths. While the nurses gave sponge baths and had seen all sorts of "immodest things," hospital policy was for men who were able to help those who needed more assistance. Victoria found the policy not only ridiculous, but dangerous. When she'd expressed her opinion during a meeting, the shocked hospital staff had struck down her idea that a nurse or VAD be present at all times. Slipping while getting in and out of the tub was common, but Victoria figured they would wait until someone was seriously injured before changing the rule, as seemed to be the way things worked here.

"Good morning!" She kept her voice soft as many of the men were still sleeping. She didn't subscribe to the military method of waking the men to the piercing sound of a bell, as many of these men would not be returning to active duty. Those who were, she reasoned, would do well with a break in structure and would far rather awaken to the sound of a woman's voice. Some of the patients were already dressing themselves the best they could. Others of those awake were awaiting help.

Victoria went to the large floor-to-ceiling windows and opened the heavy, deep-red, Roman-style velvet drapes to the dawning morning outside. Dust motes whirled and eddied in the air, looking like tiny sun-dipped Milky Ways. "Good morning, good morning," she trilled a bit louder.

Some of the men groaned while others answered in kind. The library was spacious with floor-to-ceiling bookshelves on two walls. All but a few books had been packed away, and the shelving was used to hold supplies. A large marble fireplace warmed the room.

Many of the men had never seen a room as luxurious as this one, she mused, let alone lived in one. But all the things that made the home rich and lovely also made it hard to keep clean, and she and the housekeeping staff were hard-pressed just to keep it dusted.

She walked between the iron beds and put the towels on the end of the beds of those men who would be bathing this morning. They alone would be excused from being dressed before breakfast.

"I don't see why I have to dress," a sergeant grumbled as he strained to pull himself up. "It isn't as if I'm going anywhere."

"Maybe if you're lucky, you can take a turn in the garden," she told him briskly, reaching out a hand and gently pulling him upright. One of his feet had been amputated just above the ankle and he was having trouble adjusting. Because Victoria knew he would be leaving for home within a week, she tried to get him to do as much as he could for himself.

He reached for an olive-green shirt hanging on his bedstead. "I would hardly call myself lucky, miss."

She heard the pain in his voice, and though she sympathized, she could not afford to vocalize it. Going home would be difficult enough; he didn't need to be coddled. "It could be worse. You could have no legs at all. At least you will be able to get around."

"She has a point," a voice said from several beds down. "Quit your whining."

The young sergeant shoved his arms into his shirt, his jaw tight. "And who are you to tell me to quit whining?" he called back.

"A man with no legs, you young fool."

That shut the sergeant up, and Victoria gave a wink to the man who had spoken. He would be going home, too, but had adapted surprisingly well to his new situation. "I can see my wife and hold her with two arms, and I don't have to go back to hell," he had told Victoria. "The way I figure it, life isn't too bad."

His bravery humbled her.

The rest of the morning passed quickly. Breakfast, baths, assigning tasks, changing dirty linens, and fetching took all her energy, and by the time someone came to spell her, she was exhausted. She tucked a book under her arm and left for lunch gratefully.

The VADs and nurses usually took their meals in the servants' hall, which was clean and spacious and certainly nicer than the servants' hall at Summerset. The cook patted her back and told her to sit, she would bring her plate, but Victoria shook her head. "I'll take mine outside, if you don't mind. I want to get the last of the sun before the rains come."

She balanced her bread on top of her stew and carried a cup of tea out to the garden, where several soldiers lounged in the sun. Some of the neighboring women had shown up and were writing letters or reading to them, and Victoria found a quiet spot in a corner of the garden with a small iron table and chair.

She ate the hot, tasty stew with relish, savoring each drop and reading her book, a collection of sonnets by Elizabeth Barrett Browning. She was trying to commit some to memory, but finding time was more challenging than it used to be. The exercise kept her from worrying about Kit, whose departure to the front had been delayed by some sort of training. He wouldn't tell her what it was, and she didn't pry. The less she thought about his going off to war, the less time she spent lying awake at night, her stomach churning with anxiety. As terrible of a tease as he was, his absence made her life far less intriguing than when he might show up at any minute, ready for some sort of adventure.

"Victoria?"

She glanced up, a bit annoyed at the inter-ruption, but her eyes widened at the sight of the young soldier in front of her. "Edward!" She leapt up and was about to wrap him in a hug, then realized he had a cast on one arm and a brace on one leg. She satisfied herself with putting both of her hands on his shoulders. "Whatever are you doing here?" she cried, then blushed, taking in the sight of his crutches. It was obvious what he was doing here.

His mouth twisted in a wry grin. "I heard this was the place where they patched Humpty Dumpty back up so I thought I would make a reservation." His cavalier tone was edged with pain.

Her chest tightened. "I'm so sorry you had a great fall."

He shrugged and then grimaced. "I'm one of the lucky ones. They're going to patch me back up and send me back to the front."

"Would you like to sit down? Are you hungry?" She pulled out a chair.

He sat with a sigh and propped his crutches up against the table.

"Is it so very bad?"

The bleakness of his blue eyes told the tale and her stomach knotted, thinking of Kit, Colin, Sebastian, and the rest of the Clever Coterie.

126

"Bad enough," he said. "You know, our fathers often spoke of going off to war as if it were a romantic, noble thing, but it's not really. Of course, we should have known better after Sebastian lost his father in the Boer War. But we didn't. We thought it would be one more adventure that we could write home about. But it's not. It's filthy and wretched, and just when you think you can't stand the tedium anymore, your mate is blown up just feet from where you're standing."

Victoria gasped.

His handsome face fell into contrite lines. "I am so sorry, my dear. I shouldn't be telling you all this."

Victoria reached out on the table and squeezed his hand. She didn't know Edward that well, but it seemed that war had made all the little societal niceties crumble. Maybe honesty would take their place.

"I am just so dreadfully sorry that you and all our friends have to see this. Summer picnics were so much more to our tastes, weren't they? Has war always been so destructive?" Victoria clapped her hand to her forehead. "Do I sound impossibly naïve?"

"You sound charming, as always. And I think war is more destructive because our weapons are more destructive. But let's not talk of war. I will have to talk about it soon enough when I rejoin my regiment. Let's talk of other things. Like our friends and pleasant picnics under the trees. You know I think of that time often, how beautiful it was." He glanced at her out of the corner of his eye. "And just how is Kit anyway?"

She ignored the look. "Fine, last I heard. I haven't seen him for a couple of weeks. Apparently he's getting some kind of specialized training somewhere outside of Bath, for what I know not. He's supposed to be getting a quick leave. I'm sure he'll land on my doorstep, hungry and ready for trouble. Have you heard from your friend, the one who was sweet on Daphne? What was his name?"

"Albert?"

"That's the one. Albert." Her diversion was successful and they spoke of other mutual acquaintances until Victoria had to return to her patients.

Edward's nurse, a young woman Victoria only knew by sight, came and collected him. After saying good-bye Victoria finished the rest of her shift, strangely depressed. Even praise for her first solo day by one of the nurses couldn't lift her spirits. Seeing one of her friends join the ranks of these previously anonymous broken men only further underlined how devastating war really was. She didn't even bother to chat with the kitchen staff on the way home, but instead just met her driver down the block as usual.

When she'd first begun working, she'd had Pete,

her driver, drop her off in front of Blackmore Manor, but after a few snide comments from the other VADs, she'd asked him to drop her off and pick her up off-site. She'd tried walking it, but an asthma attack at the halfway mark convinced her that it was just too far.

Eleanor visited her mother on Tuesday nights, and Susie took Tuesday evenings off and wouldn't be home until late. Victoria wondered what Susie did on her evenings off, but had as yet been unsuccessful in prying it out of her. It must be something juicy, but tonight Victoria was too tired and too disheartened to figure it out. At least she had Nanny Iris's visit tomorrow to look forward to.

The driver dropped her off in front of her flat and she trudged up the stairway. Coming home wasn't as nice without a warm fire and some hot tea to hearten her and drive off the chill. The scent and feel of winter's bite hung in the air, and she shivered to think about all those soldiers at the front. Or fronts. So many countries were at war, she sometimes lost track.

Just before she reached the landing, she looked up. It took her several moments before her eyes made sense of what she was seeing, but then it came to her in a welcomed rush that left her breathless. "Kit!"

He was sitting with his back against her door, his eyes closed. His head jerked up at her voice, and a tired smile lit up the handsome features of his face. "Am I dreaming? Is it really you? 'Now I will believe there are unicorns.'"

She held out her hands to help him up, joy bubbling up in her chest. "'We are such stuff as dreams are made on, and our little life is rounded with sleep.'"

He laughed as he arose. "Just when I think I might have you stumped, you throw it back in my face."

She laughed. How wonderful it was to see him! "I just finished rereading *The Tempest* again."

Unlocking the door, she went into the flat and he followed.

"Where's Susie?" he asked, shrugging out of his warm woolen peacoat.

"Night off. I think she has a lover."

He raised an eyebrow. "And Eleanor?"

"At her mother's. If you start a fire in the sitting room, I will make us some hot tea. Or would you rather have a brandy?"

"Tea is fine."

He turned into the sitting room while she continued down the hall into the kitchen. After starting the water to heating, she pulled out a tray and added the cups and saucers and the sugar. As neither of them took cream, she left it off and added the egg-and-cress sandwiches Susie had left in the icebox. Eleanor would just have to forgive her for giving Kit Eleanor's share.

Once the tea was ready, she added a pot and a plate of the chocolate biscuits she knew he had a weakness for.

Another overwhelming gale of happiness overcame her when she entered the sitting room and saw him standing over the fire, an intent look on his face.

"You've gotten better at starting fires," she teased.

"If I told you once, I've told you a thousand times: the chimney wasn't drawing properly." He grinned. "I miss that room. You have no idea how many times I close my mind and try to remember all the good times we had there."

Victoria smiled at the memories. When she'd first moved to Summerset after her father's death, she'd longed for a place where she could escape. She'd found a room in the closed-up wing of Summerset and had made it her own. The first time Kit had found her there, she had screamed, but their friendship had really begun there in that abandoned study.

His eyes took on a sentimental look and she quickly held the tray up. "I hope you're hungry; look what I've got for you!"

"What a little domestic you're becoming. Next thing you'll tell me is you can make your own bed."

She snorted. "I can. I learned how in prison."

He hooted. "I'd forgotten about that. What other useful things did you learn in Holloway?"

"How to dump a pot of hot tea over the heads of those who annoy me. Now, be a dear and take the tray, will you? I'll pour us tea and thereby shatter any illusions you may have about my domesticity."

He took the tray from her hands and she cleared the books from a side table. "What? You were never taught how to pour tea in hopes of luring in an innocent young man?"

"You're forgetting that I was raised by a man. He neglected to teach us the finer art of being useless."

"Ouch. I think you just slandered your entire generation. Thank you," he said, taking the cup of tea she poured.

"Not my generation, just my class. Susie and Eleanor can both cook, and trust me, that's a far better skill than pouring a fancy tea."

"So you're learning to cook?"

"Don't be silly." Victoria took a seat in one of the wingback chairs nearest the fire.

"It's hard to be anything but silly or to take you seriously while you have that ridiculous cap on."

She put a hand to her head, realizing that she still had her VAD headgear on. She set her tea down and took the cap off, inadvertently loosening some of the pins that held up her hair. She took them out as well and then quickly recoiled her hair and pinned it into a messy knot on top of her head. "There, that feels much better anyway."

Her breath caught from the look of longing she caught on his face before he turned back toward the fire. She picked up her teacup and a sandwich. "Oh, why don't you sit down," she snapped, her heart dipping with frustration. She had been so happy to see him, and now he was going to ruin it by getting all soppy.

He raised a quizzical eyebrow. "Rough day?"

"No, you just make me nervous lurking about." She added in a milder tone, "Sit and eat."

"I didn't know you suffered from nerves." He sat and took a biscuit. Dunking it into his tea, he took a bite and stared moodily into the fire.

She blew out her breath in exasperation and fell into silence. He'd been her best friend for over a year, but she still didn't understand him. "Oh!" She sat up straight. "Guess who showed up at the hospital today? Edward!"

The look he gave her was unreadable. "Did he come for a visit or was he injured?"

"Injured, sadly. Why would he come to the hospital for a visit?"

Kit shrugged. "He seemed a bit smitten with you last summer."

Her jaw dropped. "Oh, please! You've gone beyond silly into the realm of Never Never Land. Perhaps you've been concussed while off in the war." She dismissed him with a wave of a hand.

Rather than get angry, he laughed. "I only wish

I were in Never Never Land. You would make a charming Wendy."

"I most certainly would not! Imagine me taking care of children. The Lost Boys wanted her to be their mother. Could you see me as someone's mother?"

She realized her blunder then when Kit looked at her, his blue eyes burning. "Maybe, Maybe not. You certainly couldn't be any worse than my mother."

She jerked up straight. Certainly, she had been right to not trust him. "Have another biscuit and stop your nonsense."

"So you're not the motherly type. But I could see you as Tinker Bell. And don't you think I'd make a dashing Peter Pan? Second star to the right and straight on till morning and all that."

He sounded tired and she shot him a look. He was thinner, even though it had only been a month since she had seen him, and shadows darkened his eyes. Pity and tenderness stabbed at her.

He stood and poked the fire, and the sadness on his face was more than she could bear.

She joined him then, placing her hand on his shoulder. "You need to get some sleep. Would you like me to call my driver? He can take you to your mother's house."

He reached up and covered her hand with his own. He didn't look at her, and shadows from the flame of the fire flickered across his face. "I'm not going home. I have to return directly to headquarters. I had an errand to run and am leaving for Calais on the ferry in the morning. I only had a few hours."

His hand tightened on hers and they stood silently as the light from the windows dimmed around them. Victoria knew she should move to light the lamps—standing in front of the fire and holding his hand like this was dangerous, he might get the wrong idea—but she was strangely reluctant to break the spell. "Are you being sent to the front?" she asked quietly.

The look he gave her was unreadable. "I've been handpicked for *other* duties."

Fear shot through her and she didn't have to ask what duties. He wouldn't be able to tell her, and she could imagine the type of duties a young man with a perfect grasp of the German language would be asked to do.

"When do you have to leave?" she asked instead.

He glanced at the large clock over the fireplace. "I should go to the railway station in a couple of hours."

Victoria tilted her head back and looked at his profile. He'd always been handsome, in his own way, with his dark-auburn hair and sharp blue eyes. His features were more intelligent than conventionally handsome, but looking at him, she realized that Kit had changed. Whereas his mouth had often been twisted with a cynical derision or his eyes mocking, he now looked pensive and unsure. Less cocky.

Or maybe it was just a trick of the light.

He finally turned to her, and warning bells went off in her head, but she couldn't move, couldn't break the spell that his burning blue eyes seemed to cast over her.

She swallowed, knowing that he was going to kiss her. He had kissed her once before, but it hadn't meant anything then. But this was different. This meant something. This was going to count. She knew it in the way he bent his head purposefully toward her and the way her toes curled. She cursed herself for a weak fool as she tilted her head back to meet his mouth, but she couldn't seem to stop herself.

And then they were kissing, his lips moving against hers. When his arms slipped around her and pulled her close, she didn't resist. Instead, her arms snaked up around his neck and she let herself be completely filled with Kit, and it felt so incredibly right.

One of his hands tangled itself in her hair. The pins she had so haphazardly stuck in fell completely out, and the mass fell down her back. He broke off their kiss, gasping, and then, pulling her off her feet, held her close and buried his face in her neck.

"Victoria," he murmured against her hair. "My

wonderful, maddening little minx. I love you so. Please tell me you love me. Please say you'll marry me."

A tremor ran through her body, the mention of marriage shocking her out of her enchantment. How could she have let things go so far, especially on the eve of his departure?

She pulled out of his arms and took a deep breath. Twisting her hair back with one hand, she looked around wildly for her hairpins. Why was it so dark? What utter folly!

"Oh, Kit. Why do you have to keep bringing that up? Just like a scratched record on a gramophone." She cried out, frustrated and utterly confused, her head spinning, "Where are my damned hairpins?" She flicked on a lamp.

"I take that as a no." His voice was cold.

She blinked at the sudden light and winced at the stark expression on his face. His hands clenched into fists at his sides, and the eyes that had burned so warmly just minutes before now regarded her icily. She wanted to put up a hand to block the chill that came from them.

"Of course it's a no! It's always been a no. I don't want to get married. Why do you think anything's changed? You're the one who wants to tie me to you like some sort of a pack animal! And now . . . now you're leaving, and you're taking advantage of my . . . my . . ." She stopped. He was taking advantage of her melting heart, her confused mixture of anger, sadness, and deep affection. But how could she put into words what she could barely understand herself?

He reached out to grab her arms—then lowered his hands. "You're right. You haven't changed a bit. You're just as contrary and immature as you have always been."

"I'm contrary? *I'm* contrary?" She was practically screaming now, but she didn't care. She felt as if she was on the verge of tears, her frustration and confusion pushing her to her breaking point. "What lunacy! You're the one who keeps asking me to marry you in spite of how many times I repeat the word *no*. Why can't you just let us continue to be friends? Why do you have to spoil everything by bringing marriage into every conversation?" *And by kissing me like that,* she wanted to scream, but stopped short.

Kit stared down at her, and pain flashed across his face before it was replaced with a look so emotionless, she shivered and turned away from him. He turned and picked up his coat, which he had flung over the back of a chair.

"You needn't be worried, Victoria. I won't bother you by asking again." He put on his coat and walked out the sitting-room door.

She hurried to the doorway after him as he walked down the hall, still scrambling for something to say. She wanted him to stay; he couldn't leave like this. "Kit!"

But he didn't even pause, his shiny army boots keeping to their measured time.

"Kit!" she called again, fear churning in her stomach.

"Good-bye, Victoria." The door opened and shut and Kit was gone.

How dare he just leave?

She whirled around and ran back into the sitting room. Rushing to the window, she saw Kit's dark form walk into the night until he was lost in the shadows. The desolation she felt in her heart knocked the breath out of her lungs. Suddenly, in that moment, she understood the enormity of her mistake. The failing of her stubborn pride. She'd grown so used to their comfortable dynamic—his unconditional love for her and her playful refusal of him—that she couldn't see how much she'd been hurting him. And she hadn't left any room for her own feelings to truly come through.

But he was gone and this time he wouldn't be coming back. The reality that she might never see him again suddenly hit her like a brick wall. He was heading off to war, and this was how she chose to leave things between them? With so much left unsaid?

As the truth settled into her heart, she wanted to scream.

She loved him.

She loved him with every fiber of her being

and in her childish stubbornness had failed to distinguish between what her head and her heart had been telling her. Sinking down in front of the embers of a dying fire, Victoria covered her face with her hands and wept.

CHAPTER NINE

P rudence resisted the urge to hurry up the steps to Victoria's flat and instead took them one slow step at a time. She wasn't that big, really, but her balance was off and she felt as if she could topple over at any moment. Part of it had to do with the light corset she still wore so that her clothing would fit. Katie's mother, Muriel, had tried to show Prudence how to let the waists of her dresses out, but had given up in despair and told her she would do it for her. Until they were done, Prudence had to wear the corset even though putting it on was like torture and she apologized to baby Horace every time she did it.

She didn't even know why she had come to visit Victoria so late at night and without sending round a note to make sure her friend would be here. She had been trying her hand at a simple pud when she suddenly had a feeling that Victoria needed her. She'd had that same feeling on another occasion when they were growing up together, and Victoria had suddenly collapsed from a breathing episode, but it had been years since Prudence had felt the urge that now compelled her to go to her sister's side. Victoria was in much better health these days; Prudence didn't know what it could be.

Finally reaching the landing, she knocked on the door, hoping her instincts were wrong and Victoria was just fine. That hope was shattered when an old woman, whom she didn't know, opened the door.

Prudence frowned. "Is Victoria here?"

The old woman peered at her. "Rowena? Oh. No. I can see it's not. You must be Prudence."

Prudence nodded, her cheeks heating. Something about how the woman spoke let her know that she knew all about Prudence's illegitimate heritage and, what's more, didn't much care.

"Come in, child. She is resting in her room."

"What's wrong?" Prudence asked, alarmed. "Is she sick?"

"Sick in the heart, which has affected her body, more's the pity."

Susie appeared and gave Prudence a hug. "I'm so glad you're here," Susie whispered, taking Prudence's coat. "The timing of your visit couldn't be better." Her thin features were pinched with worry, and Prudence felt a stab of fear.

She hurried back to Victoria's room. Eleanor was standing next to Victoria's bed, wiping her brow with a damp cloth. Prudence set her purse down on a small side table and hurried to her friend's side.

Victoria's eyes were closed and fine tracings of blue veins stood out starkly against the pale skin of her temples. "What's wrong?" Prudence whispered to Eleanor.

Eleanor nodded her head toward the open door, and Prudence followed her. Eleanor turned. "I think she caught something at the hospital, but there is something else going on as well. I ask her what it is and she just turns her head away. She won't talk about it with either me or Nanny Iris. I'm terribly worried about how thin she's becoming."

So that was Nanny Iris. As Victoria's friend and confidante, she would know all about Prudence's past. Prudence put that thought aside. She had other things to worry about right now. "That's been her pattern. She's so slender that any kind of sickness pushes her over the edge into emaciation. How long has she been like this?"

"About three days. The doctor has been to see her but says she just needs rest. She has had a fever on and off, but nothing too dangerous."

"And you didn't call for me?"

Eleanor shook her head. "She didn't want to tell you or Rowena."

"Her and her secrets." Prudence shook her head and opened the door. "Well, let me talk to her. I'll see what I can do."

Her heart constricted as she looked down at Victoria's wan features. Carefully, Prudence sat and took up her friend's hand. It was hot and dry and impossibly small.

Victoria's eyes fluttered open, but it took a moment for her to focus on Prudence's face. When she did, she smiled. "They sent for you even though I told them not to."

Prudence shook her head. "No. I came on my own. I knew something was wrong."

Victoria's hand gave Prudence's a feeble squeeze. "You always did know when I needed you."

"They tell me you're sick and won't get out of bed, but that isn't like the Victoria I know and love." Prudence kept her voice light, trying not to let Vic see her anxiety. She looked so small lying there in the big bed, the fine linen sheets and lace coverlet covering a body that was more like a child's than a grown woman's.

"The Victoria you know and love wouldn't ever be as stupid as I have been."

Prudence spied the trembling of the girl's lips and prayed that Victoria was ready to share whatever was keeping her from fighting her illness. Prudence bent and kissed the girl's cheek. "Tell sister all about it, my darling. You'll feel ever so much better."

Tears streaming down her cheeks, Victoria did exactly that.

"He didn't even look back as he left," she whimpered when she reached the end of her tale.

"And you haven't seen him since?" Prudence asked gently. She'd met Kit before, of course, but couldn't equate the narcissistic, cultured, and rather blasé young man she'd met with the passion Vic was describing.

Victoria shook her head. "I don't even know where he went, where he's stationed. He wouldn't say."

Spent, Victoria laid her head back while Prudence watched. She'd never seen her little sister like this. Prudence couldn't judge just how worried she should be.

"Write him a letter," she told Victoria. "Write him and tell him how you feel."

"I can't! He won't listen, not after the way I treated him . . . and I don't even know where to send it."

Prudence stood up. "He may not listen, but at least you will have tried. Since when have you ever not at least tried to get what you wanted? This way you at least have a chance to make things right. Why risk losing such an important friendship"—she hesitated, wondering if she should go on, then added cautiously—"or such a great love over this?"

Victoria sniffled. "Do you think I might still have a chance?"

Prudence's heart ached at the thread of hope she

heard in Victoria's voice. "He asked you to marry him. He says he loves you. If he truly loves you, he won't let an argument stop him from being with you. And if he does, then he isn't worth it after all."

Victoria sat up, and Prudence plumped up the pillows to support her back. "You don't know Kit," Victoria said, sounding a bit stronger. "He can be prideful. Stubborn. And I know I hurt him badly this time. Perhaps even more than . . . more than I hurt myself."

"See you when you get back!" Albert yelled over the engine of the latest French SPAD aeroplane Rowena sat in. The French had let the English "borrow" the fighter in an attempt to build parts for it. Mr. Dirkes had his engineers pore over it for several days before sending it back to Hastings and then home. Though she'd made several runs for Mr. Dirkes, she had never flown a fighter, and the new SPAD, with its long, tapered fuselage and streamlined nacelle mounted in front of the engine and the propeller, was one of the best. As excited as Rowena was to fly a new aeroplane, the thought of the machine gun inside the nacelle churned her stomach.

Once she got the go-ahead from Albert, she eased the throttle forward and made a smooth takeoff. She checked her instruments, which were far more advanced than in the Flying Alices, an aeroplane only used for training now because they were almost obsolete. Practically every time she climbed into the cockpit of a new aeroplane since the war broke out, something had been added, changed, or improved. The added center struts in this aircraft gave it a concrete feel, and she played with the pedals to see if it would flex in the wind. Nothing. Solid as a rock. After checking her flight log and compass, she turned toward Hastings and enjoyed the smooth ride.

Flying for Mr. Dirkes made it a joy to get up each morning. Rowena felt she was finally doing something that had meaning and purpose. Her uncle had surprisingly been on her side . . . though the conversation with her aunt hadn't gone so well.

"So now I not only have to worry about my son dying in a ditch somewhere, but also about my niece flying into a mountain. How simply wonderful for me," Aunt Charlotte had said.

"I'm not going to crash into a mountain, Aunt Charlotte. I am far too skilled a pilot for that," Rowena had answered.

Aunt Charlotte had snorted. "And we can add that to the list of sentences I never thought to come out of your mouth, my dear."

Sometimes Rowena wondered if Aunt Charlotte meant to be funny or if it was simply her bitterness.

Rowena's case was bigger than usual because

she would be staying overnight in Hastings. Sebastian was to meet her this evening, and they were going to spend the next day in Brighton. It would be different off-season, of course, but she would get to see him. At least that was the plan. As with anything, plans were subject to military discretion. Rowena had been incredibly lucky with the aeroplanes and had never had a moment's trouble with them, though seasoned pilots warned her that it was only a matter of time.

But not today, she exulted, climbing above the cloud cover. Not today. And this evening she would see Sebastian, a thought that buoyed her spirits almost as much as the flight itself.

She recalled the last letter she had received from him, a letter filled with words that had touched her and opened her heart to the possibility that her friendship with Sebastian was blossoming into something more meaningful. He had written:

My dear Rowena,

Of course, my brilliant, brave girl would be flying aeroplanes all over England for the military. I would expect nothing less. Please be careful, always remembering how many people love you, myself included. Our future children also wish you to take care. . . .

Myself included . . .

The thought of Sebastian's loving her warmed her chest, and for the first time, she felt that she could love him back. It might not be the same wild, passionate love that she'd felt for Jon, but it would be based on far more than a love of flight and physical attraction.

As always, the time passed swiftly and before long she was winding downward to make a landing. She had never been to Hastings before and hoped it was a good field.

It wasn't. She made a smooth landing, but immediately after her wheels touched down, the aeroplane veered to the left and her shoulder was slammed into the edge of the cockpit. The machine jerked to an inelegant stop, and her neck snapped forward painfully.

The aeroplane shuddered. "Blast!" she cried once the engine stilled. Not waiting for the men she saw running toward her, she undid her harness and carefully stepped out onto the wing before leaping to the ground. *Please don't let anything be broken,* she prayed, taking careful inventory.

One of the two men reached her. "Don't you know the hangar is over there?" He spotted her face and his mouth flew open.

"What the hell were you thinking?" the other yelled from behind her.

The voice broke over her like the swell of a

tsunami and she turned as her pulse pounded in her ears.

Jon.

He saw her then and skidded to a stop, shock registering on his features before his face shuttered, becoming impassive.

Rowena froze. She couldn't think. Couldn't function. She knew she should be explaining herself, but her lips felt curiously numb.

"What is a damn woman doing piloting a plane?"

"Shut up, Parker," Jon finally said. "What happened?" he asked, avoiding her eyes.

Trembling inside, she nodded toward a sinkhole in the field about the size of one of her wheels. "I hit that when I landed." She gestured toward the hole. "The aeroplane leapt out of control."

Jon and Parker walked over to the hole. "Looks like a giant gopher dug this one, Wells."

Jon nodded. "Let's get someone out here to fill it up, eh?" He turned to Rowena. His eyes flickered ever so slightly as they grazed over her. No one except Rowena would be able to tell that her presence had shaken him to his core.

Good.

The last time she had seen him, he'd been walking away from her. Let him see and remember what he'd walked away from.

"Did Dirkes send you?"

She nodded. "I'm ferrying aeroplanes for him

because there aren't enough pilots available."

He nodded. "I figured it was something like that. Do you have a bag?"

Rowena nodded, and he leapt easily onto the wing and fished out her leatherbound flight log and satchel. He jumped back down, handed her the book, and started across the field toward the hangar and outbuildings of the base.

She followed with a worried glance back toward the plane.

Jon must have caught her concern. "Don't worry about it. If there's anything wrong with it, we'll fix it. The French are too busy to quibble much anyway."

"There won't be any." She peeped sideways at him as they walked. His profile was the same. Strong jaw and nose, same thin, perfectly formed mouth. She shivered, remembering how many times that mouth had been on hers. His shaggy, strawberry-blond hair had been trimmed short, and he wore his well-made uniform with ease. She swallowed; the sight of him still took her breath away. It also ushered in a rush of feelings more confusing than the images in a kaleidoscope. Carrying her bag, he marched furiously across the field as if he couldn't wait to deposit her at headquarters.

He probably couldn't.

She firmed her chin. That was just fine with her, but she was under no obligation to make it easy for him. "I saw Cristobel the other day. She misses you."

His long legs faltered for a moment at the mention at something so personal, and Rowena felt a twinge of triumph that she had rattled him. She also felt a ripple of pain. After all these months, it still hurt to know he couldn't possibly have loved her as much as she loved him. She'd never have walked away the way he did. It made her angry that he still had power over her, that seeing him still hurt her terribly. It meant a part of her still loved him. Yet how could she, when she was committed to Sebastian? And when her love was stained with so much hurt and anger? Her eyes swept down to the ring on her finger, Jon looking at her from the corner of her eye.

He said nothing at the mention of his little sister, and Rowena fought an urge to slap him. Instead, she took refuge in being aloof and coldly professional.

"I believe Mr. Dirkes is going to start building SPAD-like aeroplanes," she said, just to say something.

"I'm sure he will, as that's the reason he borrowed it. He could build aeroplanes day and night from now until Easter and still not fulfill the contracts the government has given him."

The tautness of his tone shivered down her spine. Why was he behaving so coldly? What had she done to merit such hostility? *He* had walked away from *her*.

He escorted her around the hangar to a square where temporary buildings had been erected in a hasty attempt to build a base. The tension between them was so uncomfortable that Rowena was relieved when they reached headquarters. Jon saluted the commander. "Miss Buxton has brought in the SPAD from the Dirkes factory, Colonel Atkins. There was a problem with the landing, but the aeroplane is in one piece and we are fixing the problem."

The colonel nodded. "And I trust you are in one piece as well, Miss Buxton?"

She nodded. "I am very well, thank you."

"When Douglas Dirkes called and told me a young woman would be delivering the aeroplane, I have to admit I was quite surprised. Seeing how lovely you are only increases my amazement at your accomplishments. Mr. Dirkes must have a great deal of confidence in your abilities, Miss Buxton."

She smiled, not daring to look at Jon. "He knew I had a good instructor."

"May I be dismissed, sir?" Jon asked abruptly.

"Of course, Lieutenant. And good luck."

"Thank you, sir."

Rowena felt her body deflate when Jon slammed the door behind him. Just like that, he was gone.

Again.

The colonel said something, and with effort Rowena dragged her attention back to him. "Pardon?"

"I said I will have someone drive you to the inn in Hastings. He said you had a ride back to the factory tomorrow, correct?"

Rowena nodded. "I'm actually not going back to the factory right away. My fiancé is meeting me this evening and we're going to spend the day in Brighton before he takes me back."

"Very well, then." The colonel led her out into the square where his own motorcar had been pulled up. His hand lingered on her elbow for a little longer than necessary, but Rowena was used to that. Most of the men she dealt with had been away from their sweethearts for far too long.

She kept her composure, chatting to the private who drove her into town and to the innkeeper, who asked if she would be down to dinner. She assured him she would and was expecting company. Then she went upstairs on legs that shook more than mere exhaustion would have warranted. But not until she shut the door behind her and sat on the slender, white, organdy-covered bed did she let the tears that had been building up during the scant fifteen minutes she had spent in Jon's presence surface.

All of the old insecurities, anger, and heartbreak came rushing back, but even as she wiped her face with a handkerchief, she knew the difference between the tears of last spring and the tears of today. Whereas once her tears had been born of fury and grief, now they were born of regret and the thought of what might have been.

Rowena took a deep, shuddering breath before going into the small water closet and splashing her face with cold water. She changed out of her flying clothes. The uniform she and Mr. Dirkes had discussed had never materialized, and Rowena was thankful. She far preferred her warm woolen split skirt, much like the kind one wore for bicycling, a heavy woolen sweater, and the new leather jacket Victoria had sent her from London with a note that contained a stanza from Percy Bysshe Shelley's poem "To a Skylark":

Higher still and higher
From the earth thou springest,
Like a cloud of fire;
The blue deep thou wingest,
And singing still dost soar, and soaring
ever singest.

Rowena kept the note in the pocket of her jacket and wore it every time she flew.

She slipped into a simple gabardine suit with pleats in the front and back of the skirt and a row of tiny tortoiseshell buttons going up the front of the jacket. She'd chosen the gabardine because the material traveled well and took little fuss. She'd also brought an automobile coat, as she and Sebastian would be driving to Brighton in the morning and then on to Summerset tomorrow night.

Unsure of what time Sebastian would be getting in, she decided to go for a short walk to stretch her legs. Sitting in an aeroplane was wonderful, but not exactly comfortable. She buttoned up her automobile coat and checked her face in the mirror. Her eyes were still puffy, and though she preferred going bareheaded now, she picked up the small taffeta hat she wore in a roofless motorcar. She arranged the netting designed to protect her face to hide the redness of her eyes.

Like Brighton, Hastings was a fishing and resort town, and the shops and buildings catered to the upper classes. Unlike other resort towns, the place did not have a sad and lonely feeling as if abandoned by tourists, but rather a sense of relief as if the locals, mostly fishermen and their families, were glad to be rid of the lot of them. She walked along the promenade and noted that though many of the shops were already shuttered for the winter, others were doing a brisk trade among the locals.

She spotted an open bookshop and decided to go find something to read. Losing herself in a book would be a welcome distraction. Perhaps she could find a place to have tea and read until Sebastian came.

The shop was old and cluttered and smelt of both the sea and old books, which wasn't unpleasant, and Rowena's spirits lifted as she browsed. An old man with an even older top hat sat behind the desk reading. He had barely glanced up when she entered except to bid her good afternoon. He and the striped tabby cat sitting on the counter next to him both turned away as if she were no longer of any interest.

The Jane Austens tempted her, but then she spotted E. M. Forster's *Howards End*. She'd read *A Room with a View* and adored it, but hadn't yet read this one, though it had been out for several years.

Rowena was paying for the book and was just about to leave when the bell above the door tinkled. Recognition jolted through her body. Jon.

"I thought I would find you here," he said quietly.

Trembling, she took her change from the old man and turned toward the door. She brushed past him without acknowledging his presence and went out into the chill autumn air.

He followed her as she continued her walk at a brisker pace. "The question is why you were looking for me," she said without looking at him.

"I thought we should talk." His voice was low, and though she ached to see the look on his face, she kept her eyes straight ahead.

"I have little to say. The time for talking passed

months ago." She spat the words at him like pebbles thrown into a pond.

"Maybe I want to talk to you. Maybe I want to apologize."

She clutched her purchase tighter to her chest as pain stabbed at her heart. "Or maybe you just want to draw me in, only to cast me aside again. I was such a fool!"

He grabbed her elbow. "It wasn't like that and you know it. Rowena, stop!"

She stopped then, breathing hard, and tilted her head back. "I don't know what it was like. I loved you. You said you loved me. We became lovers and you left. Tell me your version."

He took a deep breath. "Maybe I was hasty last spring."

"Maybe?" She couldn't believe her ears. *Maybe?*

The blue of his eyes glittered and it felt as if he were looking straight into her soul. "I made a mistake, Rowena. I'm so very sorry."

Rowena could almost hear the carefully constructed wall she had built around herself cracking like the shattering of ice across a pond. She shook her head denying his words. "No. It's too late. I'm to be married."

Jonathon's mouth tightened. "To Sebastian?"

She nodded.

He took her hand in his and removed her glove. He stared at the antique diamond ring she wore on her finger. "This isn't you, Rowena," he said, his voice urgent. "You keep trying to be like your family, and you're nothing like them. You belong to the skies and you know it. How are you supposed to fly all hemmed in? Lord Billingsly is not going to want his wife winging through the skies of England."

She shook her head and pulled her arm away. "You're mistaken. My uncle bought me a Vickers. My fiancé has already started building a hangar to house it." Her voice grew harsh. "You know nothing about me or my life. You made rash judgments on what you thought you knew about us, and you were wrong."

She started to walk away, but again he reached out and grabbed her arm. "Perhaps. But I wasn't wrong about you loving me. I wasn't wrong about loving you."

His jaw worked and she didn't know whether to trace the line with her fingertips or slap him. She did neither and instead stared up at him, confused thoughts fluttering in her mind. A woman passed by and Rowena realized they were standing on a sidewalk.

She turned away and hunched her shoulders as if protecting her heart. "I would have died for you, but you wouldn't fight for me. You walked away from me because I was a Buxton, and no matter how imperfect we are, I am still a Buxton. Could you honestly say that my last name and the wrongdoing my uncle committed against your family won't always separate us?"

Their eyes clashed, and part of her longed for him to say that it didn't matter, that he would love her forever. Would she be willing to walk away from her life for him once again?

The answer was far more complicated now than it would have been just a month ago.

Then he looked away and let go of her arm.

Disappointment knotted her stomach before she gave herself a mental shake. Had she really expected anything else? "Now if you will excuse me, I have to go meet my fiancé."

This time he didn't try to stop her. As before, he stood and watched her walk away. But this time her heart was only bruised, not shattered.

CHAPTER
TEN

S ebastian was waiting for her by the time she got back to the inn. A slow smile spread over his handsome face when she walked through the door. Part of her wanted to hurl herself into his arms. Sebastian meant safety, and his love for her would salve her wounded pride.

But was that fair to him?

"I was going to call out a search party, but wasn't sure where you would be."

Jonathon had known exactly where to find me.

She gave a small smile. "I went to a bookstore and found a place for tea and scones and read the afternoon away. It was lovely."

"I'm glad you had a good day. How was the flight?"

The question warmed her heart. "It was good. Nothing out of the ordinary." She removed her hat and blinked up at him. Sometimes she forgot how handsome he was. He leaned down and kissed her right there in the lobby, his lips lingering against hers. No fireworks, but she had been burned by fireworks before and was quite happy with warm, tender, and safe.

"What was that for?" she asked.

"Just because." His dark eyes smiled down at her. "You know I worry about you every time I know you're going up." He helped her off with her coat.

She smiled. "I know. That's why I tell you as little as possible."

"And I thank you for that. A friend of mine will be joining us for dinner. I ran into him at the base. I could hardly turn him down. I think you'll like him."

She shook her head. "Of course I don't mind. I didn't bring anything dressy, though. There just isn't enough room in the cockpit for luggage."

He grinned. "I hardly think that is going to be a problem. You're lovely no matter what you wear."

"Wonderful. Just let me take my things up to my

room. Go ahead and get us a table. I'll be down in a few minutes."

She nodded to the clerk and climbed the stairs to her room. Turning on a light, she laid her coat and her hat on the bed, then went into the water closet. She stared at herself in the mirror. Redness lingered about her green eyes.

Her day hadn't been lovely, it had been terrible.

She hadn't brought any cosmetics with her to hide the lingering traces of her tears. She rarely used them anyway. Elaine and Victoria both thought them great fun, but Rowena considered them a bother. She could certainly use some rouge and kohl now, she thought. Anything to lessen the tense pallor of her complexion.

Wetting a cool cloth, she laid it over her eyes and pinched her cheeks until they glowed. Better. She would tell Sebastian and his friend she was tired. It was preferable to telling her fiancé that she'd had her heart battered about by another man.

The restaurant attached to the inn glittered under heavy crystal chandeliers. A green-and-gold carpet on the floor echoed the green of the wallpaper and the gold trim on the china and crystal Waterford glasses. Giant potted palms almost reached the high ceiling, and the fronds cast shadows on the walls, creating intimate little corners for diners wishing privacy. Like almost everything else in Hastings, the inn catered to the upper classes and produced a dining experience as agreeable as anything one could find in London.

The waiter led her now to one of those cozy nooks. She felt quite out of place in her simple day suit, among the other women in their finery. To her relief, the place was nearly empty this time of year.

Sebastian and his company stood when she came in, and the waiter helped her with her chair. Once sitting, Sebastian introduced her to his friend Reggie, who in turn introduced her to Lord Phillip Byron, an old college friend of his he had run into and invited to dinner. Reggie was an officer in Sebastian's regiment and clad in his uniform, while Lord Byron was dressed in black tie.

After introductions, the men talked amongst themselves as if they weren't quite sure what to say to her. Rowena looked around and felt rather out of place beside them in the fine dining room. Over the past few weeks, she had begun to feel almost as if she were one of Mr. Dirkes's crew. They didn't exactly treat her like one of the men, but they were used to her comings and goings and she was no longer a novelty. The men at the factory and at the Plymouth and Hampshire bases knew her as Ro, the woman pilot. She couldn't help but prefer that identity to her current status as Sebastian's wellborn and plainly dressed fiancée.

The waiter served their soup from a white, shell-shaped tureen, and Reggie, tall and lanky, leaned forward, his homely face alight with interest. "Sebastian tells me you are quite a good pilot. However did a young woman such as yourself get into something like that?"

Her eyes flickered over to Sebastian, who was talking to the waiter.

"I had a friend who was a pilot. He took me up in the aeroplane and I fell in love. My uncle bought me my own Vickers biplane for an engagement present and I took lessons. I'm licensed, you know." She said this last bit with pride. It was quite the feather in her cap being one of few licensed female pilots in Britain.

The pale, freckled man in black tie, who had nodded stiffly at their introduction, raised an eyebrow. "I find it difficult to believe that Lord Summerset would allow his niece to fly an aeroplane."

Rowena stiffened. She'd met many men like Lord Byron—men who seemed by turns repulsed by her activities and dismissive of them. "Do you know my uncle, then, that you would know his preferences?"

The man stiffened at her words, and Sebastian broke in smoothly. "Byron here sits on the House of Lords with your uncle."

Rowena nodded at the waiter, who ladled a fragrant, clear consommé into one of the gold-edged bowls. "So, Lord Byron, you know my uncle well then?"

Uncomfortable now, he had to admit that he didn't know her uncle very well at all. Rowena gave him a dismissive shrug, which only inflamed him.

"I do know he seems fairly conservative," he said, giving her a bold stare.

She laughed, though she really wanted to toss her soup at him. If she were Victoria, she probably would have. "As I said, he is the one who bought me the aeroplane." Rowena turned back to the friendlier man. "Are you interested in flying, Captain Crowley?"

The moment passed, but Rowena had seen the malevolent look Lord Byron had shot her and shivered. Oysters were next, and then an excellent foie-gras terrine served with small triangles of toast, but Rowena had a difficult time eating with Lord Byron's gimlet eyes on her. Sebastian seemed oblivious to the tension, but Reggie talked nonstop and included Rowena in the conversation.

Over the poached cod with asparagus, Lord Byron finally attacked. "I knew I had seen you before," he said, his voice full of suppressed glee. "I saw you earlier, talking to a young man in uniform." He glanced at Sebastian to see how he would take this salacious news.

Sebastian, bless his heart, continued eating as if he didn't have a care in the world.

Rowena had never cared for him so much as she

did at that moment. "Yes, I had stopped to buy a book and ran into an old friend of mine."

She felt Sebastian's eyes on her and cursed herself for not telling him before.

"It was quite the day for running into old friends, wasn't it, Reggie?" Lord Byron's thin upper lip curled. "I hope it was as pleasant of a *coincidence* as mine turned out to be."

Rowena's chest tightened at his words, but she refused to rise to the bait. He was the kind of worthless, privileged nobleman who did little but gossip, look down his nose at others, and cause trouble. Her father had detested those sorts of people and had brought up his daughters to avoid them, too.

"Yes, how fortuitous for us that you were able to join us for supper." Sebastian made it clear by the tone of his voice that it was most definitely not fortuitous. Reggie looked miserable.

The talk moved on, but she felt the gentle, comforting pressure of Sebastian's knee against hers. She would tell him about Jon as soon as supper was over.

After their rhubarb pudding with clotted cream, Sebastian claimed fatigue and Reggie quickly feigned exhaustion as well. Lord Byron gave Sebastian and Rowena a stiff nod and the two men took their leave.

Leading her by the hand, Sebastian took Rowena to an unoccupied corner of the lobby and they sat on a red velvet settee. "I'm sorry I didn't tell you earlier," she burst out. "I didn't know you were going to be blindsided by that."

He held her hand in his and for a long moment didn't speak. Then he asked in a low voice, "Was it Jon?"

She nodded. "He is stationed here. I didn't know until I landed the aeroplane. I'd never been here before, so I had no way of knowing."

Sebastian continued staring at her hand. Finally he reached out with his finger and twirled the ring on her finger. "For several months we both considered our unintentional engagement a convenience. You were in love with Jon, a man you could not acknowledge in public, and I was getting over a bruised heart and an even more damaged ego. When I asked you to make our engagement real, I told you I wanted to do so because I thought we would make a good team and because it was better than ending up alone, but that was a lie."

Startled, she looked up into his face. His velvety black eyes searched her face. "What do you mean?"

"I wanted to make our engagement real because I had . . . I had begun falling in love with you."

Rowena's mouth fell open in shock, and her heart began to pound. She began to stammer out a response, but Sebastian put a gentle finger over her lips. "No. Don't speak. Just listen. You've told me in private that you hate how indecisive you are, but I see it differently. I see a woman who loves deeply and is afraid to hurt the ones she cares for. I see a woman of fire and passion whose eyes light up when she speaks about flying. And I see a woman who is as heartbreakingly beautiful as a goddess and yet curiously without vanity. For those reasons and many more, I love you. What I felt for Prudence was only a fraction of what I feel for you, and even though I know you don't feel the same way, I would be willing to spend my life trying to make you happy."

She stood frozen in place for a moment as his words washed over her. How different they were to Jon's confusing mix of coldness and hesitant affection, and how comforting to hear a profession so definitive, so without conditions. She clung to him then, burying her face in the lapel of his uniform, not caring what the other patrons might think. Jon's judgments of her would always be clouded by her family, whereas Sebastian saw only her. He'd even turned her faults into something good and honorable. "Thank you," she said, unable to say more.

Sebastian kissed the top of her head. "With that said, I do want you to know that I won't hold you to our engagement. I want you to be very, very sure that marrying me is what you want. If Jo—" He stopped then as if unable to complete his rival's name. "If someone else would make you happier, then I want you to be with him. Our parents' generation had too many unhappy marriages, don't you think? I don't want to mimic their mistakes. There are more important things than wealth or status."

The words reminded her of her father's, and the affection she felt for Sebastian deepened. She started to speak again but he shook his head. "Please don't. Just think about what I said. Let's spend tomorrow together, and then I will take you back to Kent. If you still wish to be married, we will do so the next time I have leave. Let's not put it off anymore. I don't need a big wedding, do you?"

She shook her head and he bent to kiss her lips. She longed to give her whole heart to Sebastian, but kept getting muddled by the image of Jon. As she made her way to her room, she fought to calm her thoughts so that she could hear what her heart was telling her. But unfortunately, her heart seemed as befuddled as her mind.

It took only a few days for Victoria to gain back her strength, and she credited her recovery to the combined efforts of the equally doting Eleanor and Nanny Iris. *Why have I never thought to live with a nurse before?* she wondered as she went about her duties at the hospital. Between Eleanor's eagle eye and Nanny Iris's herbal concoctions, Victoria felt stronger than ever. Of course, she was now heeding Eleanor's advice to get plenty of rest and moderate exercise, though she felt rather silly doing the calisthenics Eleanor had prescribed for her.

She tried not to think of Kit too much and knew it was unrealistic of her to expect a letter so soon. If he was on the kind of mission she thought he might be on—scouting in enemy territory or some other type of clandestine work—he might not be able to get his mail for weeks.

So she kept her mind occupied by throwing herself into her work. She wasn't sure if it was nursing that fulfilled her so or that she was using her herbal knowledge for a concrete purpose, but she awoke each morning with the satisfaction that she was truly making a difference. Victoria now knew that she needed to work for the betterment of others in order to feel complete. It wasn't surprising considering her upbringing. If that made her a do-good, then so be it.

"Miss Buxton, Nurse Baxter wishes to speak with you in her office when you have a moment."

Victoria hid a worried frown. The nurse's tone made it obvious that she thought Victoria was in trouble and relished the prospect. Victoria finished the bed she'd been making and hurried to the office. To Nurse Baxter, *when you have a moment* meant "immediately."

When Victoria arrived at the study, she discovered that Nurse Baxter wasn't alone. One of the staff doctors and a slim, well-dressed woman were standing in front of the matron's desk.

"Oh, excuse me," Victoria said, backing out of the room.

"Come in, Miss Buxton. I called you here to meet Dame Katharine Furse. She is the head of the Voluntary Aid Detachment. And, of course, you know Dr. Vidal."

For a moment Victoria was speechless, unsure of how to greet the estimable Dame Furse. Her upbringing would have her curtsy, but that seemed out of place under the circumstances.

Dame Furse remedied the situation by reaching out and grasping Victoria's hand. "It's so nice to meet you, my dear."

"Likewise, Dame Furse." Victoria nodded at the doctor.

"Dame Furse is looking to take several VADs to France with her for a pilot program. You do know that VADs are not traditionally dispatched to the front, don't you?"

Victoria nodded and Nurse Baxter continued, "Last month, she took two VADs with her to inspect the nurses at the front. She wouldn't allow them to nurse, but rather assigned them duties in the canteens. After an attack by the enemy, these young women were pressed into nursing duties and acquitted themselves very well."

"I was most impressed and believe that VADs have something valuable to offer to our soldiers and our wonderful nurses at the front," Dame Furse said.

"Yes, ma'am." Victoria swallowed, so in awe she could hardly breathe.

"She came to us looking for a likely young woman to round out her team, and both Dr. Vidal and I agreed that you would be an excellent choice."

Exhilaration burst forth and Victoria felt almost dizzy. Of all the VADs in the hospital, they had selected *her*. Victoria imagined herself as a proverbial Florence Nightingale—Eleanor had the book *Notes on Nursing* by Miss Nightingale, and though Victoria, who far preferred her novels and poetry, had only skimmed it, she thought going to the front sounded incredibly exciting. "Thank you, Nurse Baxter. Thank you, Dr. Vidal." Victoria had a difficult time even forming the words.

Katherine Furse smiled. "They have told me your knowledge of plants and healing herbs is second to no one's and you have a wonderfully sunny attitude, which I'm afraid you might find tried at the front. But they have also told me something which concerns me a bit."

Victoria's heart sank. They found out about her internment at Holloway Prison. They wouldn't take her because she had been so very stupid. Would her foolishness follow her around for the rest of her life?

"They told me you suffer from chronic asthma."
Victoria closed her eyes for a moment.

"I don't wish to take someone if it will compromise her own health. Plus, we will not have the time nor the resources to care for you."

"You won't have to," Victoria burst out. "My asthma is mostly controlled. I have a nebulizer that works very well when I have an attack, and I have learned how to lessen the number of attacks I have with herbal teas and tinctures." She looked from Nurse Baxter to the doctor and back to Dame Furse.

Victoria swallowed. It was so important that she say this properly. "I spent much of my childhood bedridden with my asthma. I worked very hard to become healthy and have learned how to take care of myself. I've also worked at not allowing asthma to define who I am. But in some ways it has. I am much more conscious of what it's like to be bedridden because of my experiences. So while I don't like to think that asthma formed me, it did. I am a better aide because of it."

She could say more, but kept her mouth shut. If they didn't understand after all of that, there was nothing she could do.

"Very well put, Miss Buxton. I think you'll do just fine. Can you be ready to leave for France within a week or so?"

Victoria felt a surge of triumph as well as a wash

of nerves. *I am going to nurse in France!* "Of course."

Dame Furse took a packet of papers from a small leather valise. "Here is the paperwork, Miss Buxton. Please talk it over with your family and drop them off at the VAD headquarters by the end of the week. We need to get you processed as quickly as possible." She handed the papers to Victoria and held out her hand. "Welcome aboard, Miss Buxton."

Elated, Victoria shook her hand, then hurried up the stairs to the library to finish out her day. If only she could tell her father! He would be so proud of her. *Wait until I tell Kit. . . .* But then a sick feeling settled in the pit of her stomach at the thought of Kit. She shoved him out of her mind. It had been a week since she had sent him a letter, apologizing profusely and confessing her love for him for the first time. It seemed fitting to do it in writing, though she knew she was a coward for her inability to say it in person. She had yet to receive a response. He may not have gotten it yet. She clung to that hope, for there was nothing more she could do. Now she simply needed to focus on being the best aide she could possibly be. She had been given a way to make a real difference, and she couldn't squander it now, no matter how much her heart ached.

CHAPTER
ELEVEN

Dear Prudence,

I have decided the worst thing about the war is the absolute tedium of my daily routine. Don't get me wrong, I enjoy working with the horses (though I've decided that mules are just about worthless), but my routine is the same day in and day out. In reality, I am little more than a glorified stableboy in a uniform. I shouldn't complain, but it's a little hard to think that my former unit is out doing something while I do nothing.

Prudence bit her lip at the implied criticism. Andrew hadn't mentioned her actions since he'd left, and he'd dutifully written to her once a week to let her know he was safe, but he did include little jabs such as this one to let her know he had yet to fully forgive her. It always hurt, but she would take the pain as long as he was safe. His anger was bearable as long as he was alive.

She blinked back the tears once more at the way they'd left things between them and continued reading.

I enjoy the camaraderie of the other men and sometimes we play cards into the night. It's better than trying to go to sleep listening to the distant artillery and mortars at the front. If you didn't know better, you would think it was thunder, except for the sure knowledge that legions of men on both sides are being blown to bits.

I am sorry, my dear, I shouldn't share this with you in your condition. I pray you are healthy and well. Take care of yourself and baby Horace.

Love,
Andrew

Disappointment flooded through her at the matter-of-fact tone of his note. Absent were the words of love that had filled the letters he'd sent to her from training, an era that now felt so long ago. Now he told her of his trouble with the horses and his boredom. Occasionally a personal thought on the horrors of war would come through, but other than for his admonishment to take care of her health, he might have been writing to his mother.

She was alone and with child and she needed his love to sustain her now more than ever. She laid her cheek against the paper and tears came to her eyes. She missed him so. She just wanted things to go back to the way they were before.

Inside her the baby turned and a bittersweet happiness rose up. She had done what she could to make sure their child would be raised with both parents. She placed her palms against her stomach in wonderment. This child would be loved.

Bringing out her stationery box, she sat back down at the table and chewed on her lip. Thus far, her notes had been conciliatory, but not overly so. Maybe she needed to be clearer. Maybe her subtlety was lost on him.

My darling Andrew,

Thank you for your notes. I look forward to your weekly letters more than anything and I am often overwhelmed with joy when one comes in the post.

You would laugh at how plump I am getting. I think your baby wants to come from my belly fully grown or at the very least ready for nursery school. At this rate, I will be as large as a house by the time he is born. But I have seen a nurse and she has proclaimed me as healthy as the horses you care for, so please don't worry yourself on that score.

But now I must bring up something unpleasant. I have avoided it thus far because I felt I should only give you words of encouragement while you are away, but I find I cannot avoid it any longer.

I know what I did, and by that I mean, asking for someone to intervene on your behalf, seems as if it were underhanded and sneaky, but trust me, my darling, it was done out of love. What would happen to me or your child should something happen to you? Can you imagine little Horace never knowing his father? I don't say this to tug on your heartstrings, but to let you know my motivations, because such a thought almost broke my heart and I knew I must do whatever I could possibly do to prevent it.

I know and understand your assertion that other women are losing their husbands and other children are losing their fathers because they don't have contacts to pull strings to keep them a little safer. I understand your feelings that this is not fair, but my love, I don't care. Maybe that is unpatriotic of me, but though I feel sorry for those women and children, their children are not Horace, and I could not bear it if our son did not know the warmth of his father's love. How could you expect me not to fight for our child and our future children as you wanted to fight for all of England's children?

And how can you hold such feelings against me?

Please, my darling, cease your coldness against me and offer me forgiveness and words of love. If not forgiveness, please tell me you understand why I did what I did. It would mean so very much to me to know that your love for me has not been lessened, even if your trust in me has.

Your loving and faithful wife,

Prudence

Wiping her eyes, she folded the letter and put it in the envelope. She knew it was rambling, certainly not the finest prose the world had seen, but she'd done her best to let him know how she felt without backing down from her decision to step in on his behalf. Because she would never apologize for trying to keep him safe.

Restlessly, Rowena wandered the halls of Summerset, wishing she hadn't let Sebastian and Mr. Dirkes talk her into taking a break. They both claimed she was working too hard and insisted, claiming that no one benefited from an exhausted pilot at the helm of such valuable machinery. So here she was, once again idle in her own home and hating every minute of it. Idleness only reinforced in her that in spite of her newfound happiness, her life was still missing something. With an intuition that was foreign to her, Rowena was convinced that it wasn't a man she missed, it was Prudence. But whenever Rowena thought about actually trying to remedy the situation, her stomach twisted into knots at the fear of rejection. And Prudence had every right to reject her.

So Rowena prowled the halls looking for something to keep her hands and mind occupied.

Aunt Charlotte had tried to interest Rowena in doing calls with her, but hadn't insisted when she'd refused. Aunt Charlotte seemed to understand that with an engagement and her new employment, Rowena had grown beyond the confines of paying calls.

Even Cousin Elaine seemed to be bucking her mother's authority and had gotten out of calls by claiming she was ill. Her mother's mouth had puckered as if she had sucked on a particularly sour lemon, but she hadn't insisted. It seemed that even life at Summerset wasn't immune to the changes that war had brought to Britain.

Elaine came up behind Rowena and slipped her arm through hers. "Remember the fun we had last Christmas? Do you remember the firecrackers?"

Rowena smiled, remembering how the Coterie had fanned out and lit dozens of firecrackers in the grand ballroom at the very moment the Christmas-tree lights were flicked on. The ensuing mayhem amongst the gentry in attendance had been priceless. Then she sighed. "I wonder where everyone is now."

Elaine echoed her with a sigh of her own. "I know that Kit, Seb, and Colin are all safe. I got a letter from Colin just yesterday, and he told me that both the Harris boys were killed at Ypres. You didn't know them well, but they went to prep school with Colin and Seb and attended several of the Summerset hunts. Colin sounded rattled. I guess you never get used to losing friends so suddenly, even when you're constantly surrounded by death. . . ." Elaine shook her head, as if to rid her mind of such gruesome images. "You know about Edward, of course. Victoria said he is about to be sent off to France again."

"Victoria should be arriving in Calais today. She won't be able to tell us where she's at. Just somewhere near the front." Rowena asked, "Are you sure you don't want to come riding with me?"

Her cousin shook her head. "Thank you, no. You love riding much more than I do to want to ride in November. I won't be taking to the saddle again until spring has sprung." Elaine waved her off.

Rowena had sent a note to Cristobel yesterday and hoped the girl would be able to come out today. Rowena didn't know when she would be back at Summerset and wanted to find out how the girl was faring . . . and perhaps how Jon was faring, as well. She thought of that emotionally turbulent afternoon often and still found it all as utterly confusing as she did then.

She and Sebastian had had a wonderful day at Brighton sightseeing and had toured the aquarium, played in the deserted arcade, and eaten fish and chips in the streets like urchins. He didn't mention their previous conversation, but instead showed her what their life together might be like.

It warmed her heart that he was giving her so much room to breathe despite that she could at any moment trample on his pride—or his heart. She couldn't deny her affection for Sebastian, but her feelings for him still didn't match the passionate love she'd felt for Jon, as violent and devastatingly painful as that love had ultimately been.

But what if Jon could truly offer himself to her? Did he even deserve another chance after all he'd put her through? *No, he does not.* Nor could she trust him again the way she once had. So what was to stop her from giving her heart to Sebastian, who deserved it so fully? She shook her head, wishing she knew the answers to her questions.

Frustrated, she spurred her horse into a gallop, trying not to look at the ridge where she'd met Jon after his aeroplane crashed.

She guided her mount over a fence and splashed across a stream. She slowed when the barn came into view. Cristobel loved to gallop, and Rowena wanted to give her horse a chance to breathe before what would no doubt be a hard ride.

Rowena raised her hand in a cheerful greeting, but faltered when she spied Cristobel's tear-streaked face. Her heart slammed against her chest. "What's wrong?" she cried, reining her horse next to Cristobel's.

"George was killed in Ypres. We just got word."

Thank God it wasn't Jon. Rowena tried not to let the relief show on her face. For Cristobel, who had already lost so much, losing her brother had to be devastating. "Oh, my dear, I'm so sorry. How is your mother?"

"She is holding up. Being brave." Cristobel sniffled. "It's just made worse because William is already in France and they sent Samuel to Africa and Jon . . ." The girl stopped and Rowena couldn't help herself.

"And Jon?" she prompted gently.

Cristobel's mouth tightened and she nudged her horse into a walk and Rowena followed.

"Jon came home last week. He asked his commanding officers to send him to France. He says he can't train people to go die any longer and wants to go fight. Mother begged him to reconsider, but he was adamant. He said he could check on William that way, but he's just so angry all the time now."

Cristobel glanced over at Rowena, but Rowena wouldn't meet her eyes. "I'm sorry." Rowena didn't know what else to say.

Cristobel looked down at her hands. "What if they all die? What if it's just Mother and me left at Wells Manor forever? How could I ever get married and leave her?"

"I'm sure that won't happen."

Cristobel nodded, but looked unconvinced. The reports on the war were grim, and the major battles left few families unscathed.

Rowena's stomach clenched. Who would be next to join the swiftly mounting body count this wretched war had already claimed? Sebastian or Jon? She knew she couldn't ever be with Jon again, but still, she couldn't see a world without him in it.

CHAPTER TWELVE

Victoria walked through the hospital, trying not to stumble from sheer exhaustion. Dame Furse apparently had the inhuman ability to stay awake for days on end without the need for sleep, but Victoria felt as if she had been awake for weeks. In reality, they had landed in Calais yesterday afternoon and had taken a train into Beauvais just last night. They'd had to wait for several hours for the train because the one they were supposed to take had been conscripted for military use. Victoria had half expected they would stay overnight in Beauvais after a day of travel, but it wasn't to be. They had then climbed aboard a transporter wagon and rode a number of jolting miles to Chantilly, where the hospital was located. Now, instead of showing them where they would be staying, Dame Furse had one of the French nurses give them a tour of the hospital.

Victoria glanced at the four other women who were also on Dame Furse's VAD team. Two were older women and two were about Victoria's age. They all looked just as drained as she felt.

The hospital had hastily been built just outside Chantilly proper. It comprised half a dozen buildings with wooden floors, canvas walls, and tin roofs, none of which kept the cold out. Victoria shivered in spite of the woodstoves burning every twenty feet or so. They had gone through four of the buildings, each set up almost identically. As far as Victoria could tell, they were distinguished according to the wounds the soldiers in each had sustained, but she was too fatigued to be sure.

"Do you have any questions?" the French nurse asked in heavily accented English. She glanced at her wristwatch, clearly wishing she were somewhere else.

"Just one," said the Yorkshire VAD on Victoria's right. "Where are our beds and bathrooms?"

Victoria barely refrained from applauding.

The nurse laughed. "Not here, silly goose. You will be staying at a boardinghouse in Chantilly. You won't live here . . . it will just feel like you do. Come. Let us go see your boss. Perhaps she will take pity and take you to your beds, *oui*?"

Oui, oui, please, Victoria thought. They sat on a bench as Dame Furse and the head of nurses talked. After one of the women fell asleep sitting upright, Dame Furse finally seemed to notice the state of her contingent. Victoria thought she spied disappointment cross the handsome older woman's face, but couldn't be sure. Was the woman even human?

They piled into a wagon that took them and their luggage back into Chantilly. It would be the only ride they would get to and from the hospital unless they could beg one off the soldiers going in those directions. Otherwise they would be expected to walk, no matter what the weather. The walk wasn't so bad, less than a mile, and Victoria had often walked twice the distance to Nanny Iris's home, but never after working a ten-hour shift.

She had a fleeting impression of a clean, rather cramped home turned into a boardinghouse by an enterprising Frenchwoman, before she was shown to a small room with two beds a mere twelve inches apart. She would be sharing with the young Yorkshire girl who had spoken up at the hospital. Victoria couldn't remember her name and was too tired to care. After washing up in a small communal bathroom down the hall, Victoria collapsed on her bed and fell asleep fully clothed.

It seemed only minutes later that Victoria was

awoken by a loud rapping on the door. She sat upright and blinked. Her neighbor squealed, rolled out of bed, and got stuck in the narrow pathway between their beds.

"Breakfast in ten minutes!" a voice called.

Victoria wanted to cry.

After fishing the Yorkshire girl out from between their beds, they reintroduced themselves and took turns in the bathroom. Because both of them were still in their uniforms from yesterday, they made it downstairs on time.

The boarders were each given a large, round bowl of coffee with thick cream and a warm piece of bread with butter and jam. Victoria wolfed it down and, after wrapping herself in her coat and scarf, followed the other drowsy women out the door and down the road.

"How did I get here?" she whispered to herself as she and her roommate, Gladys, trudged down the road.

"I keep hoping I will wake up and it will be just a bad dream," Gladys whispered back.

"Hush, girls," Dame Furse said from in front of them. "You must never forget that we're in a war zone."

That snapped Victoria to attention. The reality of the past twenty-four hours stood in stark contrast to her romantic expectations. What was she doing in a war zone? Why had she thought this would be a great adventure? She was no wiser than the young men she'd met in the hospital in London who told her they'd had dreams of honor and glory as she dressed the stumps of their missing limbs.

The routine of the hospital wasn't much different from what she had done back home. The similarity calmed her anxiety, and soon she was laughing and joking with the patients. Those who were able to muster a laugh. Some just stared at the ceiling looking at no one and nothing, and her heart ached for whatever their empty eyes were seeing. Others spoke nonstop about their experiences at the front, and Victoria's stomach turned at the images they invoked, of tripping over scattered body parts in the field, of gut-wrenching dysentery, and of grown men crying out at night, racked by nightmares and over-whelmed by their own mortality. By noon, her feet ached and her mind was spinning. She walked two tents over to the mess hall, more eager to sit down than she was to eat.

Gladys was already seated when Victoria went through the line and got her food. The soup looked watery and smelled strongly of onions and garlic, but was served with a generous hunk of bread. Balancing the soup with the bread on top with a cup of strong coffee, she joined Gladys at the table. Gladys's eyes were puffy and red and she stared at her soup with distaste.

"Are you okay?" Victoria asked.

Gladys shook her head and took a deep breath. "I was assigned to triage, and the men were coming in straight from the field hospitals." She paused and Victoria saw her battling tears again. When Gladys got herself under control, she continued, "I can't believe anyone survived the ride in. Limbs looked as if they'd been sawed off at a woodmill. There was so much dirt. So much blood. I was cutting clothes off of men."

Gladys fell silent and stared at her hands. Victoria wrinkled her nose at her own food, her appetite diminishing. Instead of picking up her spoon, she put her arm around Gladys. "I'm so sorry. Do you want to trade assignments?"

Gladys shook her head. "No. They'll be reassigning us every day. I don't want Dame Furse to think I can't deal with the work. If we work out well, then they'll be bringing in more VADs to help the nurses. From what I've seen, they can use all the help they can get out here."

"I've noticed that, too. They do seem to be shorthanded." Victoria prayed she, also, could handle all the jobs she was assigned, physically as well as psychologically. So far she'd survived a grueling morning without so much as a sign of a breathing episode, but she knew that some of the horrors these nurses were exposed to left mental scars much deeper than any physical wound ever could.

She was given the opportunity to prove that she

could rise to any challenge the next morning when she was assigned to triage. According to the nurse in charge, the fighting had slowed because of the bad weather, but was heating up again as both sides wanted to get their last licks in before the holiday. Horror crawled over Victoria's skin like spiders as a wave of wounded were brought in. These men had not only been injured but had suffered from exposure to some kind of poisonous gas that Victoria was unfamiliar with.

"It's xylyl bromide," one nurse said grimly. "The Germans have started shooting grenades loaded with it into the trenches. It burns the skin, as well as the eyes and throat. So far, the blindness it causes has been temporary. Treat the skin like you would any burn, and place cold compresses over the eyes."

Horrified, Victoria swallowed hard and did as she was instructed. Her mind could hardly fathom a world where men would toss canisters of poison gas at one another.

Victoria was aghast at the steady stream of casualties that passed through the triage tent, but she soon tucked her shock—and her modesty—into the far reaches of her mind as she cut clothes off men and washed their open wounds. At moments, though, she couldn't keep her revulsion at bay and had to retch into a bedpan set to one side just for that purpose.

She soon forgot if she had even washed her

hands between one patient and the next, and in all the filth she wondered if it would make much of a difference anyway. What was an actual field hospital like if the patients were coming to her in this condition?

One man was so still she wondered if he was even alive. His face was black with dirt and smoke and his leg was missing below the knee. Pieces of shrapnel peppered his ribs.

The nurse took one look and shook her head. "I don't know how these men survive. They have to really want to live to endure this. Wash him up, and if he's still alive when the doctors are ready for him, we'll take him into surgery." She nodded toward the pack that had come in with the solider. "See if you can find out who he is and fill out some of the paperwork before we take him in, all right?"

Victoria nodded. She cut his pants off his body, her stomach churning at the look of his leg. Helplessness swept over her. She poured alcohol over the wound and he didn't even flinch. As she sponged off his face, she frowned. He looked familiar. Could he be a member of the Clever Coterie she hadn't known very well? Her cousin Colin had so many friends . . .

Once she'd done everything she could for him, she knelt next to his cot and rummaged through his pack. Most of it was army issue, but then she found a picture that had been folded and creased.

She unfolded it and stared, confused, at the pretty, dark-haired woman who stared back at her so somberly. It took her a moment, but then she cried out and clapped a hand to mouth.

Prudence.

Victoria stared at the man who lay so still before her. Andrew. It was her best friend's husband whose life was ebbing away.

No. Oh, no.

She leaned close, her heart pounding in her ears. "Andrew, you must hear me. It's Victoria. You are going to make it. I am going to take you to Prudence, I swear. You have to hold on."

She took his hand in hers and called for the nurse. "This is my sister's husband," she cried out, her voice cracking in her frantic desperation. "We have to get him into surgery right away."

The nurse put a hand on her shoulder. "As soon as the doctors are finished with the surgery they are working on, we will get him in."

Victoria nodded shakily. She knew they couldn't get him in any quicker. She only prayed it would be quick enough.

Rowena grabbed her satchel from the motorcar and waved her driver on. If she was to be truly independent, she would have to learn how to drive. But Mr. Dirkes had kept her so busy she hadn't had the time. He had opened another plant near Surrey, and both factories were now running at full capacity. She was making aeroplane runs all over England. She hadn't run into Jonathon again, but heard about him via the military grapevine. According to gossip, which was surely as popular a pastime among soldiers as it was with Aunt Charlotte and her set, he was known for his fearless flying, and between him and his gunner, they had shot down four German aeroplanes. Rowena tried not to think of what else the gossips said—that as reckless as Jonathon Wells was, he would either become an ace or get killed before the spring.

She waved to a couple of the other pilots coming out the door. Mr. Dirkes was right. As more military and political heads saw for themselves just how valuable aeroplanes were to the war effort, demand had increased. They were sending their own pilots to pick them up because Rowena and the other pilots couldn't keep up with demand.

"Where are you headed?" she called as they passed.

"Across the Channel," one of them called back, and Rowena frowned. That was new. They usually flew the planes to the main naval ports and the boats ferried them across. The fighting must be heating up if they were flying them directly into France.

Mr. Dirkes was on the telephone when she walked into the office, and he waved at her to sit. She took the wooden seat across from his large, cluttered desk. Photographs and pencil drawings of aeroplanes in various stages of production decorated the walls. Books of all sorts were stacked haphazardly on every available surface. His office might look cluttered and disorganized, but Rowena would bet that he knew where everything was.

He hung up and smiled. "You're always a sight for sore eyes, Miss Rowena. Like a breath of fresh air."

Her eyes narrowed. "You're being especially nice today. Why?"

"I'm always nice to you, my dear. Besides, I feel bad to have called you out on Christmas Eve. You should be at home attending balls or whatever you posh bastards do on high holidays."

Rowena smiled at his jovial bluster. "Christmas is a sad affair this year, I'm afraid. No one is much in the mood for making merry with Victoria and Colin and most of our friends gone." She changed the subject. "Where are you sending me now?" She held her breath praying he wanted her to fly across the Channel. She had yet to fly over water and longed for an opportunity. For Rowena, flying over the Channel had become a personal test of her piloting skills. It was also an indicator of Mr. Dirkes's confidence in her.

His tone changed from teasing to brisk. "I'm actually going to need you to make several runs in a very short amount of time. You'll get Christmas and the day after off, of course. But we're going to be running you nonstop after that."

She straightened. "Where to?"

"Here."

Her eyes flew open. "What? I'm confused."

"The Germans have been putting a great deal of pressure on our transport ships. They've sunk two in the last several weeks—both were transporting aeroplanes to France. We're bringing aeroplanes from our western naval bases back here and then flying them to France. As you know, pilots are in short supply so I am going to need to step up your schedule."

She nodded, excitement running through her. "Of course. When will I be taking them across the Channel? When we have them all assembled here?"

He shook his head. "No, lass. I'm not sending you into France. The crossing is too dangerous."

She stiffened. "What do you mean it's too dangerous? I'm one of the most experienced pilots you have left."

"That's not the point."

"Then what is the point? You're always saying adapt or die—"

"It won't do you any good to use my words against me! I'm not about to risk your life."

"But you'll risk the life of other pilots? And you know very well I'm risking my life every time I fly."

He shook his head, and Rowena's chest hollowed with disappointment. "I'll not do it. I believe in women's suffrage more than most men and you know it, but I'm drawing the line and there's nothing you can say."

She knew there was no use in arguing. He wasn't going to let her cross the Channel. Even though she knew it was childish, she crossed her arms and glared. She couldn't help it. She'd proven her worth and her skill, and yet she was still being held back because of her sex. She'd never been as militant about suffrage as Victoria, but for the first time she had a real grasp on where the anger stemmed from.

Rowena knew she could cross the Channel. She'd even flown over Ben Nevis once. The air currents of the Channel couldn't be any trickier than those of that mountain, for God's sake.

"I'm going to have Albert pilot you to Liverpool. It'll be faster than driving. Of course, you won't be able to sleep much this way . . ."

His voice held a question and she nodded firmly. "I'll be fine."

He sent her to their navigation man, who already had the flight charted for her. "You shouldn't have a problem as long as the weather holds," he said in a thick cockney accent. "Be careful crossing the Central Plains. The wind could get tricky."

She nodded and joined Albert, who was preparing for their flight.

"You got everything?" he asked.

She nodded and tucked her hair back into her flight jacket before putting on her leather helmet and goggles. He helped her up into the plane, touching her no more than necessary, reminding her of those fools back at the barn who had given her such a hard time. She'd never told anyone how they'd treated her. Somehow the entire incident shamed her, as if it were her fault, even though logically she knew it wasn't. It just seemed best if she tried to put it out of her mind.

The aeroplane took off smoothly, and Rowena found herself relaxing in a way she couldn't when she was doing the flying. Albert turned the nose of the aeroplane in the direction they would be going for almost four hours. The iciness of the wind took her breath away, and she was doubly glad for the thick wool that lined her leather jacket and the scarf she had wrapped securely around her neck. Rowena wasn't often in the front of the aeroplane as a passenger, and she settled back to enjoy the novelty of flying without responsibility.

Albert kept below cloud cover for quite some time, so Rowena watched as the artificial shapes of London gradually changed to a patchwork quilt of fallow fields, farms, and villages. When a strong wind caused the aeroplane to pitch, Albert climbed upward, and Rowena's view of the world turned gray and misty. Her anticipation built as they climbed, and when the mist began to sparkle and clear, she wanted to cry out in exultation. She would never tire of the miraculous moment of clearing the cloud cover into the wide-open blue. The experience reinforced why she loved to fly.

The rest of the flight passed quickly, and she was soon getting ready for her own flight back. She'd never been to the Liverpool Naval Base before, so Albert stuck close to her, and no one gave her any trouble. She was both grateful for and annoyed by his presence—grateful that no one dared to question handing a valuable BE2 over to a woman and annoyed that she needed a man by her side to do a job she was fully qualified for.

Rowena did a quick inspection of the BE2 and nodded at the soldiers helping her. Albert had just taken off and she didn't want to linger. If the weather was going to change, it would do so in the late afternoon, and she wished to be as close to Kent as possible. She didn't want to be out after dark anyway. She'd done it once before, but didn't much like it. Landing almost blind was dangerous.

By the time she finally got the aeroplane in the air, Albert was a speck in the sky. She shrugged. Fine, if he wanted to race so badly, she would just let him win; she wasn't used to the BE2 but she liked the way it felt. The wing warping gave it positive control, but its response time was a bit slower than that of the SPAD. But what it lacked in acrobatic prowess, it more than made up for in solid grace.

She hoped the winds would remain calm. Flying a new aeroplane through a storm would be perilous, even for her.

The first leg of the trip went smoothly. She kept the aeroplane low, unsure as to how it would perform at higher altitudes and unwilling to take a chance with the weather so erratic.

The wind picked up over the Central Plains, and worry knotted in the center of Rowena's stomach. By her calculations, she wasn't even halfway to Kent and the sun was sinking fast. Either that or the clouds that had blown up were obscuring it. It began to sprinkle, and soon the rain was whipping her face. She was going to have to land some-where soon. . . . She kept wiping her goggles, but still had trouble seeing. It looked much as it did when she would go bathing at the shore as a child. She had to land immediately.

Afraid that she was going to run into a hill if she flew straight along the ground, she kept the aeroplane going in smaller and smaller circles until she wound her way to the ground. Her visibility increased and she breathed a sigh of relief. She could see no trees.

The wind was worse the closer she was to the ground, and it buffeted her aeroplane back and forth. She fought to keep the machine from overturning. This close to the ground, if she caught the wind under a wing wrong, she could be slammed into the earth. Sweat trickled down her forehead in spite of the chill creeping through her body and numbing her fingers and toes.

Rowena had always known in the back of her mind that flying was dangerous. Aeroplane crashes were common, though in many cases the pilot was able to glide the machine close enough to the ground so as to avoid sustaining life-threatening injury.

But not always.

The largest threat came from hitting obstacles as one landed, such as trees or buildings. Suddenly, for the first time since she'd first installed herself in a cockpit, that threat felt all too immediate.

But she couldn't let her confidence waver. She had to get the aeroplane safely to its destination. Dirkes was, for the most part, a modern man, but he wouldn't hesitate to take her off the roster if she wrecked an aeroplane, Rowena reminded herself. Not only was it a valuable piece of machinery bought and paid for by the Crown, but his sense of protective chivalry would kick in and he would ground her for her protection. She'd be damned if she was going to lose everything now. Not after she had worked so hard to win the respect of Mr. Dirkes and the men in his employ, and especially not after she'd achieved a level of self-respect that buoyed her spirits. She could never return to her old life now that she'd experienced what it was like to have a real purpose, to rise to a challenge and face it head-on, to awake in the morning ready for tasks infinitely more consequential than dressing for luncheon.

The ground had never before rushed up to meet her so quickly. Her stomach flew up into her throat, and the landing jarred her so badly she cried out and bit her tongue. Hard. The taste of fear and blood filled her mouth as she brought the aeroplane to an abrupt halt. She sat in the cockpit, battered by the wind and rain, her heart pounding in her ears.

As she slowly caught her breath, relieved to be on the ground despite how harsh a landing it had been, it dawned on her that she was still in danger and could die of exposure if she didn't find some kind of shelter.

She looked around but saw only empty space. No trees or rocks to huddle under, thankfully. Had there been a tree . . . she shuddered to think about it. Briefly she thought about seeking shelter under the plane, but quickly discarded that idea. An idea came to her and she grabbed her valise and left the cockpit and made her treacherous way to the passenger pit. It was directly under the upper wings and therefore more protected against the elements.

Taking her long driving coat out of the valise, she scooted as far down onto the floor as she could and draped the coat over the top of the pit.

The material wasn't waterproof, but it was heavy and would hopefully keep her dry for a bit.

Not that she could be considered dry by any definition. Keeping the coat from blowing off with one hand, she pulled her wet goggles off with the other. She dropped the goggles to the floor, but left her leather cap on to help keep her warm. Still holding her driving coat in place with one hand she felt into her valise until she found her change of clothes. She wiped her face with her linen blouse, then stuffed it down the front of her leather jacket to help insulate her body.

Reaching back into the valise, she then took the extra skirt and wadded it up to make a pillow. Tucking one side of the coat under the pillow, she laid her head against it to keep it in place. With one coat arm tied around one of the rigging wires, it kept out the wind and the rain.

At first she shook with cold and fear as she thought about how close she had come to crashing the aeroplane. Soon, however, her body heated the small space and she was, if not warm, at least not quite so chilled. As she subtly rocked herself back and forth to keep warm, she couldn't help but let a troubling thought creep into her mind: *What would Victoria do if I died?* It was just the two of them now that their father had died. They had Aunt Charlotte and Uncle Conrad, of course, but just as Summerset, no matter how beloved, could never replace their Mayfair home, their uncle's family could never replace their own little family. She, Victoria, and Prudence were the only ones left that remembered what a happy house they had been raised in.

Prudence.

Rowena's heart ached and her cheeks heated with shame as she once again thought of how she had treated Prudence and how she was still taking the coward's way out by avoiding her. She knew Prudence was angry, but wasn't facing the conflict and being yelled at better than losing her sister? She resolved to go to Prudence the next time she was in London and beg her forgiveness. Prudence might never absolve her, but at least she would have tried.

Rowena felt as if a weight had been lifted off her shoulders. Closing her eyes, she settled herself more comfortably against the seat and waited for the storm to pass.

CHAPTER THIRTEEN

Prudence went about her morning chores, her heart as heavy as her steps. Instead of spending the holidays with a loving husband, she was alone, wondering if her husband still loved her or would ever forgive her. Muriel and Katie had invited her to spend the holiday with them, and rather reluctantly she'd agreed. She almost felt that she should stay home alone, that she should be punished for what she had done—as if not hearing from her husband for weeks now wasn't punishment enough.

But finally she decided to join Katie, Muriel, and their borders for a festive, albeit feminine, Christmas. She planned on going over as soon as she finished the washing. No one else in the building would be doing their clothes on Christmas, and she would have the basement to herself.

As always, the dank basement gave her chills, and doing the wash drove her wild with impatience. She couldn't imagine what it was going to be like to add nappies. She prayed that before she had too many more children they would be able to hire some help.

Her stomach tightened. If her husband returned from the war.

She pored over the newspaper obituaries with the morbid fascination of a hypochondriac studying a pharmacopoeia. She cringed whenever she read the names of young men she had known growing up. She wondered if they had married and what their deaths would mean to their families.

Pushing her morbid thoughts from her mind, she rinsed the wash and ran it through the wringer. She consoled herself with the knowledge that at least Andrew wasn't on the front. He was as safe as he could possibly be, given the circumstances. Prudence rolled the items into small wet packets and put them all in her laundry basket. Going up and down two flights of stairs took a lot more of her energy than it used to.

She climbed the stairs, mindful of her steps. She wasn't too large yet, though it did look rather as if she had a rugby ball under her skirt, but her balance was off and the last thing she wanted was to take a tumble down the stairs.

Once back in her flat, she strung the line across their small living area and added a bit more coal to the fire. Prudence was to bring a plum pud for dinner, but knowing her rudimentary cooking skills, Muriel had instructed her to buy the pudding premade and simply boil it at home. After checking to make sure plenty of water was in the pot, she walked to the window and stared down at the street. Occasionally, a motorcar would pass, probably taking its occupants to a family holiday feast somewhere.

Restlessly, she drummed her fingers against the cold glass, wondering why she felt so jittery. She blew on the window, watching it fog up and then disappear as the room grew warmer. Even though she'd originally been relieved to have somewhere to go for Christmas, now she found herself wishing she could just stay home.

You're just being contrary, she chided herself. The pregnancy was doing it to her. She looked down. "Stop it, Horace," she told her rugby ball. "You're not even born and you're making your poor mama cranky." She caressed her stomach lovingly. "I'm sorry, Horace." She sighed. "None of this is your fault."

A posh motorcar rolled up in front of the greengrocer below her flat, and she watched it curiously. Surely the driver knew that stores were all closed today?

A woman stepped out and Prudence gave a small, joyous cry. She'd know Victoria's diminutive figure anywhere. She was about to turn away from the window when a wash of cold swept over her as if she'd been caught in an ice storm. She knew something was wrong by the way Victoria's fine head tilted to look up at her window. Prudence swallowed and raised a hand before turning toward the door.

What was Victoria doing here? Last she'd heard, Victoria was going to be spending the holidays in a hospital in France. Had she returned early? If so, why wasn't she at Summerset with the rest of the family?

Rowena.

Prudence's stomach dropped. Rowena had probably crashed in one of those stupid aeroplanes she was always flying about in. Why had such reckless folly even been allowed? But more important . . . why had Prudence been so hard-hearted? What if she never had the chance to tell

Rowena that she loved her, in spite of being so angry with her? Because she did love her, of course she did.

She reached the door just as Victoria stepped onto the landing. Panic tightened Prudence's throat at the sight of Victoria's white face and worried blue eyes.

Prudence's hand fluttered to her throat. "Is it Rowena?" she asked in a whisper.

Victoria shook her head. "Oh, my dear, you are going to have to be strong."

Prudence clutched at the doorjamb, not wanting to hear whatever was going to come out of Victoria's mouth next.

"It's Andrew, he's—"

Prudence screamed and black spots erupted in front of her eyes.

"No!" Victoria cried out, grabbing hold of Prudence.

Prudence let Victoria lead her to the chair next to the stove. Clutching Prudence's hand, Victoria said urgently, "Don't panic, Pru. He's alive, but just barely. He'll be all right . . . eventually."

Prudence collapsed into the chair and closed her eyes as she clung to Victoria's hand. He was alive. That was all that mattered. "You said *eventually*. What is wrong? Where is he? This wasn't supposed to happen! Not in the remount depot." She looked at Victoria, begging her to say differently.

"I'm so sorry. He volunteered to take a string of mules to an encampment near the front. An enemy scouting group must have stumbled right over him."

Prudence's heart chilled as she imagined the scene in her head. "He was shot?"

Victoria nodded. "Several times."

Prudence whimpered. "How badly?"

Victoria didn't mince words. "It's bad. He was shot in the side, but the bullet went straight through, thank God. It was the other wound that almost killed him."

Prudence strangled Victoria's hand with her own and waited.

"Be strong, Prudence." Prudence breathed in deeply. "Andrew lost his leg."

Dizziness overcame her and she shut her eyes, strangling a scream about to erupt once again. If she started screaming, she didn't know if she would ever stop. Everything they had worked so hard for was gone. How could he be a veterinarian with only one leg? Teach Horace how to play ball? He'd lose his job at the docks, at the very least, although she realized that there had never been a guarantee it would be waiting for him when he came back from the war.

She put her hands over her face and wept. Her fault. All her fault. She had interfered and look what had happened. She had manipulated fate. This was God's way of punishing her, and poor

Andrew had to suffer for it. "Where is he now?"

"He is at the hospital where I worked before leaving for France. I had to pull some strings to get him in because it's for officers, but I think it's the best place for him."

Prudence's head jerked up, her heart pounding. "He's here? In London?"

Victoria nodded. "Yes, I've come to fetch you. He needs to see you. He's not well."

Prudence stood. "No, of course not. But he'll be fine?"

"The doctors say so, but . . ."

Prudence stiffened. "But what?" What else could there possibly be?

Victoria hesitated. "It's going to be a long recovery. Both in body and in spirit."

Prudence nodded. It would be fine. As long as she could be with him, he would be fine. He was alive, and unlike so many other men with lesser wounds, he wouldn't be going back to the front. "Can I see him?"

Victoria nodded. "My driver is waiting outside to take us to the hospital."

Prudence rose to get her things, but then froze as her baby fluttered inside, as restless as his mother.

"Are you all right?" Victoria asked anxiously.

Prudence bit her lip and nodded. "I think so."

She buttoned her coat tightly and added a scarf. Just before she walked out the door, she took the pud off the stove. She would send word to Muriel and Katie later. They would worry otherwise. Her mind took care of all these details, but inside, her grief raged like a storm and the hands that picked up her handbag and locked the door so carefully behind them wanted to pound on the wall in desperation like a child.

Calmly, she followed Victoria to the motorcar and climbed inside. Calmly, she asked the right questions concerning his wounds and his recovery. Apparently, Victoria had found Andrew quite by accident when he was coming in from the field dressing station. He had burned with fever from an infection in his leg. They had thought he wasn't going to make it, but he had rallied and pulled through. As soon as he was strong enough to move, Victoria had made all necessary arrangements and asked for and received permission to travel with him. He was, after all, her brother-in-law. She grinned at Prudence when she said this, but all Prudence could muster in return was a grateful squeeze of Victoria's hand.

The drive to the hospital passed in a blur, and it seemed to Prudence as if only moments had passed since Victoria had stepped out of the motorcar and looked up at Prudence's window. The hospital neighborhood seemed familiar, and seeing her quizzical glance, Victoria nodded. "The Bronsons lived near here. We used to go bicycling with the Bronson sisters, remember?"

Prudence remembered, but that wasn't it. The

connection came to her and her cheeks burned with shame. Near here, she had run into Sebastian, and after some angry words he had kissed her and she had let him, even though she had been married to Andrew. It had never happened again and would never happen again. In fact, that incident helped her realize how much she truly loved her husband.

Who was at this very moment lying in a bed, missing his leg.

As they walked through the mansion-turned-hospital, she reminded herself not to break down in front of her husband. *Be brave,* she told herself. *Don't let him see your horror, or how over-whelmed you feel at the prospect of caring for both a new baby and an invalid husband.* She just wanted to show him how much she loved him and how sorry she was that her actions had led to this unspeakably horrible fate.

The room Victoria led her into looked as if it had once been a music room or perhaps a sitting room. Seeing the iron beds and the bedpans against the red-and-gold silk wall coverings was obscene.

And then she saw nothing except Andrew. She wanted to scream his name and run to him, but instead walked sedately to his side. His eyes were closed and her heart wrenched to see how gaunt he'd become. His fine muscular body, honed by years of farmwork, lay wasted under the thin blankets. She tried not to look at the place where his leg should be. Her own legs trembled and she sank to her knees onto the floor next to the low bed. Gently, carefully, she traced the veins on the top of his hand. When he didn't move, she picked it up and pressed her lips to the palm, willing him to open his eyes.

Tears made a silent trek down her face and onto the bed as she waited, choking back her silent sobs. At last he awoke. His eyes were unfocused at first and then zeroed in on her. Her heart had fallen for the kindness in his hazel eyes before she'd even realized that she loved him. They regarded her now, fuzzy with pain and morphine, but they were still his. As he blinked his eyes into focus, they filled with tears and she pressed his hand against her damp face.

"Look at the pair of us, turning on the waterworks," she said, trying to force a laugh into her voice.

He shook his head a bit and managed weakly, "I'm . . . sorry. For this. This wasn't in our plans."

She gave a sob. "Oh, my love, the plan was for you to come home alive, and that you have done."

"But not all of me."

His voice, ragged with grief and anger, was almost unbearable to hear. Prudence's stomach clenched.

Victoria set up a screen around his bed, but it gave them only the illusion of privacy. Prudence realized their conversation could be heard by the other men in the room and she dropped her voice.

"Your heart is unharmed and you have two arms to hold me and our child." She tried to be firm and practical, but a tremor shook her voice. His eyes searched her face and she met his gaze. He must not see that she was as horrified and heartbroken as he was.

He broke from her gaze and stared at the ceiling. "Whoever heard of a one-legged veterinarian?"

She swallowed back her tears. "You're only missing part of a leg, my love, and we'll cross that bridge when we come to it. Right now, we have to get you well and healthy, so you won't miss Horace's entrance into the world."

His eyes softened at the mention of their baby, and she filed that away. If talking about their baby made him feel better, she could use that to motivate him to do the hard work of getting healthy and learning to live with his infirmity.

His eyes fluttered and she knew the visit had tired him already. She leaned forward and kissed his forehead. A ghost of a smile crossed his face as he put his hand gently against her belly. Again her tears arose, but she blinked them back. "I'll be back after you've had a bit of a rest, all right?"

He nodded, lines of weariness creasing his face.

Victoria poked her head around the screen, her eyes damp as well. "The doctor wants to see you before you go."

Prudence squeezed Victoria's hand in gratitude

and love. Thank God Vic had been there for Andrew. Thank God. Otherwise . . . no, Prudence wouldn't allow herself to even consider what could have happened otherwise.

She let herself be led into a small drawing room that hadn't been changed since the home had been converted into a hospital. The walls were papered in blue with a pattern of white velveteen fleur-de-lis. A heavy, gilt mirror hung above a white-marble fireplace so draped in royal blue velvet that Prudence wondered how they built fires in it without setting the whole house ablaze. French period furniture stood stiffly around the room, making Prudence curious about the people who'd lived here. Were they really so in love with French revivalism or did they just have terrible taste?

"Here." Vic handed her a warm, damp cloth. "You can clean yourself up a bit."

Prudence gave a wobbly smile. "Do I look that bad?"

"Ah, Pru, you could never really look bad." Victoria tilted her head sideways. "All right, you do look rather like a wrung-out mop, but an attractive one nonetheless."

Prudence gave a halfhearted laugh, and satisfied, Victoria set off to find the doctor. Prudence stepped in front of the gilt mirror and stared at herself. Her red-rimmed eyes and nose sat in a face swollen with pregnancy. Victoria was wrong. She looked horrible. She wiped her face and repinned her hair as best she could without a comb. The door opened behind her and Vic introduced her to Dr. Sanborn, an older gentleman with silver-white hair and mustache. Instead of a white coat he wore an open black jacket with an old-fashioned watch chain strung across the vest.

"It's very nice to meet you, my dear." His eyes fluttered momentarily to her waist and then back up to her face. "Please take a seat. Miss Buxton, could you please bring Mrs. Wilkes and me some tea?"

They sat in two rather uncomfortable chairs set in front of the fireplace. "My apologies for the chill of the room. We always seem to be a bit short-staffed. I usually like to have a fire going for the families and visitors. It makes a room so much cozier, don't you agree?"

Prudence opened her mouth to answer, but the doctor was off again, talking at a brisk pace that made her feel as if he brooked no nonsense. Of course, he was probably used to dealing with hysterical relatives and was giving her no chance to respond that way.

"Besides his obvious injuries, your husband was also beset with an unusual fever. At first we thought it was from the infection in his ankle, and indeed it was horribly infected, but once that cleared up, he kept spiking odd cyclic fevers. Our only thought was he contracted some sort of strange virus that we were unaware of."

Prudence licked her suddenly dry lips and wished Vic would hurry with the tea. "Is it gone? The fever, I mean?"

"It seems to be. He hasn't had one in over a week."

A thought struck her. "Why wasn't I informed of his injuries? I know he had to stay in France until he was strong enough to move, but it seems I would have received some sort of notification."

The doctor shrugged. "I think you should ask Miss Buxton. Perhaps, considering your condition, she wished to be with you when you learned the news."

Prudence nodded. That sounded like something Victoria would do.

"Now about his other injuries, I know it's difficult for you to comprehend his luck at this point, but because he lost the bottom half of his leg, the knee joint is completely functional."

The doctor beamed at her as if he had just given her a gift, and Prudence shook her head in confusion. "I don't know what that means."

"It means that he will have the ability to bend his leg, Mrs. Wilkes. With the advances they are making in prosthetics, he will be able to walk much more normally. He may not even have to use a cane once he is used to the prosthesis. He will always have a limp, but he'll be able to walk much more normally than if the cut had been made above the knee."

Prudence wanted to share his enthusiasm, but her insides were so knotted, she could only nod.

That seemed to satisfy him. "His prognosis is good, but much depends on his attitude. And unfortunately, what we have seen from many veterans missing limbs is that they tend to slip into a type of despondency. It's important to keep his spirits up. Physically, he is going to be weak for quite some time, so I don't imagine he will want to start on working with his prosthesis until he is stronger. Probably not until March at least. He will be fitted then."

Prudence took a deep breath digesting that. "How long will he be in the hospital?"

"Let's just take that a day at a time, shall we? It's difficult to tell. If all goes well, I would hope to have him home by February. He'll see a specialist before he leaves. Don't worry, he is going to receive the best of care, it has all been arranged."

Her mind spun at this new reality. Doctors, prosthetics, specialists. This was going to cost a fortune. How much would the army pay? Then what the doctor said sank in and she frowned. "What do you mean, it has all been arranged?"

He looked puzzled. "The Buxtons, of course. Lord Summerset sent a note saying all expenses concerning Andrew Wilkes were to be forwarded to him."

Shock swept over her and her chest tightened so

much she couldn't breathe. She gasped for air and the doctor leapt to his feet. "Mrs. Wilkes? Are you quite all right?"

Prudence's head spun and she gripped the arms of her chair willing herself to stay upright. Closing her eyes, she did as Victoria always did when she was having an asthma attack—she counted to three and took little breaths. After a few moments of this she was able to breathe normally. Dr. Sanborn was holding her by both shoulders.

"I'm all right now. Thank you." Could this be true? What could provoke such a random act of kindness from the man who'd cast her out as if she were nothing but a reminder of his family's legacy of shame?

The doctor sat down, a concerned look on his face. "Has this ever happened before?"

Prudence shook her head.

"I'm sure this has been a shock for you, but because of your condition, I do worry. Taking care of an invalid is difficult work, and it may adversely affect your pregnancy. Do you have someone who can help you? Friends? Miss Buxton would be perfect, but she is scheduled to go back to France within the week. Is there anyone else?"

Prudence shook her head.

"You'll need to hire a nurse to help when he comes home. That's all there is to it. She doesn't have to be with you full-time, but you will need to get rest, Mrs. Wilkes, for the sake of the baby. If you like, I can send one of our nurses over a few times a week and bill Lord Summerset."

Prudence's stomach churned. "No. Thank you. I just remembered someone who could possibly help."

He nodded. "Very well, Mrs. Wilkes. Now would you like to check in on your husband once more before you leave?"

He rose and Prudence took that to mean that the meeting was over. She stood carefully and thanked Dr. Sanborn. Victoria came in and took Prudence back through the house to where Andrew still slept. She stood for a moment, watching her husband's still form. He had always been an active sleeper, moving his legs, tossing, giving the occasional snort. To see him lying there so still and white, his kind features hollowed out, only drove home how grave the situation was. She couldn't look at his missing leg. Her limbs trembled and she felt sick to her stomach.

She swallowed, nodded at Vic, and, taking a deep breath, turned away. She hated leaving him like that, but the doctor was right. She needed to think of herself, too. Besides, she very much needed to have an unpleasant word or two with Victoria.

CHAPTER
FOURTEEN

Victoria chattered all the way to the motorcar knowing that if she paused for a breath, Prudence was going to let her have it, and she could guess why. Dr. Sanborn had no doubt told her that Uncle Conrad was going to pay for all of Andrew's medical expenses beyond what the army paid for. Given their history, Prudence's pride likely made her bristle at this charity, despite how necessary it was. So Victoria chatted inanely, which seemed obscene considering they had just left Andrew lying so helplessly in that iron bed all alone.

Though Victoria wasn't an expert in pregnancy, Prudence didn't look well at all. Even before Victoria had told her about Andrew, Prudence had looked drawn and pale, and her eyes shadowed. Surely most pregnant women didn't look that way. Of course, Victoria hadn't seen many expecting women. Most women of her class entered their confinement about five months into their pregnancy.

As they climbed into the motorcar, Victoria, out of the corner of her eye, saw Prudence turn, her pretty mouth compressed into a flat, unattractive line. She probably wouldn't appreciate Victoria's telling her that when she made that face, she looked rather like a disgruntled parakeet.

Aware Prudence was about to talk, Victoria jumped in with "Are you hungry? Would you like to go to dinner?" Then it hit her: it was Christmas Day. "Actually, nothing is open. Would you like to go to Katie's house after all? I'm sure they wouldn't mind us being so late. Not after they learn . . . no? All right. We'll go to my flat then." She held up a hand to forestall Prudence's protests. "No, I'll not hear another word. You are not to be left alone. You are dead on your feet, and I believe Susie and Eleanor are both home so we'll make a real party of it." Victoria forced a smile.

She sat back suddenly, drained. The day was taking its toll on her, as well. She'd hardly left Andrew's side for the past two weeks, and all she could think of when she'd landed in England was staying upright until she found Prudence and took her to Andrew. The relief of finally achieving her goal had given her a burst of energy, but it was waning now and she was tired all the way to her bones.

Victoria leaned back and closed her eyes, hoping Prudence wouldn't chastise her too much.

"Victoria?"

She braced herself. "Mhmm?"

"Thank you for bringing him home to me."

Victoria's throat tightened. Without opening her

eyes, she held out her hand and Prudence reached for it. "Of course."

They rode the rest of the way home in silence. Victoria knew better than to think that Prudence had forgotten or that she wouldn't have to answer for her actions, but it seemed for now Prudence just needed her support.

The flat was quiet but warm when they arrived. Victoria hadn't come home after settling Andrew at the hospital; she had gone directly to Prudence.

"Susie?" she called. "Eleanor?" Victoria was desperate for Eleanor to take a look at Prudence and tell her if she looked as she ought.

Susie came rushing out of the kitchen and into the long hallway, her eyes saucer-round in her thin face. She was wearing a red dress, with short lace sleeves, and her hair was dressed in a softer fashion than she usually wore it.

"Oh, Miss Victoria! I didn't know you would be home today. Why didn't you send word, miss?" Her eyes slid back toward the kitchen.

Victoria saw Susie fidgeting and knew the girl was so flustered for some reason beyond Victoria's sudden arrival. She was just too tired to figure it out. "I didn't know when I would be back. What's going on Susie? Where's Eleanor?"

"Miss Eleanor said she was going to visit her mother after her shift, but that she wouldn't be too late. We decided to have just a simple Christmas supper of creamed haddock and mash. I can easily make enough for you and Prudence, as well. Though begging my pardon, Prudence looks as if she should sit down."

Victoria turned. Susie was right. Prudence was swaying on her feet. "Come into the sitting room," Victoria urged. "Please get a roaring fire going in the fireplace, Susie. I'll put a kettle on for tea."

"Oh, miss, that's fine! I can do both, really. You look all done in yourself. Just sit and I'll put everything to rights. I was just a bit taken aback by your sudden appearance, that's all."

Victoria frowned, but let herself be persuaded. She really was bushed. She collapsed in her favorite chair while Susie busied herself by fussing over Prudence. She tucked a throw over Prudence's legs and then grabbed another for Victoria. Victoria felt herself relaxing. Her father had always been ambivalent about having servants and had compensated them handsomely and treated them like members of the family. Victoria followed suit and, like her father before her, had been rewarded for her benevolence.

After starting a roaring fire, Susie disappeared to make the tea.

"How are you feeling?" Victoria asked Prudence a bit anxiously.

"Like I could sleep for a week. I may not make it back to the flat tonight."

"That's all right, dearest. You can borrow some of my nightclothes and sleep in the extra bed."

Prudence nodded. "Why did you do it, Vic?" she asked suddenly.

Victoria stiffened. Just when she thought she was going to avoid talking about it tonight. She took a deep breath. "I have a confession to make."

Prudence gave an inelegant snort. "I'll say."

"Hush now and listen!" Victoria frowned at Prudence. "Don't interrupt."

"I hardly think you're in a position to make demands."

Victoria kicked off the blanket wrapped around her legs, feeling suddenly overheated. "I'm going to go see what is keeping Susie with that tea." She beat a hasty retreat into the hallway, then froze. Susie was pressed against a man and kissing him with a passion that showed a certain experience. Victoria's mouth hung open. "Susie!"

Susie leapt away from the man as if he'd suddenly turned into a pillar of salt. "I'm sorry, Miss Victoria. I didn't know you would be coming home." She clapped her hand over her mouth as if she knew she'd said the wrong thing, and Victoria raised an eyebrow. "I mean, Gareth, Mr. Johnson, had no place to make merry, and since you were gone and Miss Eleanor was out, I thought, I mean . . ." Susie folded her hands and looked down at the ground. "I'm sorry, Miss Victoria."

"You should be," Victoria said.

"I'll turn in my resignation."

The man looked stricken, and Victoria turned

her attention from her maid and to the man standing in her hallway. He twisted his cap in his hands and appeared to be older than Susie by about ten years. He was small, barely taller than Susie, but stood erect. "What do you have to say for yourself, Mr. Johnson?"

He lifted his chin just a bit and looked her in the eye. "I'm only sorry for entering your home without meeting you first, miss. But I'm not sorry for kissing Suzanne, if that's what you're talking about. We haven't done anything unseemly. I love her and would marry her, if she would have me, but she keeps saying no, that she's too young to know her own mind and won't let me make it up for her."

Victoria blinked and Prudence came up behind her. "What's going on?" she asked bewildered.

Victoria waved a hand. "Ask Susie, I barely know myself."

Susie introduced her caller proudly, and again Victoria was impressed with his poise under extremely awkward circumstances. He turned to her. "I would hate for Suzanne to lose her position on my account, miss. My family lives in Yorkshire and she didn't want me to be alone on Christmas. She was just being kind."

"I wouldn't fire Susie for this, though I wish she hadn't felt it necessary to hide you. I was just thinking how wonderful she is and how lost I'd be without her."

For the first time a look of resentment came to his blue eyes. "I suspect you would do what other posh ladies do and hire yourself a new maid. But I'll be off now."

He nodded at Prudence and Victoria and squeezed Susie's hand. "I will see you next Wednesday evening like always."

She gave him a nod and he left.

"So that's what you do on your days off!" Victoria said accusingly. "You sly fox!"

Susie tried and failed to hide a smile, clearly pleased with her beau. Just then the teapot whistled and she waved Prudence and Victoria back toward the sitting room. "Go sit, I will bring us some tea and biscuits. You both look knackered."

They had barely resettled into their chairs when Prudence attacked. "You have a confession?"

Victoria sighed. She might as well come clean. "When you asked me to go to Colin, I didn't. I went to Uncle Conrad."

A look of hurt crossed Prudence's face and Victoria felt wretched. "Why?"

"Because you don't go to the flautist when you want a symphony, you go to the conductor. Uncle Conrad has more power and connections than Colin will have for years and years. I knew that he could get the transfer done, where Colin wouldn't be able to."

Prudence looked at her hands. "Oh, Vic. You know how he feels about me."

"And you know how *I* feel about you. You're a Buxton. Not only were you raised like a Buxton, but you have as much Buxton blood as I do."

Prudence shook her head. "That's not the way the world works. At least, not your world."

Prudence's words were as bitter as wormwood, and Victoria went to her. Kneeling next to her chair, Vic wrapped her arms around her friend. "It's not my world and it's changing, you know it is. Uncle Conrad bought Rowena an aeroplane. How much more proof do you need?"

Prudence laughed and sniffled at the same time.

Victoria tilted her head back. "Pru, he didn't even hesitate. Just said, yes, of course he would. And then when I wrote him about Andrew, he wrote back saying to send him any expenses the army didn't pay."

Prudence stared into the fire, and Victoria watched the light from the flames play across her fine features. "What am I going to do, Vic? Everything has changed."

Victoria laid her head in Prudence's lap. "You'll love and care for your husband and your baby the best you can, just like you would if he had both feet. And take one day at a time, just like the rest of us."

Victoria thought of Kit, fighting in some far-off place, and wondered if he ever thought of her. She wondered what would happen if he really was behind enemy lines as she suspected and

226

something happened. Would his family be informed? Would Mrs. Kittredge even think to tell Victoria if something had happened? Worry gnawed at her stomach. She still hadn't heard from him, which worried her even more. Kit wasn't known for his silence. Clutching Prudence's hand, she suddenly prayed with all her heart, *Please let him be all right*. Even if he hated her for the rest of his life. Even if he never spoke to her again.

Just as long as he is all right.

Please don't let our angry words be the last words we ever have.

Rowena stood in front of Mr. Dirkes. She knew she looked a fright, but she hadn't wanted to take time to clean up. In retrospect, she probably should have. She'd spent the entire night curled up in the aeroplane, and when the morning had dawned, bright and clear, she had flown back to the factory. Her clothing was wrinkled and damp, and her hair a tangled knot.

Mr. Dirkes took one look at her and began blustering, "Do you have any idea how worried we were about you when Albert showed up without you behind him? I was about to send out a bloody search party. What the hell were you thinking?"

She took a deep breath and remained calm. No doubt he spoke in exactly the same manner to his men. "I was doing my job, which was to bring the

BE2 back to you in one piece. I got a later start than Albert, and he must have missed the storm. I had no choice but to land somewhere and wait it out." She raised an eyebrow. "Unless, of course, you wanted me to risk bringing the aeroplane through the storm?"

His red face matched his hair, and he looked as if the vein in his temple were going to blow. "Don't be impertinent! Where did you stay?"

"In the aeroplane, of course. It was too nasty to try to find shelter, and besides, what was I supposed to do? Present myself on the steps of some stranger's house and ask for accommodation for the night on Christmas Eve? Not to mention leaving a valuable aeroplane unprotected for hours."

He scowled and Rowena hid a smile. She was far too reasonable, and it was annoying him. She crossed her arms and waited for a reply. This was almost fun.

"Fine. You should go home for Christmas. You've earned a rest, and I know my nerves have."

She tilted her head and gave him a saucy smile. "Aren't you going to tell me I did the right thing?"

"No!" he barked. "And happy Christmas!"

She laughed and held her arms out. "I'm perfectly fine, see? Now, don't we have more aeroplanes to move? Why are you sending me home?"

He slammed a fist on the desk. "Why can't you just do as you're told? I told you that I was giving you a couple of days off. Now, come along. I'm taking you home to be with your family. Come back the day after tomorrow and we'll finish moving the bloody aeroplanes."

She saluted him and he grunted as he grabbed his coat and a bag. He must be spending Christmas with the Wells family. She wondered if Jonathon was allowed home for Christmas but refused to ask. It was no longer any of her business, no matter what he'd said on that sidewalk in Brighton.

She settled back into Mr. Dirkes's Silver Ghost and closed her eyes. A rest did sound wonderful, and Aunt Charlotte and Uncle Conrad would worry if she didn't show up for Christmas supper. Of course, it would take them almost four hours by motorcar, and that was only if they didn't blow a tire. She'd barely get there in time to make herself presentable before supper.

Rowena woke up some hours later, groggy and disoriented. At some point Mr. Dirkes must have stopped and tucked a driving blanket around her because she was warm even in the chilly car.

"I thought you'd gone and turned into Sleeping Beauty," Mr. Dirkes said.

"Where are we?" she asked, looking around. The sun was low in the sky, and barren, twilit fields surrounded them.

"About an hour on the other side of Cambridge. It won't be long now."

Rowena stretched and rubbed a hand over her face. Every muscle in her body ached from her night in the aeroplane, and falling asleep in the car hadn't helped. Her hair stuck to the side of her face, and she was fairly sure she had never been this long without brushing her teeth.

Mr. Dirkes handed her a flask and a cheese sandwich. "I didn't think to bring water, but the brandy should cut the thirst. Probably do you good, but don't tell your aunt and uncle."

She took a long pull off the flask and gasped a bit at the burn. "Thank you." She smiled at the shock on his face.

"Well, now, you are a pilot, aren't you? No, keep it," he said when she tried to hand it back to him. "You need it more than I do."

She took a hungry bite of her sandwich. "I don't know when I ate last."

He grunted. "You better start taking care of yourself, missy. Jon will kill me if anything happened to you."

The bite of sandwich stuck in her throat and silence fell between them. "Jon and I haven't been together for a long time, Mr. Dirkes. I'm engaged to someone else, as you well know."

"Huh. So you both say, but I know how he feels about you, and I can't think as your feelings have changed all that much, no matter whom you're engaged to."

He sounded cross and Rowena was silent for some time before answering, "I don't know how much you know about what happened between us, but Jon left me, not the other way around. I was shattered. Sebastian helped me put the pieces together, and I'm not likely to turn my back on that, and I have learned to love him very much." Tears pricked at her eyes, but she knew it was true.

Mr. Dirkes reached over and patted her hand. "I'm sorry, lass. I shouldn't have opened my big mouth. Please forgive me. And after the mess I've made of my own life, I'm the last person who should be handing out romantic advice so freely."

Rowena turned to look at him in the darkening motorcar. "You've never married?" She'd always wondered about Mr. Dirkes's being single. He seemed like the kind of man who should have a family of his own.

He shook his head. "No. I lollygagged around, and by the time I was ready to ask my love to marry me, she had gone south on a visit and ended up marrying an Englishman."

So there *had* been a romance in Mr. Dirkes's life. "She never came back?"

"Oh, she came back some years later with three strapping lads and about to issue another. It was clearly too late by that time."

Her heart felt bruised and tender for this kind

man who spent so much of his life alone. No wonder he lavished attention on Jon and his siblings and treated her like one of his own. A suspicion came to her and she mulled it over while she finished her sandwich. Finally she turned to Mr. Dirkes and asked him point-blank, "It was Mrs. Wells, wasn't it?"

He was silent, and though she could no longer see his expression, she knew she was right.

"I love her still," he said softly. "That's why I never married. I couldn't settle, you see, for someone who would only be second best."

Rowena felt the gentle rebuke and said nothing as they turned into Summerset's tree-lined drive. "You should ask her to marry you now. It's not too late."

He chuckled. "Don't think I haven't thought of that myself, lass."

They pulled in front of the entrance to Summerset and Rowena handed him the flask. "For courage. And good luck."

He took it and nodded. "I'll be back day after tomorrow to pick you up." He paused as Rowena gathered her things. "It's not too late for you either, you know."

She smiled as she climbed out of the motorcar and didn't answer. Instead she just said, "Happy Christmas, Mr. Dirkes." Then she turned toward Summerset.

CHAPTER
FIFTEEN

Aﬆer Mr. Dirkes drove away, Rowena snuck around to the servants' entrance. If she could possibly manage it, she was going to sneak up to her room without being detected and ring for a servant to draw her a bath. Even though the plans for the evening were far simpler than in previous years, Rowena knew that Aunt Charlotte's closest companions would be there in force. They should still all be dressing for dinner, a tradition that was becoming as scarce as men under thirty.

The servants' entrance led down under the great house where the wine cellar, servants' hall, kitchen, pantry, and the butler's and house-keeper's offices were located. The predinner bustle of the kitchen reached Rowena as she tiptoed down the long hallway past the various doors on either side. Her stomach rumbled at the scent of roasting meat and freshly baked bread. Even a world at war couldn't halt the steady array of delicacies coming from the Summerset kitchen.

She and the other girls had often come down here when they played hide-and-seek or to escape the heat. Not until she was older did she realize how much the servants disliked their trespassing on their domain.

"Miss Rowena!" Mr. Cairns's voice could not

have been more shocked than if he had found the Queen sneaking past his office.

By his voice, Rowena knew she must look much worse than she thought. She gave the Summerset butler a sheepish grin. "Good evening, Cairns. Could you please have one of the maids run me a bath? And have someone inform Lady Elaine that I am up in my room. I want to surprise my aunt and uncle when I appear for supper."

The butler sniffed. "Very well, miss. Do you need someone to help you dress?"

She shook her head. "Lady Elaine will help me."

As she started to move, a gentle cough stopped her. She turned back. "Yes, Mr. Cairns?"

He nodded toward the servants' stairs, and she gave him a conspirator's smile. "Thank you, Cairns."

Rowena slipped up the stairway and poked her head out into the hallway. The coast was clear and she hurried down the hall to her room. Sighing, she took off the men's patent-leather shoes she wore whenever she flew. It was much easier to work the pedals in them than in any of the heeled shoes she usually wore, and dancing slippers weren't practical—her feet would freeze at that altitude.

With a knock on the door a maid Rowena hadn't before seen came into the room carrying a tea tray.

"Mr. Cairns said you might want some tea while waiting for your bath?"

"Yes, thank you, you can put it over there." Rowena nodded toward a small table in front of the small, white-marble fireplace. She handed the maid her jacket.

"Would you like anything else, miss?"

"No, thank you. Oh, wait. I'll need my clothes laundered and pressed by tomorrow night." The maid nodded and went to start Rowena's bath. With distaste she kicked off the split skirt she'd been wearing for over forty-eight hours. Aunt Charlotte had had bathrooms installed in all the family bedrooms and several of the guest bedrooms. Summerset had been one of the first country houses with both electricity and central heating. As traditional as she was, Aunt Charlotte did love her creature comforts.

Rowena sighed with relief as she slipped into the hot water. She'd like nothing better than a good long soak, but knew that she was already going to be late joining the others in the sitting room.

"You do like to cut things close, don't you, Cousin?" she heard Elaine say as she came into the room. "You do know Mother is already fit to be tied because Victoria isn't coming for Christmas. I think she would have had an apocalyptic fit if you hadn't shown up."

Elaine's hands were on her hips. She was already dressed for dinner in an intricately whorled and beaded black gown with short lace sleeves. All of England, it seemed, was now in mourning and everyone wore black.

"Well, I haven't shown up yet. Still have to dress and do my hair without collapsing. Could you please pick me out something to wear? Something simple with no corset."

"Well, aren't you the rebel? First you take a job flying aeroplanes and now you've tossed your corset!"

Elaine winked and then her eyes went wide. "Good God! What happened to your shoulder?"

"What shoulder?" Rowena looked down and gasped. The pale skin of her upper arm and shoulder had turned a brilliant shade of purple surrounded by an evil-looking black. She wiggled it back and forth and winced. She was so sore all over she hadn't even noticed.

"All right," she said, "the dress must also hide that. I don't want to tell your parents I hurt myself making an emergency landing and spent last night by myself in a field."

Elaine's eyebrows skyrocketed upward. "You do lead the most interesting life," she murmured, leaving the room.

Rowena certainly did. But it was far, far better than the gray sadness that had marked most of the past year. At least now she was doing something.

She finished washing and rinsing her hair and climbed out of the tub. She dried off quickly and took another towel for her hair. The maid had started a fire.

Elaine shook Rowena's underthings at her. "I take it you still want to wear a chemise, right? Or do you plan on going nude under your dress?"

"Maybe I am. When did you get to be so demure?"

Elaine laughed. "I choose my rebellion carefully, Cousin. I am only defiant when I'm sure Mother won't see me."

Rowena slipped into her lawn underclothes and shimmied into the fine lace dress Elaine had picked out. "She would see your bloomers maybe?"

Elaine snorted as she did up the long line of buttons in the back. "I wouldn't doubt it. I think she has the maids spy on me."

Rowena quickly began toweling her hair. "Does she really?"

"Of course."

"Whatever for? You've never given her reason to mistrust you, have you?" Rowena twisted her head to see her cousin's face.

Elaine smiled, a little grimly it seemed. "I had a bit too much freedom in Switzerland. Mother never got over it."

When they had dried Rowena's mass of dark hair as well as they could, Elaine ran a brush through it and twisted it back into a simple French roll. "There," she said, observing her efforts. "Now let's go, before Mother sends out a search party."

"Do they know I'm here?" Rowena asked as they hurried out the door.

"I'm sure Cairns has let them know by now."

When Rowena entered the sitting room, she saw that this was indeed the case. Aunt Charlotte, dressed completely in black, resembled nothing more than a spider lying in wait.

"Be careful," Elaine whispered with a smile curving her lips. "She's been in a foul mood all day. She can't reconcile herself to the fact that it's her least favorite child she has to spend Christmas with."

"Shhhh," Rowena said, before turning to face the room. "Aunt Charlotte! Uncle Conrad! Happy Christmas."

"I was beginning to doubt that you were going to make it, darling." Aunt Charlotte's cultured voice sounded brittle, and Rowena could see that worry over her son had left new wrinkles in her forehead and a tightening around her mouth that had never before been there. She kissed her aunt's cheek with renewed tenderness. No matter how frighteningly cold Aunt Charlotte could be, no mother should have to worry about her son in a far-off war.

"I would move heaven and earth to spend Christmas at Summerset," Rowena assured her aunt while kissing her uncle.

"Well, that is more than I can say for your sister, but then she always was a strange little thing.

Rather like a bird, always fluttering here and there. I actually would admire her passion if it wasn't so annoying."

Rowena raised her eyebrows. That almost sounded like a compliment. Of course, Victoria always dared more with her aunt than either Rowena or Elaine, and her aunt seemed to have developed a grudging respect for that.

"Of course, I am rather put out with her right now."

A footman balancing a silver salver offered Rowena a glass of mulled wine, and she took it with a smile. "And why is that? What has she done now? Last I heard she was in France?"

Aunt Charlotte sniffed. "Apparently not. She saw fit to accompany our former footman back to a hospital in London. I don't see why she couldn't make her way out here for the holiday, but obviously she would rather spend it in that awful girl bachelor flat with her new friends."

Rowena detected the hurt beneath the condemnation of her aunt's voice and shot her uncle a questioning glance.

Uncle Conrad cleared his throat. "Yes, I received word from Victoria that Andrew Wilkes had been terribly wounded and Victoria was bringing him to England, where he could receive better care."

For a moment the name didn't register, but then it came to Rowena in a rush. Prudence's husband.

"Oh, no. Poor Prudence. Is he going to be all right?"

Aunt Charlotte's face took on that faraway look that she got whenever Prudence's name was mentioned, but, shockingly, Uncle Conrad faced Rowena directly. "The doctors informed me that he will recover, though he took a direct hit to both his ribs and his leg. They had to amputate his leg, but the other wounds are healing quite nicely."

"Oh, there is Lady Asquith, I must go say hello. Her son is in the same regiment as Colin. She may have news." Without another word to either her niece or her husband, Aunt Charlotte took her leave with her head held aggressively high.

Rowena watched her aunt depart. "That's horrible," Rowena murmured, thinking of what Prudence must be going through. "About Andrew, I mean. I'm glad Victoria stayed with them. Prudence must be beside herself. She's with child, you know."

Uncle Conrad's face, so like her father's, with the Buxton green eyes and firm jawline, froze.

She didn't understand him. He had gone out of his way to tell her about Andrew, but at mention of the baby he grew stiff, reticent. Was it really because Prudence's mother had been a housemaid, or was it the reminder that his father had preyed on appallingly young, lower-class girls? Or was it his own discomfort that a line of the Buxton family had been besmirched with the blood of servants? Whatever it was, Rowena's stomach churned with the injustice of it all, and she leveled an accusatory stare at him. "Yes, you are about to become an uncle again. Congratulations."

With that, she went to greet Sebastian's mother. The rest of the evening passed in a blur. The festivities were muted, of course, and there was no ball. Few young men were left to man the orchestras, let alone partner with.

Rowena slept late the next day, missing breakfast completely. Elaine smuggled some food up from the kitchen and helped her dress so they could be downstairs in time for the annual exchange of gifts.

Unlike so many grand estates that were teetering on the edge of ruin, Summerset was practically self-sufficient. It had been blessed with a long line of heirs who were not only frugal, but had an affinity for business. Paired with a long line of equally sober-minded managers, Summerset not only paid for itself, but made a tidy profit and kept a small portion of England's economy solvent.

Though the tenants and townspeople had hated Rowena's grandfather and were only marginally warmer toward Uncle Conrad, they had few complaints about the fairness of their landlord. He treated them well, and so the tradition of handing out gifts to the servants, tenants, and their children continued. While the Buxtons might not always be charitable with their own blood, they certainly wouldn't cast aside a time-honored Summerset tradition. The tenant gifts—barrels of ale, salted herring, and hams—had already been delivered. Today, they would give out the gifts for the servants and hold the party for the children. Each child had already received one gift—a pair of new shoes—because Aunt Charlotte found it offensive to see children barefoot in the winter.

The great hall, which led into the grand salon, never failed to awe and inspire Rowena, who had a hard time believing it was in a private house. The domed rotunda of the great hall's entrance looked as if it belonged in some magnificent museum. The grand salon itself was decorated with gilded rosettes, silk draperies, and a stone fireplace so immense Rowena could stand upright in it.

When Elaine and Rowena entered the grand salon, Aunt Charlotte and Uncle Conrad had already taken their seats in front of the sparkling Christmas tree in front of the dormered windows. Because there had been no Christmas ball this year, the tree in the grand salon was their only one. Rowena had noticed that, contrary to custom, a tree hadn't even been set up in her bedroom. Summerset's holidays were marred by the grief of a nation this year.

The servants were already lined up in front of the doorway. They stood chatting and gossiping as Rowena and Elaine took their places. Their job was to pass the gifts to Aunt Charlotte, who would give the female servants their gifts, and Uncle Conrad, who was responsible for the male servants. Cairns and Mrs. Harper would be standing on either side of Rowena and Elaine to whisper the name of the next servant into their ears. It seemed more personal if each gift had been chosen with a specific servant in mind, as if the lord and lady truly knew and cared for each of their servants. In reality, everyone knew that the head housekeeper and butler had chosen the gifts, and they were the ones the other servants needed to impress.

Elaine helped her mother while Rowena handed gifts to Uncle Conrad. "James, second gardener," Cairns would whisper, handing Rowena a set of pipes and a small bag of fine tobacco.

"James, second gardener," she'd repeat in Uncle Conrad's ear.

"James!" Uncle Conrad would call heartily. "The gardens looked wonderful last year. Do you think we'll win the county floral competition again?"

"I believe we could, Your Lordship."

"Wonderful! Enjoy the tobacco. May you smoke in good health!"

And on and on until all the servants had received a gift and a small word of appreciation. "Why don't they just put tags on the gifts?" Rowena whispered to Elaine after the last gift had been handed out.

"Because Cairns and Mrs. Harper want everyone to know who's really in charge. Besides, as my mother would tell you, 'This is the way it had always been done and the way it will always be done.'"

The family took tea in the sitting room to fortify themselves for the children's party. Aunt Charlotte and Uncle Conrad would no doubt put in a brief appearance and then flee, so the family would be represented by Elaine, Rowena, and Colin's wife, Annalisa, who had arrived just before tea.

"You look lovely!" Elaine said as the three entered the grand salon for the second time that day. It was true. Annalisa wore a soft, rose-colored lace gown and had tied a matching ribbon around her golden-brown hair.

"Thank you, darling." Annalisa said. "I'll not wear black like I'm a widow. It would be like jinxing Colin's safety."

The room had been transformed by busy servants during the tea. All of the fussy art objects within reach had been put away, and several tables had been loaded with the sweets and drinks that children so dearly loved—tureens of hot chocolate, stacks of biscuits and shortbreads, marzipan animals, tiny almond cakes, and sugarplums. The tenants' children, who rarely got such extravagant goodies, would make short work of them, but Rowena knew more would appear as if by magic from the never-ending supply. The children were invariably sick after . . . the trick was to get them out of the house beforehand.

"I'm glad you are staying for a bit," Elaine said to Annalisa. "It's been horribly dull here. Rather like a daily wake. No doubt Rowena is leaving me again to risk life and limb flying those aeroplanes of hers." Elaine gave Rowena an accusatory glance.

Rowena smiled. "I leave in the morning. I think you can manage without me."

Elaine's face grew somber and she turned to where Mrs. Harper was opening the doors to let in the children. "I guess that's all any of us can do until this bloody war is over, isn't it? Manage."

Rowena agreed but was soon too busy playing games with the children to think sad thoughts. The children adored her, and when they clamored for her to be the blind man in blindman's buff, she laughingly consented.

"Now, don't you all leave the room and let me stumble about alone until supper," she warned.

They promised not to as she tied the blindfold around her head.

"Make sure you can't see!" one of the children cried out.

Elaine turned Rowena around and around until she was dizzy enough that when suddenly let go, she stumbled, much to the delight of the children around her.

Cries of "Over here!" "Over here!" surrounded her, and she good-naturedly careened about the room, banging her shins on various pieces of furniture.

When the room went suddenly silent, she stood with her hands on her hips. "Oh! So we're going to play it that way, are we?" She took a few experimental steps this way and that. A muffled giggle came from her left and she lunged toward it, running headlong into something both solid and yielding. She stopped and put out her hands, confused.

Robbed of sight, it took her normally quick senses longer to figure out what she was touching. Her cheeks heated when she realized her fingers were running across a muscular chest and broad shoulders. Whipping off her blindfold, she stared into Sebastian's dark eyes. Shock propelled her to throw her arms around his neck. He held her in his arms and bent his head in a hungry kiss.

A cheer went up all around them, and Rowena broke away. Ducking her head with embarrassment, she laughed. Elaine must have sensed her bashfulness because she and Annalisa took matters into hand.

"Time for musical chairs!"

The servants filed in holding straight-backed chairs in front of them. Sebastian led Rowena by the hand to a quiet corner. Turning, he took her other hand in his and beamed down at her, his handsome face alight with the success of his surprise.

"Happy to see me?"

"Of course!" And she was. Joy, unexpected and effervescent, bubbled up in her chest. "How were you able to get leave?"

"I volunteered to escort a contingent of politicals into Calais for a meeting with the French. The opportunity only was available to me because a member of the party was a friend of my father's. I have to be in London by midnight tonight."

"So soon?" Her heart sank.

He nodded. "We are leaving in the morning. The commander told me I was crazy, that I'd be better off getting some sleep and a good meal, but I wanted to see you."

She looked at him then, truly looked at him. His eyes were shadowed with circles and he was practically swaying on his feet from exhaustion.

"And you came here . . ."

His hands tightened on hers. "I would rather be with you than sleep any day, even if only for a few hours."

Across the room Elaine played a cheerful song on the piano, and the lilting melody matched the music in Rowena's soul. Tears rose to her eyes. Jonathon had walked away from her twice while Sebastian would make any sacrifice to be with her.

Her heart, which had swelled with emotion the

moment she took off her blindfold, no longer felt torn; she no longer doubted whom she loved and whom she wished to spend the rest of her life with.

"I love you, Sebastian," she said simply, staring into his eyes.

"I've waited so long to hear those words from you." He smiled. "And I love you, too."

He bent his head to kiss her, and Rowena met his lips, no longer caring who saw.

CHAPTER SIXTEEN

Prudence gave her flat another critical once-over as she waited for Andrew to arrive from the hospital. In accordance with the doctor's wishes, she was trying to rest more and had hired a woman to come in and clean the flat for Andrew's arrival. Victoria's driver would be bringing Andrew home, and Eleanor would stay with them for the first night. They had a hired nurse who would after that come twice a week until Andrew was doing well on his own. Then she would come back when the baby came to help Prudence with whatever needed doing. Prudence prayed she wouldn't need her for long. She hated knowing Lord Summerset was paying for expenses the army wouldn't cover.

Andrew had been fitted with a prosthesis, but it

wasn't as sophisticated as the one the specialist could get him. So far Andrew was being obstinate about ordering another one, so Prudence had ordered one behind his back. Prudence knew that it went against his grain to owe anything to his former employer, and while she understood the sentiment, it pained her to see him struggling with the rather crude device he'd been fitted with, especially compared with the light, perfectly balanced one the specialist had shown her. The new one wouldn't be done for several more weeks, so she had a bit before telling him she had hidden something else from him.

She swallowed and went to the small front room they grandly called their sitting room. In the month since Christmas, their visits, beyond that first one, had been strained. Prudence wasn't sure if it was because she felt so guilty about his injuries that she hid it by being unnaturally jolly, or if it was because Andrew didn't talk about much at all. The only thing that perked him up was mention of the coming child.

She spotted Victoria's motorcar coming down the street and wiped her suddenly sweaty palms on her apron before untying it and slipping it off. She had dressed carefully for this homecoming in one of the dresses she had worn at the Mayfair home. Rather out of fashion now, it was still pretty, made out of a fancy woven wool and sporting a double row of jet buttons down the front. But watching her husband being helped out of the car by the driver, she suddenly wished she had dressed in a simpler dress.

Moving away from the window, she stood, her hands clenched by her sides as she listened to the labored thumping of her husband coming up the stairs.

I will not fall apart.

When the rap sounded on the door, she took a deep breath, then held the door open. "Come in, come in, it's freezing out there! How was the ride?"

The driver nodded. "It's was fine, ma'am. Where would you like his things?" He stood on Andrew's bad side while Eleanor stood behind them holding his valise.

"Oh, I've got it. Do you want to sit in your chair, darling?" She smiled over Andrew's shoulder at Eleanor. "It's the ugliest piece of furniture in the whole flat, but it's his favorite and the warmest."

"It may be a bit difficult for him to get in and out of on his own for a bit," Eleanor said. "But I want you to know how to lift him properly until he is more confident on doing it himself."

"I'm right here," Andrew said crossly.

"I know you are, love, and when I want to talk to you, I'll address you." Eleanor gave him a cheerful smile. "I'll be talking about you a lot to your wife, so don't get snippy every time I do. Or get snippy if you must—Prudence and I will ignore you. Won't we?"

Prudence smiled uncertainly. "Would anyone like a piece of cherry tart?"

The driver shook his head. "I'd best get home. I will be back to pick you up in the morning, Miss Eleanor."

"Thank you, Pete. I appreciate it." Eleanor waited until Pete had left before addressing Prudence and Andrew. "Can you imagine having a driver at your disposal? Everyone in the old neighborhood thinks I am quite posh now." She laughed. "I guess I am at that!"

Prudence turned to Andrew. "Would you like a piece of cherry tart?"

"I'm not hungry."

Prudence's heart dipped with disappointment. She'd baked the tart trying to show him how much she had learned while he'd been away and had fussed over the stupid thing all day. Now he couldn't even pretend to want some? She shoved the thought down and gave him the best smile she could muster.

"Oh, don't be silly, Andrew," Eleanor chastised, her blue eyes reproachful. "Your wife baked a tart special for your homecoming. The least you can do is taste some."

"Lord, you're bossy," Andrew snapped. "And you're only insisting because you have never tasted my wife's cooking. But, fine. I'll have a piece."

"You don't have to have any," Prudence said, picking up the tart.

"Give us both a big piece of the tart, Prudence," Eleanor commanded. "And put some coffee on. You and I will need to stay up late tonight to talk about Mr. Grumpy here."

Both Prudence and Andrew stared at Eleanor until she laughed. "What? I worked in a prison for years. Victoria didn't tell you how overbearing I am? Just you wait. You'll be sorry for asking me to help."

Andrew gave a sheepish smile. "I'm sorry. I'm just out of sorts."

"Don't apologize to me, just eat the damn tart."

Prudence hid a smile as she made a pot of coffee and plated three healthy pieces of tart. She almost wished Eleanor were staying indefinitely. It would be easier to face Andrew with someone else around.

After they ate, Eleanor decided that Andrew must rest, and Prudence agreed. Her husband, though not as gaunt as the first time she'd seen him, looked worn and pale about the edges.

Eleanor gave Prudence a lesson in helping her husband from a sitting to a standing position. "Use your back not your legs," she instructed, making sure Prudence's arm was under Andrew's correctly. It was the most intimate moment they'd shared in a month, since she'd held his hand when they were first reunited at the hospital. Part of her just wanted to wrap her arms around him, and the other part shrank at the thought.

What was wrong with her? It wasn't even that he was missing a limb—she just felt so terribly guilty. It ate away at her insides, and if she were to hold him and be held by him, she might just fall apart at the seams.

And falling apart wasn't an option.

Eleanor helped Andrew get ready for bed, and by the time Prudence had done the dishes, Andrew was already asleep.

"He's going to be fine," Eleanor said, coming back into the room. "He will be able to do a lot more by himself than you think, though you are going to have to make sure he doesn't overdo it." Eleanor settled down into a chair with a sigh of relief. "I've been on my feet all day."

"I'm sorry. Thank you for helping us tonight. I feel guilty asking for your help after you've worked a full day already. I don't know what I would have done if you hadn't come."

"Don't worry about it. I'm happy to help. And we have a lot to go over, so don't thank me yet. Patients who lose limbs fall into two groups, those who become completely helpless, and those who do too much on their own and end up reinjuring themselves. I believe your husband is going to fall into the second camp. He won't want to ask you for help and will get cross when you offer."

Prudence poured them both a bit more coffee

and sat across from Eleanor. "Then what am I supposed to do?"

"I tell my other families to be patient with their patient, but in your case, I don't want you to be too patient. He simply cannot be allowed to give you too much grief."

"No, I don't mind, really," Prudence interjected, but Eleanor shook her head.

"It isn't good for the baby or for you." Eleanor leaned forward, her blue eyes alight with sympathy. "I know the story behind this, so I know you must be feeling terrible right now, but, Prudence, this isn't your fault. It is happening to men everywhere. The war is not your fault, and that is why your husband is in there right now without a leg. The war. Not because you were trying to keep him safe."

Prudence gazed down at her hands. Her thoughts spun around in her head accompanied by emotions so strong she could hardly make sense of them. "I understand what you are saying," she said slowly, trying to articulate what she was feeling. "It does make sense, but . . ." She hesitated.

"But you can't help feeling the way you feel, right?" Eleanor asked, her voice compassionate.

Prudence shrugged helplessly. "How do you make yourself stop feeling something? I can't help but feel that if I hadn't interfered, he might still be whole."

"Or he might be dead. Have you ever thought of that?"

An infinite sadness washed over her. "I think of it all the time. But I will never know, will I?"

Victoria watched the black French lorry pass by the window of her cramped room with the same sense of foreboding she always felt when she saw it. The long nose with the giant grille and the enormous rectangle of windscreen glass split down the middle made it look like an immense and predatory raven. Victoria murmured:

> *Caught from some unhappy master whom*
>   *unmerciful Disaster,*
> *followed fast and followed faster till his*
>   *songs one burden bore—*
> *Till the dirges of his Hope that melancholy*
>   *burden bore*
> *Of "Never—nevermore."*

That feeling was only exacerbated because its cargo consisted of dead soldiers, picked up at some French village that had been caught in the line of fire. Whenever she spotted the lorry with its sorrowful and macabre contents, a spurt of fear shuddered through her and she thought of Kit.

She still prayed for his safety every morning and every night. She knew he was still alive as Cousin Colin had mentioned seeing him in his last letter to her. She'd read the lines over and over: *Ran into Kit not long ago. We shared a drink in the officers' tent and he asked after you and Rowena. He looks good, though thin, and is still as irreverent as ever.*

She'd been deliriously happy until she saw the postmark and realized the letter had taken four weeks to reach her. So all she knew was that Kit had been safe at some point not too long ago. She didn't know for sure if he, or Colin for that matter, was still safe. The uncertainty—the constant wondering and worrying—was slowly fraying her nerves to shreds. She didn't know how much longer she could take it.

She longed to ask Colin if Kit had mentioned her letter . . . but she thought better of it. If Kit wanted to reach out to her, he would do so. She pulled the quilt from her bed and wrapped it about her shoulders. Coal was scarce, and the only time Victoria was warm was when she sat next to the stove downstairs in the common area or when she was at work.

It was her day off, but she would probably walk back to the hospital this afternoon anyway. What else were you supposed to do in a country besieged with war but help in any and every way that you possibly could, at every waking moment? She borrowed books from the landlady and wrote letters, but invariably she would find herself wandering back to the hospital to chat with the men, to pen notes for those who could not, or to recite poetry to keep their minds off their injuries. Gladys was on duty today, so she had the room to herself, which left her both frozen and quite alone with her thoughts.

Beneath her window, she spotted Gladys hurrying up the walk. Frowning Victoria threw off her quilt and hurried down to meet her.

"Is something wrong?" she cried, coming down the stairs. The hospital staff lived in fear that the Germans would reach their hospital and they would have to evacuate. No one really expected it this far from the front, especially since both sides were waiting until spring for a big offensive, but these were such uncertain times that Victoria was always on guard, expecting the worst.

Gladys's eyes widened. "Nothing. We got our mail early and I needed a break. I thought you might like your letters."

"Oh, thank you so much!" Victoria took the proffered bundle and then frowned at her roommate. "Are you all right?" Victoria worried about Gladys, who often cried herself to sleep at night and whose pretty mouth was constantly pinched together as if she had to work hard not to scream out loud.

Gladys nodded. "As right as I'll be until I'm safe in my own bed at home. Lord, I think I'll sleep a week."

"Do you want some tea or coffee before heading

back?" When Gladys shook her head, Victoria breathed a sigh of relief. She wanted to dive right into her mail.

"No, they'll be wondering where I am if I'm gone for too much longer. Are you stopping in later?"

Victoria nodded, and her roommate turned to make the trek back to the hospital. Victoria clutched her precious package to her chest, free to read her letters in peace. "Eloise, is there any tea or coffee?"

The landlady and her young niece were already busy in the kitchen making a meal for some of the boarders. The military people usually ate at the mess hall, but a handful of boarders in the huge house were not affiliated with the army, but rather were moneyed refugees who had fled the fighting. Eloise nodded toward the woodstove. "There is still some left from breakfast, I think. If not fresh, you tell me. I make more."

Eloise liked Victoria because they shared a love of books and Victoria could converse as easily in French as she could in English.

Victoria poured her coffee and sat at the long wooden table in the kitchen. The kitchen was typically French with white tiles on the floor, an enormous porcelain double sink, low, dark-stained beams, and whitewashed walls. It was the cheeriest room in the house, and Victoria far preferred it to the formal and rather dank sitting room the guests were supposed to use.

She looked through her letters, recognizing Elaine's neat handwriting and her aunt's flowery cursive. Then her heart thudded as she read the name on the third letter.

Kit.

She stared at the neat block letters, wondering why she wasn't ripping it open. It occurred to her that she was afraid of finding out what it contained. She took a sip of her coffee and discovered that her hand was trembling.

"Is the coffee good?" Eloise asked, handing her a letter opener.

Victoria blinked and stared at the opener blankly for a moment. "The coffee is fine, thank you."

Not yet ready to face the contents of Kit's letter, she avoided it as if it were a gun shell and took up Elaine's instead. It took her several tries to actually see the letters, but soon she could almost hear her cousin's sweet, carefree voice.

Dear Vic,

The holidays were grim and sad and rather gruesome as you can expect for such a time. Everyone tried to make merry and not talk about the war because there were so many women here—wives and mothers of soldiers either recently fallen or fighting on the front. But of course, that's what everyone was thinking about, so conversation not only didn't sparkle, it was as dull as lead. Understandable, truly, but still vexing when one remembers all the good times we used to have. Especially last year when you and Rowena were with us and all the boys were here. Remember the fight at the servants' ball? There was no dancing this year, or fun at all. Listen to me complaining while you are stuck in a hospital and our boys are fighting so bravely on the front. You will think me quite shallow, and that is not the case. Well, it is, but I am not as bad as all that . . . I just wish we could go back to a time where everyone was safe.

And I saved the best news for last. . . . I am going to be an aunt! Yes, Annalisa is expecting a baby. I should have known, she has been getting so round, but I thought she was just stuffing biscuits and tea cakes into her mouth because she was worried about Colin, and honestly, she has always been on the plump side. (Like I have room to talk!) But, no, she is going to have a baby and I will no doubt be punished for my uncharitable thoughts. But at least a baby is something to look forward to, and God knows we could all use something to look forward to. I think back on my life and have so many regrets and things I would have done differently had I only known the entire world was going to change in just a few short years. But there, I am getting melancholy and I am supposed to be cheering you up.

Just remember, I love you and think you are ever so brave. I wish I were half so bold . . . if I were, I would tell Mother to go rub salt and find something useful to do with myself. But I am not, so I will remain always your incredibly bored and frivolous cousin.

Elaine

Victoria blinked back tears. Poor Elaine. While Victoria was certain that her aunt loved her daughter, Aunt Charlotte was always so hard on her. She wondered if there was any way to persuade Elaine to move into the city with her when she was finished with her stint here. Probably not. Aunt Charlotte hadn't even let Elaine visit yet. Sooner or later Lainey was going to have to stand up to her mother. Victoria just hoped it wasn't when she was around to witness the inevitable fallout.

Still unwilling to face the letter from Kit, she reached for Aunt Charlotte's.

Dear Victoria,

As I am sure my daughter told you, the holidays were a poor imitation of the festive events we used to have, but unlike my daughter, I know what propriety is, and making merry when young men are dying is not appropriate. Elaine should be ashamed of herself for complaining, but what can one expect? She is as dizzy as you are but without your intellect.

Of course, I have to wonder about your intelligence considering your behavior over the holidays. You wrote and assured me that you would come to Summerset for Christmas if you could but absolutely could not leave the hospital. Then your uncle tells me that you took the time to accompany a former employee of ours to London and spent the holiday at your flat? What sort of nonsense was that?

I must tell you, my dear, I am rather hurt by your callous actions. Could no one else accompany a sick footman? Could you not spare the time to have your driver bring you to Summerset? If only for a few hours? It would have made your uncle and cousin very happy during this dark time.

There. I have said my piece and will speak no more about it. I just want you to think, my dear, how your actions are perceived by others, that's all. I would be remiss in my duties if I did not remind you of this.

I did want to let you know that I will be spending the next few weeks in London. We are opening up the house for a time. Colin may be getting a short leave, and it would be easier for him to see us in London, and my dear Annalisa misses him so. It only seemed fair.

Perhaps you could stop and see us when you are in London. If you are not too busy.

Love,

Aunt Charlotte

Victoria shivered and shoved the letter away from her. That woman was as poisonous as a cobra. And like a cobra, her beauty didn't make her any less deadly.

Victoria stared at Kit's letter, longing and fear warring in her heart. What if he told her he'd had enough of her? That she didn't know her own mind and he couldn't love anyone so indecisive. Oh, bother. She wasn't indecisive. She made snap decisions all the time, life-changing decisions. She just changed her mind often, given that she didn't always consider the consequences of her choices. He *knew* what she was like when he'd met her and had fallen in love with her anyway. Just as she knew he was vain, irreverent, contrary, and a horrible tease. It was no wonder it took her so long to realize that she truly loved him back—the man was an absolute wretch.

Angry with herself for her lack of resolve, she snatched up the envelope and tore it open.

Dear Victoria,

She sat the letter down and rubbed her eyes. That was not a good beginning. He called her Vic, kitten, minx, or little devil, but rarely by her given name.

Eloise poured her more coffee and gave her a worried frown. "The news from home, it is good?"

"Yes, everything is fine." Victoria smiled unconvincingly.

Eloise nodded and Victoria picked up the paper again.

Dear Victoria,

I have given much thought to our situation and have come to realize that much of the fault lies with me. You are right in that I did not take you seriously when you said you did not want to marry and I kept pressing you, thinking, in my vanity, that eventually you would acquiesce to my wishes. That I could bend your will. In doing so, I put at risk a friendship I greatly value and do not wish to lose.

So I am writing with an apology. I am sorry that I did not take your desires into account nor did I see the wisdom in your original assertion that we would no doubt kill one another if we were to be bound in holy matrimony. You are so very right, my dear friend. We were not meant to be married. A friendship such as ours does not come along very often and it should be valued. I did not value it, and in pushing for more, I put our relationship at risk and for that I am very sorry.

I would very much like to rekindle that friendship with no more declarations of love, etc. Please do not worry yourself on that score, as I have been courting someone else and, in doing so, realize that the relationship I have with you was indeed platonic.

So what do you say? Can we still be the very bestest of comrades or have I ruined that possibility forever?

Your friend always (I hope),

Kit

For a moment Victoria felt as if she had been frozen. Then the trembling began. It started in her stomach and spread throughout her entire body until her teeth were chattering. She had confessed her love and it was too late. He had found someone else. No doubt he was embarrassed by her declaration, and this letter was his charitable response.

"Are you quite all right, child?"

Victoria tried to nod, but was shaking too much.

"Come sit here. You are chilled. Bad news?"

Victoria nodded as her landlady moved her to a rocking chair next to the heat and bade her niece to get a throw from the sitting room. Once ensconced in the chair, Victoria was wrapped up and given more hot coffee. Her chest tightened and she braced herself for the shortness of breath to commence, signaling an asthma attack. But it didn't come. She concentrated, wondering why her chest hurt so badly when she wasn't having an attack. Then it came to her.

Her heart was broken.

CHAPTER SEVENTEEN

Rowena sat in Dirkes's office, drumming her fingers against the arm of her chair. He had bid her to wait while he spoke to the foreman. She hadn't been in an aeroplane for a week due to inclement weather, and now that the skies were clearing up, she was eager to get back to work.

Ever since his holiday visit to Mrs. Wells, Mr. Dirkes had been an entirely new man, and Rowena planned to capitalize on his good spirits to land herself back in a cockpit. Though he'd always been jovial, since winning Margaret

Wells's hand in marriage, his cheerfulness had reached new heights.

Rowena found herself torn between being happy for her dear friend and being envious of his uncomplicated, unadulterated bliss. She prayed Sebastian would get leave soon so they could be married. She was more than ready to get on with the next part of her life.

Restless, Rowena stood and went to the door. She poked her head around the corner and saw Mr. Dirkes walking toward her, the bounce in his step a tribute to his happiness.

He must have sensed her impatience because he asked quickly if she was ready to leave.

"You're the one who kept me waiting, not the other way around."

He nodded. "So I did, lass. Forgive me for that. They are all ready for you, now."

He seemed in a hurry now to see her off and Rowena frowned. "Where am I going? Am I delivering or picking up?"

"We have someone in the field waiting to take you to Southport now. You'll stay the night up there and bring back a SPAD in the morning."

She clutched her valise and followed him out into the massive hangar where the aeroplanes were being stored. She wondered if he ever worried about being attacked. If this hangar and the accompanying factory were ever taken out, it would definitely put a wrinkle in the war effort.

Out in the field a Flying Alice was running, and a wave of nostalgia came over her. The Alices that she and Jon had loved so much were almost old-fashioned now that so many advancements had been made in aeroplane machinery.

She waved at the pilot, already in his leather cap and goggles. She wondered if it was Albert or Chuck, who also ferried aeroplanes back and forth on occasion, then decided it didn't much matter. He waved back and bent his head to peer at the instrument panel. After she strapped herself in, she yelled good-bye to Mr. Dirkes, who had a curiously smug look on his face. Really, all this happiness was almost annoying.

She signaled to the pilot behind her that she was all set to go, and the aeroplane began moving across the field. Even though she was used to the bone jarring that came with taxiing across the field, she was always glad when the lift brought relief. She relaxed as the aeroplane ascended. The morning was clear and bright, no doubt one of those strange false-spring days that occasionally came in late February or early March and lulled everyone into sweet complacency before ending with an unexpected—and wholly unwelcome—snowstorm.

When the pilot behind her leveled out, she shut her eyes, wondering why Mr. Dirkes had her staying the night in Southport. They were getting such an early start, she was sure she could get back before nightfall. But then, he'd been extra-cautious about sending her out since her emergency landing.

The loud hum of the aeroplane had lulled her almost to sleep when the craft suddenly shifted into a deep turn. She startled and looked around, wondering what the pilot was doing. When he completed a circle and dove downward sharply, she grinned. He was taking advantage of the bright blue sky and unseasonable weather to play. She understood playing.

He then pointed the nose upward and increased speed until they were soaring upward, the wind chilling her nose and cheeks. The aeroplane leveled off, once again heading north in a sedate fashion; clearly they didn't have enough petrol to do any more tricks. She turned around to give the pilot a thumbs-up and froze at the cocky grin that greeted her.

Jonathon.

Her head swiveled back around, her heart beating wildly. What was he doing? What had Mr. Dirkes been thinking? Had he thought if he could just get Jon and her together that all would be forgiven? That her fiancé meant nothing? What a romantic fool.

She could feel Jonathon's eyes on the back of her neck, but she set her teeth and refused to look back again. She squeezed her eyes shut, wondering what she was going to say to him when they stopped and where they would spend the night. What was she supposed to do if Sebastian got wind of this? This would devastate him. No. She wasn't going to hurt him.

She tried to ignore the excited fluttering in her stomach and focus all of her energy on her anger. But she was once again flying with Jon, and her thoughts whirled around her head like frenzied snowflakes, disappearing when they hit anything concrete. Her neck clenched with the effort to keep looking ahead. She crossed her arms over her chest and forced her eyes closed. If this was how she had to sit until they reached their destination, then she would do it. And she wouldn't talk to him when she got there. She would simply stalk off the field.

Of course, he did go to a lot of trouble . . . and part of her couldn't help but feel thrilled with the effort he had put into getting her alone. She swallowed. No. She couldn't think that way.

Something struck Rowena in the back of the head and she jumped. She turned around and glared. Jonathon smiled and shrugged innocently.

She turned around again, her shoulders stiff in outrage. Something tapped the back of her head again, and she forced herself to remain still. The next time she was ready, and she turned, throwing her arm around to catch whatever he was hitting her with.

But instead of catching what turned out to be a

stick, she knocked it out of his hands, and it flew over the side of the plane. Aghast, they stared at one another, their eyes wide. An object traveling at a velocity like that could kill someone.

She looked over the side of the plane and was relieved to see they were over farmlands. But still, it might hit an errant farmer. She scowled at Jonathon, but his mouth was still agape, and in spite of herself she dissolved into giggles. He began laughing, too, though a bit sheepishly.

She turned back around. She might as well relax for the time being; it wasn't as if she could step off the aeroplane. Besides, they were nearly there now. By the time they began descending, Rowena had decided that, regardless of what Mr. Dirkes had been thinking, she had no choice but to calmly and firmly rebuke Jon.

Which would surely be easier to think about than actually do. By the time the Flying Alice had come to a complete stop, Rowena's stomach bounced with nerves that had little to do with their landing, made rough by a sudden wind. Confrontation had never been her forte. Hiding her head in the sand was much more her style, though admittedly it had never solved anything and often made things worse.

They taxied to a stop, and men came running out to meet them. Rowena had met them all before and they helped her down with pleasant but professional greetings. She waited until they had ferried the plane into the hangar before turning to Jon.

"Do you mind telling me what the hell this is all about?" she demanded. So much for calm and firm.

Jon took off his goggles and helmet and she did the same. "So you've taken up cursing now? Might have expected it since you spend so much time among men. Have you taken up smoking, too? What does your fiancé think about all this?"

Her mouth fell open.

Jon grimaced. "I'm sorry. That's not how I wanted to start out our conversation."

She stared at him, saying nothing. This was his doing. The burden of explanation fell on him.

"Look, Rowena, can we not do this here? Let's go get checked in at the inn and we can go for a walk or something."

"I certainly will not go to an inn with you!" How could he even ask? She swallowed. Had he already forgotten about what happened the last time they checked into a hotel together?

The faint red crossing the fine planes of his face showed that he did indeed remember. "I didn't mean I was checking in. I wouldn't be so bold as to . . ."

"As to what? Ruin me? Funny that. I think you already did."

She turned and marched across the field. Too late she remembered her valise and turned back.

He was following her, with his bag in one hand and hers in the other. She went to snatch hers from him and he held it away from her. She couldn't chase it without looking foolish, so she crossed her arms and scowled.

"I'm just carrying your bag," he snapped. "I don't plan on ruining your reputation. I just need to talk to you someplace where it's not so public." He nodded to the men looking at them curiously.

She gave him a nod.

After checking in with logistics, she and Jon went to the motorcar the captain had lent him to take her to her lodging. She turned to him the moment they pulled away from the base.

"You wanted to talk to me, so talk. Make it fast because you are not coming in with me."

"Will you meet me for dinner?"

"Jonathon!"

He grinned at her and she realized he was teasing her. She'd forgotten how incredibly frustrating he could be.

"I'm sorry." His smile faded. "I am sorry for everything. For not having the courage to fight for you, for us. For walking away from you. For walking away twice, actually. For letting my feelings for your family come between us."

She stilled. She'd already told him it was too late. And she'd heard all of this before. Why was he doing this? "I don't understand."

He stared straight ahead, his hand tense on the steering wheel. He didn't speak for the longest time, and then he pulled up in front of the inn she usually stayed at when she came to Southport.

"What's not to understand?" he asked bitterly. He didn't look at her. "A man brave enough to face the enemy in the skies realized he's not brave enough to live the rest of his life without the woman he loves. And that woman is you. Every time I go up now, not knowing if I'm going to be victorious or defeated, I think of you. It's always been you, Rowena. And it shouldn't have taken a war to knock some sense into me, but facing the reality of death made me think hard about what's actually worth fighting for in this world. And I am fighting for you now, whether you like it or not. You are what keeps me going."

His voice caught and she couldn't move, couldn't breathe. For a moment, every fiber in her being yearned for him. Yearned to wipe away the pain she saw on his face, heard in his voice, felt in the air for God's sake, but she couldn't, wouldn't do it. It wasn't that she didn't long to, but the hurt and pain of the last ten months, the annihilation she'd felt after the last time he'd left, wouldn't let her.

Then her thoughts turned to Sebastian. His steadfast love deserved to be returned whole-heartedly.

Jon's blue, blue eyes bore into hers. "Rowena, I

know we can't go back. I know you have other things to think of, but please, please consider my words before you marry someone else. Please." He was breathing heavily.

Her heart ached for him, but she would not, could not, give him hope where there was none. For as much as she had once loved him, she now loved another. She took a deep breath.

"When you walked away from me, I was destroyed. I thought I would never recover. But I did. I did recover, and that was in part due to Sebastian. I trust him. He will never walk away from me." She paused. "And I will not walk away from him."

"So you are punishing me? Punishing us?" he cried out, and Rowena saw the desperation in his face.

"No! I rebuilt my life and my heart and I gave it to someone else. . . ." She struggled to find the right words. "I will always love you. I can't deny that. But even if I hadn't given my whole heart to Sebastian, I would never be able to trust you again. Some things cannot be undone."

She wrenched open the door and ran blindly toward the inn.

"Rowena! Rowena, please!"

She stumbled at the anguish in his voice, but kept moving forward as if her life depended on it, which, in a way, it did.

She didn't look back.

• • •

Rowena stared at the stairwell with a mixture of resolve and indecision. She hadn't written to Prudence to tell her she was coming in case Prudence forbid it, but part of her now wished she had. What would Prudence say? Would she be turned away at the door?

No. Prudence was one of the fairest people she had ever known. She would listen to what Rowena had to say . . . and *then* she would kick her out.

How could a woman who had the courage to fly any aeroplane Mr. Dirkes bade her to be so afraid of a simple apology?

A silly, senseless woman who feared conflict.

But up in that aeroplane when she thought she was going to crash, her first thought had been of Prudence. Her biggest regret. She must make amends. She had grown up missing a mother and she no longer had a father—she would not lose a sister if she could possibly help it. Her conversation with Jon had only strengthened her resolve to make things right. Time was short, precious, and not to be squandered.

All around her the cold rain fell, cascading off her umbrella. Winter was playing its final swan's song. It was time.

Taking a deep breath, Rowena climbed the steps to Prudence's flat. She knocked on the door and shook off her umbrella. No one answered. Maybe they weren't home? No. She knew of Andrew's injuries, and even though he must be walking much better now on his prosthesis, they probably wouldn't be tramping out in such a rainstorm.

She raised her hand to knock again and then paused. Maybe Prudence had seen her out the front window and wasn't going to answer the door at all?

Just then the door opened, and Andrew was on the other side.

They stared at one another for a moment. Rowena was shocked by his appearance. He had always been such a finely built man, which is one of the reasons he had been selected as a footman, but now his shoulders were hunched with pain and even his chest seemed to have shrunk.

She frantically gathered her thoughts. "Hello, Andrew. May I come in?"

Leaning heavily against a cane, he stepped aside, allowing her in. She could see that one pant leg looked shriveled, empty, and her heart clenched for him. Anger rose up in her against the war that was taking so many men and leaving still others as shadows of their former selves.

"Is Prudence home?" she managed, forcing a tight smile.

He shook his head. "No, she stepped out for a bit, but should be back soon. You're welcome to stay."

She hesitated, then, biting her lip, decided to stay. If she left now, she might never come back given her penchant for avoidance. "Thank you, I will."

"Would you like something to drink?" he asked, his face an expressionless mask. "I just put a pot of water on for tea."

His voice sounded excessively polite and Rowena wondered what he was thinking or if he really wanted to wait upon the woman he used to drive around and serve dinner to.

"That would be very nice, thank you." She kept her voice as polite as his, afraid she would sound condescending if she was overly friendly and an insufferable snob if she sounded cold. He bade her to sit and she did, suffering another attack of uncertainty. Should she offer to help or would that be demeaning? She wished she had Victoria's unassailable confidence. Her little sister was rarely at a loss for words or actions.

She watched him work until he turned and gave her a crooked smile. "I'm going to let you get your own cup. If I do it, you are liable to be wearing it, which would embarrass both of us."

The smile transformed his face, and for the first time she understood why Prudence had married him. The self-deprecating humor in his words put her at ease and broke the ice. She gave him a tentative smile in return. "How are you getting along with that?" She nodded toward his leg.

He shrugged and lowered himself down in the chair across from her. "I have my good days and I have my bad days. I've always had two left feet, and having only one doesn't make me any more graceful."

She gave a surprised laugh and he smiled at the success of his little joke.

"So why are you here?"

She startled, almost spilling her tea. She set it down on the table next to her and gave him a narrow look. How much did he know? She searched his face and realized that he knew everything.

"I have come to give Prudence a heartfelt apology and beg her forgiveness. I made a lot of mistakes, but none of it was done malevolently. I just want her to know that."

He considered her words. "I think she knows that inside," he finally said. "But you may have a hard time getting her to realize that."

Rowena took a deep breath. "I hope I can. She has been my best friend for so long. This last year has been unbearable without her by my side."

"You can tell her that." He cocked his head. "I think I hear her now."

Moments later the door flung open and Prudence hurried in carrying a bag of groceries. "Sorry I'm late. I ran into Muriel at the butcher's and—" Prudence froze as her eyes fell on Rowena.

Rowena's heart sank as she watched Prudence's mouth tighten. "Hello, Prudence."

Prudence nodded and shut the door behind her. Setting the bag on the counter, she took off the enormous black cloak she wore.

Rowena stared. "You're pregnant!"

Prudence's eyebrows raised. "You didn't know?"

"No. I mean, yes, of course I knew. I just didn't, I didn't expect . . ." Rowena shook her head, unable to express herself on how beautiful Prudence was or how it made Rowena feel to see her. Prudence had always been lovely, but with pregnancy she had bloomed, and even though her eyes held shadows, her pale skin glowed with health, her dark hair gleamed, and her green eyes, so like Rowena's own, shone like jade. "You're gorgeous," she said, and then, moved by an unnameable emotion, burst into tears.

For a moment no one moved. "Well, do something," she heard Andrew say to Prudence.

"What do you want me to do?"

Rowena covered her face and cried, feeling completely foolish.

Prudence patted her shoulder. "There now. What are you crying for? I should be the one crying. I'm as big as the Mayfair home, my feet are swollen, and I still have to make dinner. Hush now, Rowena."

Rowena sniffled. "I'm so sorry. I don't know what came over me. I've just missed you so much, and I didn't expect you to be so very pregnant. I've . . . I've missed so much . . ."

"Well, I'm still going to get bigger before I get smaller," Prudence said. "Or at least that is what I've been told. Now then, why don't you tell me why you are here? Everything is all right with Victoria, isn't it?"

"Yes, as far as I know. Can you believe she went off to nurse in the war?"

Prudence sat across from Rowena and put her swollen feet on a small stool. "It's not any odder than you flying around the skies in an aeroplane." Prudence's voice changed and suddenly sounded uncertain. "I guess I'm the only one not joining the ranks of brave new women."

Rowena's laugh ended in a hiccup and she felt like crying again. "You can't be serious. There's nothing braver than what you're doing right now."

Prudence waved a hand. "You still haven't told me what you are doing here."

Rowena's heart fell. She couldn't expect Prudence to let her off scot-free. She turned to the woman who had been like a sister for so long and took a deep breath.

"I'm sorry, Prudence. I am sorry for so much; I don't even know where to start." Rowena paused. Prudence's face had gone still. Rowena bit her lip. "When Father died and Uncle Conrad made us move, I did what I thought was best. I didn't know that you were my grandfather's illegitimate daughter, and I had no way of knowing that the family would treat you so badly." Prudence tried to interrupt and Rowena held up her hand. "No, please let me get this all out. I am not making excuses; what I did was wrong. I am just explaining what I was thinking at the time."

Rowena waited and Prudence nodded for her to go on.

She took a deep breath. Why was this so hard? "I should have known. Even if I couldn't know that you were related by blood, I should have known they would treat you badly because your mother was a servant." Rowena shook her head. "You know Father, it was his style to teach you about something and then let you see it for yourself. It would have been so much easier if he had just held up Uncle Conrad and Aunt Charlotte as examples of the worst kind of snobs, but he didn't. He wanted us to learn to see on our own, and while Victoria was astute enough to see this, I just shrugged off any misgivings I had about them. It's hard to think bad things about people you love." She looked at Prudence, pleading. "You understand that, don't you?"

Prudence tilted her head as if considering Rowena's words, and Rowena held her breath. "I suppose. Go on."

Rowena shut her eyes briefly before continuing. Andrew sat forward, his eyes watchful as if protecting Prudence. "Anyway, that was the first mistake. And then everything just sort of happened. . . ." Rowena saw Prudence's mouth tighten. "I know. I *let* it happen. I don't know why I did. I just felt paralyzed with grief—we all were—and I didn't know what to do. The longer I waited to do something, the more difficult it became. I felt that if I just waited until we returned to London, everything would go back to normal."

Rowena stopped and all three sat in silence. Outside the rain picked up and she heard it pounding against the windows in the front room and through the open door to the bedroom.

"When did you know? How long before *we* all found out did you know that your uncle had let out our home and we wouldn't ever be able to go back?" Prudence asked.

Rowena shook her head. "I'm not sure. A week maybe? Maybe less. I don't remember." She wished she could find a way to explain how those days had felt. So sad and gray. Rather like the rain outside. The grief over her father. The guilt over Prudence. It's not so much that she wouldn't act on anything, she felt as if she couldn't. "I truly felt paralyzed," she said softly. "It felt as if all the color had been leeched from my life, and not only did it take too much energy to act, I felt as if action would only make things worse. By the time I resolved that something must be done, it was too late. You were gone. And I have never forgiven myself."

Rowena hesitated. "I don't want to live the rest of my life without my best friend. I don't want to miss out on your child's life. I am sorry, Prudence. Please, please forgive me so we can be sisters again."

She searched Prudence's face. If Prudence didn't forgive her now, there was nothing else she could offer. Perhaps the pain she'd inflicted was just too deep for an apology to heal, especially after all of the time she'd let go by.

It took several moments, but at last Prudence's face crumpled and she slumped as if she had finally given up something she had been holding on to for a long time. She said nothing, but held her hand out to Rowena.

Rowena went to her then, her heart so full she could no longer speak. Tears fell down her face and she knelt, laying her head on Prudence's knee as her lap was no longer available. She knew that Prudence was crying, too, but silently, not wanting to add to Rowena's burden. Rowena felt as if she could face anything now that she had Prudence in her life again.

CHAPTER EIGHTEEN

Prudence's feet and legs throbbed, but that was nothing compared to the ache in her heart that still felt warm and tender after Rowena had left. How long had she tried to deny that a piece of herself had been missing while estranged from

Rowena? Oh, there were still things left unsaid between them. They couldn't speak of Sebastian while Andrew was there. But everything else, all the pain and confusion and betrayal, had been laid to rest, and Prudence knew she was the better for it. Especially with the baby on the way, Prudence no longer had room in her heart for bitterness and resentment.

As she sliced up the potatoes she had brought home from the grocer, she realized that it didn't much matter if they didn't speak of Sebastian. He meant little to her now. A tender memory. A fragile regret of something that might have been but was not. Andrew and Horace. That was what her world had narrowed down to right now. Andrew and Horace.

Whereas she'd at first felt trapped and, admittedly, terrified as her baby made itself known to her, she'd melted before the waves of love that wee scrap of humanity growing within her had engendered. Whenever the distance between her and Andrew grew too painful, she would shut herself in their bedroom and take out the modest layette she had put together: the soft, miniature gowns with the silky, blue feather stitching, impossibly small knitted bootees and caps, a stack of fresh, clean diapers, and the snowy-white bibs edged with lace and covered with embroidered pictures of Little Boy Blue and cows jumping over the moon, which were

Victoria's special offering. Prudence would run her fingers over these fine things and feel tremors of joy strumming through her body as from a finely tuned guitar.

She tried not to think about how many times she'd buried her face in the soft flannel receiving blankets and sobbed.

Prudence glanced toward where Andrew sat, all too often now, in his favorite chair, reading the newspaper she had brought for him. She recalled the last conversation she'd had with Eleanor.

"He doesn't move enough."

Eleanor had been blunt but Prudence had shrugged helplessly. "I don't know what to do. He doesn't talk to me like he used to. Just comments on the war news he gets from the newspapers."

"Does he go outside?"

Prudence shook her head. "Rarely. But then I don't either."

Eleanor had frowned. "Don't let his condition or yours make you a hermit. I know the weather is nasty, but you need fresh air, even if he won't go out. Has he tried his new prosthesis?"

Prudence admitted that he had not. "He keeps struggling with the cheap one. Says he prefers it."

Eleanor's nose wrinkled and she'd sniffed, "Stupid, stubborn men."

Prudence wanted to agree, but she didn't let herself. How could she possibly know what he was going through or the adjustments he was having to make? How could she fault him for anything?

She put the potatoes in the pan and glanced toward the prosthesis in the corner. The specialist, who had brought it and made sure it fit, had told her that Andrew's behavior was quite common. He said she should leave it out as a reminder to Andrew that he didn't have to suffer with the cheap one. The specialist didn't know that Andrew's distaste for the new leg was a protest against Prudence's ordering it and paying for it without consulting him.

Prudence added some onions to the potatoes and then the ground beef she had already fried. Muriel had taught her to make a pan supper when she didn't feel up to cooking anything else. Basically, she'd just cut up anything on hand, fried it in lard, and seasoned it with salt and pepper. Even Prudence couldn't mess that up if she watched it. She interchanged pan suppers with boiled suppers, which was the same concept only tossed in a pot with water and boiled until done. If Andrew got tired of pan or boiled suppers, he never said anything.

But then Andrew didn't say much of anything anymore.

"I hope you're hungry!" she said cheerfully as she put some water on to boil.

"Mhm," he answered.

"What did you think about Rowena coming

over? I think it's pretty wonderful, the way she apologized and all." Prudence didn't really want to discuss it, but she wanted him to talk to her and would talk about Rowena or anything else. Anything besides what was going on in the war.

He glanced over the top of his newspaper. "As long as you are happy with it, I am happy."

But he isn't happy, she thought sometime later as she set his plate on the table. She used to let him eat in the chair, but Eleanor had thrown a fit when she saw it, waggling her finger at the both of them.

Andrew came to the table now.

She gave him tea and then chipped off a piece of ice from the icebox to add to the water he liked to have with his meals. "Do you need anything else?"

He shook his head. "No, thank you."

Prudence wanted to scream. All the warmth she had felt from Rowena's visit had disappeared, buried beneath the frustration, anxiety, and sorrow she felt about her marriage. She laid her hand on her belly. Not a comfortable and happy home to bring a baby into.

Andrew leaned forward, a frown on his face. "Is the baby all right?" Andrew showed concern for the child, but little of the excitement Prudence felt. Occasionally, she would force him to feel the baby's movement within her, so as to see the look of wonder that would cross his face. That look kept her hope high that all would be well once the baby came.

She nodded. "Everything is fine."

He went back to eating, his eyes straying to the newspaper.

She wished she could understand why his spirits had sunk so low that he would no longer speak to her. She had even visited the Royal Veterinary College and received assurances that her husband would still be welcome when he was ready. She had excitedly rushed home to tell him, only to see him greet the good news with the same indifference with which he now greeted everything else.

Other men had lost legs and were still out living their lives the best they could. What was it? Sometimes he almost became himself with other people, but never with her. Was he still angry over her asking the Buxtons for help?

The food she was eating stuck in her throat and she took a sip of water. She might as well have been chewing on sawdust for all she cared. She set down her spoon and watched him eat.

He raised his head. "Are you not hungry?"

His carefully polite voice pierced her heart and she shook her head and asked, "What's wrong?"

He looked down at his plate. "Everything is fine. It's good."

Prudence couldn't take it any longer. "I'm not talking about the food!" she almost cried out, the careful control she'd mastered beginning to crumble. "Do you think I care about the food? What's wrong with *you?*"

His mouth twisted and he motioned with his fork to his leg. "I think that is obvious."

"I didn't mean your leg!" Her voice rose. "I meant what is wrong with *us*. Are you still angry with me for asking Victoria for help? Do you blame me for what happened to you? Why won't you talk to me? Why do I feel like you resent me so?" Hot tears began rolling down her cheeks.

Andrew turned toward her and she was stunned by the pain she glimpsed in his eyes. "What is it?" she cried.

His face shuttered again and he shook his head. "Nothing. I just . . . I look at this prosthesis and all I can think about is how you went behind my back to the Buxtons as if we were some sort of charity case. As if you don't trust me to figure things out for us, to take care of you. I didn't know when I married you that you would be so . . . oblivious to my pride. I mean, I knew we came from different stations in life, but I never thought you'd be so . . . so sneaky. And just . . . selfish."

His words fell like shards of ice between them. She wanted to cross her arms over her chest to protect herself, but the damage had been done. She sat in bewildered silence as he heaved himself upright.

"I'm not hungry. I'm going to go lay down." She

started to get up but he waved her down. "No, I'm fine. I can do it myself."

She stared at the plate in front of her, unable to watch him make his slow, painful way into the bedroom. The baby quivered inside her as if he knew things were not well with his mother. Prudence sat for a few minutes listening to Andrew in the bedroom until the flat was so quiet she could hear the ticking of the clock on the mantel.

Victoria stood on the bow of the ferry. In the distance she could see British and French battleships guarding the precious waterway between Calais and Dover. It made her feel safe. Her time in France was over and she was happy to be heading home. She'd had enough of the blood, the filth, the desperation, and the constant, pulsing fear that pervaded every moment of her day, knowing that men were dying in her care, that she, too, could die at any moment. Gladys cried herself to sleep nightly, and though Victoria couldn't blame her, she could not participate lest she begin screaming and never stop.

It wasn't Gladys's pain that scarred her; it was the men's tears. Quiet tears over their pain, or their missing limbs or comrades they had seen bleed to death right next to them. She'd held their hands and let them talk, even though she knew that had they met socially back home, they would never have used such language or described the events in such unholy detail. But somehow, when on their backs on an iron cot, with the sound of other men groaning in pain all around them, they needed a confessor. So in perfectly calm voices they shared the most unimaginable images, images Victoria saw in living color every time she closed her eyes.

She was afraid she would never unsee them.

And, always, her worry over Kit gnawed at her stomach like an ulcer.

Dame Furse and the other VADs who had gone over with her were inside. They no doubt thought her crazy to be standing out in the bracing wind, but she had spent far too much of the past few months indoors. She needed the fresh air to wipe the cobwebs from her brain.

Of course, some aspects of nursing were wonderful. The Red Cross nurses had come to appreciate the lesser-trained VADs for what they could give the men. Victoria was always in demand because she could go about her duties while reciting stories and poetry. The gratitude of the men bruised her heart with tenderness.

The white cliffs of Dover became visible on the skyline and her heart quickened. She wanted to be in her own little flat with her friends. She wanted to work in her own little hospital where the men recovered, not died. She wanted to be there when Horace was born, and she wanted to visit

Summerset, her family, and Nanny Iris on the weekend.

And she wanted to be where Kit could find her. After sobbing for what felt like days, then spending several more wanting to spit on the ground he trod upon, she realized that, if nothing else, she would rather be a friend in the fringe of his life than to do without him again. Perhaps she deserved this fate after treating him so badly. As long as he came home safely, she didn't care whom he fell in love with. Well, she did. But she would rather have him in the arms of someone else than missing from the earth, no matter how painful it would be to see her Kit with another woman. She wondered if he ever called his new lover a minx, or if he quoted poetry to her. She shook the thoughts from her head and pulled her coat tighter as the wind picked up. She looked again at the cliffs as they came nearer and nearer. She couldn't help but feel that the young woman who had left home so long ago was very different from the one who was returning. A year ago she had wanted to be a botanist, before setting her sights on teaching following her stint at Holloway. She had longed for independence, for a grand adventure. Now she was returning from the greatest adventure she hoped she would ever have, and all she wanted was to be with the people she loved, to know that they were safe. How she had changed.

But then, there wasn't an Englishman or woman alive who wouldn't irrevocably be changed by this war.

By the time she reached her flat that night she was dead on her feet. "Susie?" she called when she walked in. The warmth of the flat welcomed her. The late-March wind had been brisk and her cheeks were stinging with cold.

"You can leave the trunk there," she said to the taxicab driver, who had lugged it up the stairs. She paid him and locked the door behind him. "Susie," she called again.

Susie rushed out of the back bathroom. "I'm sorry, miss, I was cleaning the bathtub and couldn't hear you over the water. Oh, thank God you are home!"

Susie threw her arms around Victoria and she could feel water from the wet rag trickling down her neck. "Susie, you are getting me wet! Whatever is the matter?"

"It's Miss Prudence! She has gone into labor early!"

Victoria's blood froze. She whirled around back toward the door, but Susie caught her by the arm. "They're not at the flat, miss. Miss Eleanor took them to the hospital. Something was wrong."

"Which hospital?"

"Miss Eleanor didn't say. She just rang me on the telephone and told me to tell you that she was taking Prudence to a hospital to see a doctor."

Susie's eyes were as round as saucers, and Victoria wanted to shake her. "Why didn't you ask where they were going or what was wrong?" she cried. Susie's face puckered and Victoria gave her a fierce hug. "I'm sorry, of course this isn't your fault. I'm just upset."

Victoria tried to think, but fear paralyzed her. What if something happened to Prudence? She couldn't bear it.

Susie nodded, taking Victoria's coat. "Would you like a cup of tea or something to eat? You must be hungry, right?"

The eagerness in Susie's voice told Victoria that the girl was willing to do anything to distract her from her worry. Victoria nodded. "Tea would be wonderful."

Susie started toward the kitchen, then paused. "Do you think Prudence will be all right, miss?"

Victoria nodded, but the fear that had settled in the pit of her stomach said otherwise. "Of course. Prudence is as healthy as a horse. I have an idea. Why don't you let me warm up and drink some tea, and you can teach me how to make some of those lemon biscuits I like so much. We can take them over to Prudence and Andrew as soon as the baby comes."

Susie nodded and hurried down the hall, while Victoria went into the sitting room. Holding her hands to her face, she concentrated on breathing. She didn't feel as if she were going to have an asthma attack, but the careful breathing helped calm her.

What hospital would Eleanor have taken Prudence to? How had they gotten there? She held her hands out to the fire, thinking hard. "Thank you," she said absently when Susie handed her a cup of tea.

Susie was heading back out when Victoria had a sudden thought. "Did the driver take Eleanor to Prudence's house?"

"I think so. Miss Eleanor was awfully tired this evening, but she wanted to go check on the Wilkeses before turning in. She may have called for the motorcar."

Victoria hurried to the telephone. She had left the motorcar and driver at Eleanor's disposal while she was gone. Eleanor had done so much for her, Victoria felt it was the least she could do.

Dialing the telephone she'd had installed in her driver's flat, much to her uncle's disapproval, she prayed for two things. That someone would pick up and that whoever it was would know where Eleanor was. The phone rang and rang and Victoria was just despairing when someone answered.

"Hello? Hello?" Mr. Peters always sounded suspicious, as if the phone were going to blow up in his hands. Inanely she wondered if he ever got calls from anyone else.

"Yes, Mr. Peters, it's Miss Buxton. Did you take Eleanor anywhere this evening?"

"Miss Victoria, welcome home! When did you get in?"

Her driver's leisurely tone drove her mad. "Just now. Please, it's important. Did you take Miss Eleanor anywhere?"

"Well, yes. Yes, I did. I took her to Mrs. Wilkes's flat. I asked her if she wanted me to linger and she said no, she was going to stay on for a bit and would take the tube home. I didn't like it, but what am I supposed to say? It's not my business if you young ladies go gadding about on the streets by yourselves."

Victoria's shoulders slumped. Well, that was that. She'd been so hoping that she'd be able to find out something.

"So I was very relieved and surprised when I got home and my wife told me she had called again and needed to be picked up right away."

Victoria clenched the phone. "And did you? Where did you take her?"

"Mrs. Wilkes was in a bad way, and in her condition Miss Eleanor wanted her to go to the hospital—"

Victoria's breath caught, and she cut him off. "I am very sorry, but I am going to need you to come pick me up as soon as possible. I am going to meet Miss Eleanor at the hospital."

"Yes, miss." He sounded less than enthusiastic. She had no doubt interrupted his supper. But her solicitor paid him every month to be at her beck and call, and right now she was calling.

"Susie!" she yelled the moment she got off the telephone.

Susie came in, wiping her hands on her apron. "Yes, miss? Did you find out something?"

"The driver took them to the hospital, so he knows where Prudence and Eleanor are. He'll be picking me up in a few minutes. Get my coat."

Susie hurried back to the closet she had just put the coat into.

"Should I have anything?" Victoria looked around wildly. She was just so scattered.

"Do you have money in your handbag?" Susie asked.

Victoria nodded.

"Then you're good. Let me know as soon as you hear something. How many biscuits should I bake?"

"As many as you can," Victoria said, hurrying out the door. She only hoped they would be taking the treat to a happy family and not as an offering for grief.

CHAPTER NINETEEN

M r. Peters was just pulling up to the door when Victoria ran out of the building.

She got in the backseat and leaned forward, her hands clutching her bag. "Which hospital is she in?"

"West End Hospital. We stopped at London City, but it was full up with soldiers and they told us to try West End."

Victoria lapsed into silence and concentrated on keeping her breaths even to loosen the tightening in her chest.

They reached the hospital in record time, and after telling Mr. Peters that she would ring him if needed, she sent him home and hurried into the building. The familiar scent of urine, ether, and bleach greeted her nostrils. Supper had already been served, and Victoria saw aides wheeling carts of trays down the hallway. She gave the nurse at the front desk her name and was sent to the third floor. Ignoring the lift, she ran up the stairs, only to realize her mistake halfway up. Her chest tightened further and she struggled for breath. She stopped on the second landing and rested. When would she ever learn? How could she help Prudence or anyone else if she killed herself with reckless stupidity? She sat on the second-floor landing until she could breathe regularly, then made herself take the rest of the steps slowly.

The third-floor matron nodded when Victoria told her Prudence's name. "Yes, she came in several hours ago. The doctor is with her now, but Mr. Wilkes is in the waiting room. Right this way."

Victoria followed the nurse, who waved her into a small, bare room with a couch, a chair, and a table with several books and periodicals. Andrew sat on the table, resting his face in the palm his hand.

Panic rushed over Victoria upon seeing him looking so defeated. The past months had taken a toll on the man she had always seen as filled with quiet strength. But not today. His jacket drooped about his shoulders and his skin hung. All she had thought about was what losing Prudence would mean in her own life. She hadn't given a thought to what Andrew would do without her.

He won't have to, she thought fiercely, shaking a mental fist at God. *None of us will. Prudence is going to be fine.*

He was so lost in his thoughts that he didn't seem to hear Victoria approach. "Andrew," she said softly, putting a hand on his arm.

He looked up at her, his hazel eyes so shadowed they looked almost black. When he focused on her face, his shoulders heaved, and for a moment his face looked as if it were going to crumple. Then he took a deep breath and put his hand over hers. "I'm so glad you're here. She would want you to be here."

Victoria pulled a wooden chair closer to where he sat. "What happened?"

"She hasn't been feeling herself all week. Eleanor was coming almost daily, and Prudence was laying down a lot, which didn't seem normal to me. The baby isn't supposed to come until May."

He paused and scrubbed a hand over his face. "She started complaining about having pains this afternoon, and we didn't notify the doctor because we didn't think it was time. Well, that and the fact that it isn't easy for me to go anywhere. We figured we would wait for Eleanor."

He buried his face in his hands. "By the time she came, Prudence was doubled over in pain. Eleanor ran to the pub to telephone the driver. I felt so helpless. When he came, I couldn't even help my own wife down the stairs."

He broke down then. Victoria had seen men cry before, many times, but this was different. This was someone she knew and cared about and who had always been so strong. His sobs testified to his love for Prudence, his fear, and his helplessness. Victoria had learned that when men cried this way, it was because they needed to, so she didn't try to stop him, but merely let him know she was there by keeping a hand on his shoulder.

When he finished, he nodded at her. "My apologies. I shouldn't have broken down like that."

"It's no wonder," she said in her nurse voice. "You have had a horrible scare. Have the doctors said anything?"

"Just that the baby is coming and there is no way to stop it." He paused and his jaw tightened. "It's too early and there's a chance, a strong chance, the baby won't survive. They . . . they don't know about Prudence."

For a moment the room swirled before Victoria's eyes, and she closed them quickly as if to shut out the ugly truth he had just given her. The urge to cry out rose up inside, and she pressed her lips together tightly to hold it back.

Her eyes flickered open. The strong electric light overhead, the ugly heavy furniture, and the bare wooden floor, all took on a surreal quality that made her dizzy. She sprang up and paced back and forth, her head spinning. "There has to be something someone can do. I am not just going to stand here and leave the fate of my nephew in someone else's grasp."

She whirled around. Andrew's helplessness showed in the defeated slump of his shoulders. But simply accepting the way things were went against every fiber of Victoria's being. No matter how intimate she'd become with loss and death while nursing in France, a lifetime of fighting against her asthma had left her unable to admit defeat.

"It's my fault," Andrew said, his voice so quiet, she barely heard him.

Shock ran through her. "Of course it's not your fault! How could you say that?"

"It's true. I let her take care of me, instead of taking care of myself. I took my own misery, my own pathetic sense of worthlessness, out on her while I should have been assuring her of my love and affection. I should have tried harder. I should have been there for her, supporting her, loving her. If our child dies, if she dies, I will know exactly who to blame."

Victoria shook her head and sank down at the table next to him. Exhaustion permeated every bone and muscle of her body. She'd spent last night packing and then traveled all day. She could barely think coherently, let alone find a way to help Andrew.

"I don't know exactly what is going on between you and Prudence, but I do know that after what you have been through, what you're describing isn't unusual. And no one is more understanding than Pru. Plus, add a coming baby into the mix and no wonder you both were having a hard time. Whatever happens, Andrew, please know that it isn't your fault. You mustn't think that way or you will be no good to her at all."

Andrew stared off into the distance, and Victoria wondered if he'd heard her at all. Or if her words could make a difference.

"I was so surprised when she said she would marry me," he said as if talking to himself. "Someone like her, so fine and beautiful. One could tell she was a real lady, born and raised. So smart and refined. It didn't matter that she was sitting there in the servants' hall, I could just tell. Everyone could."

He looked over at Victoria. "That's even before

I knew about her blood. It seems obvious now, looking at her and Rowena together."

Victoria nodded, smiling at the image of Ro and Pru together. She'd grown up with them under the same roof and still never seen what was right before her eyes—they truly were bonded by blood.

Andrew continued, "I thought I was going to lose her. Lord Billingsly was smitten, I know he was. It would be hard, I know, for a lord to marry someone with Prudence's background, but I know he would have. Someone like Prudence? Of course he would. So when she sent me a note . . ." He shook his head. "I was the luckiest man on the earth the day she married me. And I always tried to make it up to her for marrying beneath herself. To be worthy of such a woman. To take care of her, to provide for her. I didn't even care that she couldn't cook. But I never felt good enough for her, and when she went behind my back to ask for your help, it was such a blow. She doubted me." He paused. "It was as if she had finally realized what I've known all along . . . that I'm unworthy of her."

Victoria tried to interrupt, but Andrew shook his head. "And then I lost my leg and I wasn't even a whole man, let alone a worthy one."

Victoria put her hands on the table to keep from hitting him in the arm. He wasn't Kit. He probably wouldn't understand. But she was so angry. Why were men so stupid? "You're right. You're not worthy of Prudence. But I don't know any man who is. She is one of the best women I know."

She leapt up from her chair and paced again. "But she chose you, and you can't just give up because you don't think you're worthy or you lost a leg. What do you—" Victoria was about to give him a good tongue-lashing when the door opened. "Eleanor!"

Seeing Andrew struggling to get to his feet, Victoria leapt to his side and helped him up. She understood. Whatever the news was, he didn't want to be seated when it came.

"How is she?"

Victoria shivered at the stark naked emotion in his voice. This man would be destroyed if anything happened to his wife.

Eleanor frowned and shook her head. "The baby turned and, thank God, seems to be coming normally. It's strange that a baby would turn this late in labor, but there you have it. But if the doctor's calculations are right, the baby is still much too early. But she is quite large so it may be all right."

Victoria detected the uncertainty in Eleanor's voice and fear shot through her.

"*May* be?" Andrew asked.

Victoria swallowed and glanced at Andrew, who had turned white. Eleanor squeezed his arm. "Andrew, there's nothing you can do right now and Prudence is a strong woman."

"Can I see her?" Victoria and Andrew both asked at the same time.

Eleanor shook her head. "No. The doctor said no visitors, and that Prudence needs to rest as much as possible. If it were up to me, I would let you both in, but it's not. I'm lucky he is allowing me to stay as I don't work here, but luckily I went to school with his nurse."

Victoria's heart sank.

Eleanor regarded the two of them and her mouth twisted. "Okay. I will wait and see if the doctor takes a break. If he does, I will let you both in for a moment."

Victoria gave her an excited hug. "Thank you so much."

"Thank you," Andrew said simply.

"No promises, though," Eleanor warned as she left the room.

As she opened the door, Prudence's screams echoed through the hallway and Andrew cried out and started for the door.

"No! Stay here!" Eleanor said, running down the hall.

Andrew and Victoria clung to one another as the screams subsided to low moans.

Andrew swayed on his feet and Victoria led him back to his seat.

He buried his head in his arms on the table, and Victoria decided not to bother him. Like her, he was barely keeping it together. Instead she went over to the couch and sat heavily, her body trembling with exhaustion and dread. She shut her eyes against the glare of the light. *Please God,* she prayed. *Please don't let anything happen to her.*

Victoria was aware of the passage of time the moment she opened her eyes.

She looked around, completely confused. Hadn't she spent last night in the boardinghouse in France? Or the night before? She sat up.

Prudence!

How could it be possible that she had slept?

She turned her head, but even before she spotted the empty table, she knew she was alone. She stood, staggering a bit as her muscles cramped. Andrew must be with Prudence.

Victoria swallowed and moved toward the door as if in a dream. Her heart thudded in her ears—the only sound she heard in the night-hushed hall. Her limbs were as solid and cumbersome as stone as she inched her way toward the room she'd seen Eleanor enter earlier. Fear almost paralyzed her. Would she would find Prudence and Andrew celebrating the birth of their child, or grieving its loss? Or, at the worst, would she find Andrew alone? She reached the doorway just as she heard voices.

She grabbed on to the doorjamb as dizzy relief overcame her. Prudence. Taking a deep breath, she peered around the corner. Prudence's eyes were closed, and her long, dark hair was spread out, lank and matted, against a white pillow. Andrew sat by her bedside, his hand clinging to hers. For a moment Victoria's heart cried out, fearful the baby had been lost, but then she realized that Prudence's face held a peace that Victoria had never before seen and her lips were curled at the corners.

"There is nothing to forgive, my love," Andrew said, his voice low. "The fault was mine. I volunteered for the duty in rebellion against you. I put myself in danger knowingly because I was being a fractious child instead of a good husband."

With her eyes still closed, Prudence raised his hand to her lips. "You're right. There is nothing to forgive. We have both made mistakes. It's just important that we learn from them." She kissed the back of his hand, smiling. "We may be flawed, but as long as we love one another, all will be well."

Victoria's lip trembled. She couldn't see Andrew's face and Prudence still had her eyes closed, but the contentment that surrounded them made her heart swell.

How she yearned to have that for herself. Not the baby, but the love. The comfortable, secure, steadfast love that had bloomed between her sister and this man.

Kit.

And to think she had thrown away her chance at a love like this. What folly. What lunacy. What had she been thinking? And now she might never see him again.

"You know, eavesdropping is just bad manners," Eleanor whispered, causing Victoria to jump. "Come. Let them have this moment. I have something more interesting to show you anyway."

"Is the baby all right?" Victoria asked as Eleanor led her down the hall.

Eleanor nodded. "Apparently Prudence was further along than the doctors had thought. The baby is still small, but not dangerously so, as long as care is taken."

"This baby will have the best nurse and the best care under the sun," Victoria vowed.

"Thank you so much for everything you have done!"

Eleanor laughed. "I didn't do anything. Prudence did all the work."

Victoria shook her head, unable to explain for the tears clogging her throat.

Eleanor led her to a room where Victoria was handed a cap and an apron.

"Be careful," Eleanor warned.

Victoria began to roll her eyes, but the sight of a nurse dressed in head-to-toe white, holding a tiny bundle in her arms, completely shut her down.

"Would you like to hold Margaret Rose?"

The nurse's voice was appropriately gentle for this quiet kingdom. Apparently not many babies were born in the hospital as only four bassinets were in the room and all appeared empty. The nurse tilted her head toward a rocker, and wordlessly Victoria moved toward it. Once she was seated, the nurse gave her brief instructions.

"Let your arm curve like this. Don't let her head bobble, and don't get up."

Victoria nodded, and then her arms were full of Margaret Rose. Though it was not the boy Prudence had been expecting, Victoria couldn't imagine a more beautiful child than this one. Warmth spread through her chest as she stared. How had she made it almost twenty years on this earth without ever holding a baby before? Her arm curved around the bundle naturally, and the weight felt both light and satisfyingly heavy.

The baby's eyes were closed, and her dark sweep of lashes cast a shadow against skin so pale and fine it looked almost translucent. With her eyes, Victoria traced the gentle curve of the baby's cheek and the well-defined bow of her upper lip. Tears stung Victoria's eyes with a tenderness so fierce she would have started to sob if she weren't so frightened of waking the child.

"I will always take care of you," she whispered. "You are going to be my favorite, little Maggie Rose, but let's not tell any future babies that, all right? Let's keep it our little secret."

The baby shifted and Victoria tightened her arms around her. A song she didn't realize she knew came unbidden to her mind. It couldn't have been from her own mother, who had died when she was as small as the child in her arms. It must have come from Prudence's mother. She sang softly:

Sleep, baby, sleep,
Thy father tends the sheep.
Thy mother shakes the dreamland tree
And down fall pleasant dreams for thee.
Sleep, baby, sleep,
Sleep, baby, sleep.

CHAPTER TWENTY

Rowena walked through the hangar, a bounce in her step. If she could whistle, she would. She hadn't felt this light and irrepressible since before her father died. Or maybe she had never felt this way. She was on her way to what would surely be another glorious flight, and April was behaving just as a spring should with gloriously balmy days interspersed with drenching rains that turned all of England into a patchwork quilt of brilliant greens. *Spring can only be truly appreciated by air,* she thought.

But more than just the changing season buoyed her spirits: Sebastian would be getting leave soon, and they were to be married. The wedding plans this time around were simple, and Aunt Charlotte had acquiesced to everything Rowena suggested.

Rowena assumed Aunt Charlotte had begun to worry that if they didn't wed soon, it wouldn't happen at all, but she needn't have worried. Rowena was as sure of her decision as she was about her love of flying.

Rowena waved at one of the men who noticed her passing, but didn't stop. She wasn't sure where Dirkes was sending her, but if it was a long trip, she would want to get started early. Recently, and unofficially, the army had been using her to transport men about England, as well. They were usually high-ranking men that needed to be somewhere in a hurry, and since Rowena was there and so incredibly reliable . . .

She grinned, remembering one self-important toff who'd been completely demoralized by having to fly with a woman. Most were so terrified of flight it didn't matter who was piloting the aeroplane, but this man clearly resented its being a female. He'd sat in the aeroplane stiffly, torn between his desire to show his disdain and his survival instincts, which told him not to insult the person with his life in her hands.

After they'd landed, she'd left him out on the field to figure out on his own how to unlatch his harness.

She opened the door that led to the offices, hoping to catch Mr. Dirkes alone. She wanted to again beard the lion in his den about crossing the Channel. With each passing week she was feeling more and more confident that he would eventually be forced to give in. Because of the change in the weather, the fighting was once again heating up. Aeroplanes were playing an ever-increasing role in the war effort, and production had been trebled. The armed forces needed every pilot they could get for the fighting, and sooner or later he would be forced to admit that she was needed for ferrying aeroplanes across the water.

Today, she was going to make sure it was sooner.

The office door was open and Mr. Dirkes was sitting at his large, cluttered desk. For once he wasn't rapping out orders into the telephone or writing in his famous chicken scratch across aeroplane schematics. Instead his hands were folded across his broad waistline and his face was turned toward the window.

"What? Has the war ended? Does the world no longer need aeroplanes? Is that why you're lollygagging about?"

He turned toward her and Rowena sucked in her breath. Mr. Dirkes was an older man, but his ruddy good health and vibrant personality always gave the impression of his being younger. Today, however, all the joy that usually lit his face was gone and its lines were pronounced. He looked as if he had aged twenty years since she'd last seen him.

"What is it?" she cried.

"Oh, lass. It's a sad day. The saddest day you could imagine."

The trembling began in her heart and spread throughout her body. She knew. Without even hearing him say the words, she knew.

"Jonathon."

Fumbling, she made her way to a chair and sat. With her hands twined in her lap, she waited.

He nodded once. "His mother just sent word. His aeroplane went down during a dogfight over eastern France. They found the aeroplane, but not his body. Or I should say, what was left of the aeroplane."

Rowena gripped the arms of the chair. "It was a bad crash, I take it?"

"Not sure. The plane had been purposely burned."

Relief coursed through her body, making her dizzy. "He's alive then. I'm sure of it."

"Or at least he was when the aeroplane crashed. French troops in the area are looking for him, but have seen no sign. They have, however, seen many signs of German scouts."

She leaned forward, her neck and shoulders tensing. "He is fine. Jon is smart and he was raised in the country. He has good instincts. He would know how to survive out there."

Mr. Dirkes took a deep breath. "That is what I told his mother. Thank you for reaffirming my hopes."

Rowena nodded. At least Mr. Dirkes was reassured. Rowena felt as if she were going to fall apart at the seams and crumble into a helpless heap on the floor.

They both sat in silence for several minutes, the enormity of their mutual fear paralyzing them.

Mr. Dirkes shuffled some papers on his desk and cleared his throat. With effort, Rowena focused.

"I ran into a woman you may have heard of," he said. "Marie Marvingt."

Rowena tried to remember where she'd heard the name before, but her shock made it difficult to rein in her thoughts. Then it came to her. "The French aviatrix?"

He nodded. "The French government is allowing her to fly in combat missions against German bases." He paused as if waiting for a reaction, but Rowena was numb. "If they are allowing a woman to do aerial combat missions, there is no reason why I shouldn't allow you to ferry our aeroplanes across the Channel."

Rowena blinked. "Are you serious?"

He sighed. "I'm afraid I am. The need has never been greater. Besides, I'm afraid the government is going to lure you away from me with the promise of more exciting missions, like taking off from a naval ship, if I don't loosen my reins on you at least a little bit."

She expected to feel triumphant at the news, but she felt nothing. Knowing he was watching her carefully, she mustered a smile. "When would you like me to start?"

He stared at her for a moment. "Actually, I was going to have you start this morning. We're in a bit of a bind, and both the French and British are losing planes quicker than we can make them. They have been breathing down my neck for more aeroplanes, but I am running at capacity now. I need more workers, but so many men are fighting . . ."

"Hire more women."

"I've already thought of that. I would like you to help me interview women next week, if you would."

"If you'd like. I really don't know anything about hiring."

"It would be helpful regardless. Now, do you think you can fly today after . . ."

"After hearing about Jon, you mean? Of course. I'm not going to fall apart, if that's what you think."

If only she felt as confident as her voice sounded.

It seemed as if only a few minutes had passed before Rowena was preparing to start her aeroplane, but it had been more than an hour. Mr. Dirkes made Albert go over the flight plan with her until she had it memorized. They would be flying the latest SPADs into Dover, refueling, and then crossing the Channel to a naval base in Calais.

"Follow Albert. He is under strict instructions not to leave you this time. There's no place to make an emergency landing in the Channel."

Rowena glared. "You do realize that I have only had to make one emergency landing and have never broken wood, like most of your other pilots?"

"Well, today isn't the day to start. And for the love of God, avoid all other aeroplanes, even if they look like ours. They've been bombing Dover like they want to pound it to dust, and I don't want you caught up in that." He paused and wiped his forehead with a handkerchief. "I don't know what I'm doing by letting you fly into a war zone. You'd best go before I change my mind."

Rowena gave him a fierce hug and climbed into the SPAD. She gave Albert the go-ahead. Even though she had taken off from this airfield dozens of times, this time felt different, and she took it even more seriously than she usually did. She was on a mission of import and one that could be dangerous. This was not a flight to be enjoyed, but one that demanded she have her wits about her. She wished she could feel a greater sense of excitement. After all, she'd earned this. But somehow the thought of Jonathon, alone and perhaps wounded, leeched away her sense of triumph. She shoved the thought out of her mind and ignored the sick lurching of her stomach. Any distraction could get her killed.

Keeping one eye on her instruments and one on Albert in front of her, she flew to Dover without incident. Not until she was over the city and saw the rubble and pits from the recent bombings did the immediacy of the war and the danger of her current mission truly hit her. Hard.

She could be killed. There were men in the sky, *her sky,* who would do whatever they could to shoot her down. Her chest tightened. The thought was both surreal and sobering.

She climbed out of the aeroplane, her muscles stiff. The break in Dover would be short. Long enough for her to get a drink, use the WC, and fuel up. Albert waved to her and she joined him.

"I need to go talk to Major Rayne. He coordinates transportation and can tell us about weather, wind, and how hot the action is right now."

She was about to ask what he meant when it dawned on her. Fighting. He meant fighting. Sweat trickled down the back of her neck.

Major Rayne was rugged, older, with a tidy mustache and a Yorkshire accent. She focused as he spoke of the weather and coordinates, but shied away from talk of the war, dogfights, and the increased pressure on maritime travel.

"You may have difficulty getting back," he warned. "The government has been sporadically shutting civilian travel down if they don't think it's safe, and quite frankly right now it's not safe."

Rowena raised an eyebrow. "You mean they will let us go over by aeroplane, but not return on one of their boats?"

Major Rayne's mouth twisted wryly. "That's about the extent of it."

"But we're doing military work," she protested. The last thing she wanted was to get stuck in France.

"But you're not official military. The ban doesn't last for long. It's open right now. We had several ferries come over this morning with both civilians and nurses. I just wanted to make you aware of the situation."

After several more minutes, Albert and Rowena were ready for the flight. Rowena replaced her goggles and gave the men starting her propeller the thumbs-up. As the engine caught, it roared to life, and she nodded at Albert, in the aeroplane next to her.

Albert went first and she followed him. They both took off smoothly, circled once, then headed east out over the open water. The beauty of Dover's green fields against the white of the cliffs and the blue of the ocean caused Rowena's chest to ache. She could have stared at that scene forever, but turned her eyes to the instrument panel and then toward the back of Albert's plane, flying steadily about one hundred feet ahead of her. The clouds bloomed fluffy and white just above them, but they remained on the fringe. They didn't want Rowena to lose sight of Albert, but they wanted to be able to use the clouds as cover should they spot an enemy plane. Of course, the enemy could use the clouds as cover while they attacked, as well.

As much as she tried to avoid the troubling news of the war, Rowena had learned much simply by listening to men discussing their aeroplanes, including the mounting machine guns on them. Mounting them to the front was dangerous as the bullets could, and would, damage the propeller. The race to create aeroplanes with firing power was heating up, and Mr. Dirkes was on the cutting edge of trying to figure out an efficient way to take down German reconnaissance aircraft. The Germans had already come up with such a design that seemed to work.

Rowena shook her head, trying not to think of the German advantage. She needed to focus on completing her mission because the British army desperately needed these aeroplanes. She wondered about the men who would fly them. No doubt they would be photographing Germans on the ground, trying to build a complete mosaic map of the German's trench system.

No wonder the enemy wanted to shoot her down.

Rowena stretched her neck from side to side, tension stiffening her muscles. There was so much she didn't want to think about right now. Couldn't think about. Jonathon. Sebastian. The war. She took a deep breath and stared at the tail end of Albert's Vickers until it mesmerized her.

She was concentrating so fully on the aeroplane ahead of her that she didn't even see the other plane until it was almost wingtip to wingtip with her. Startled, she glanced upward knowing he must have come out of the clouds she was flying under.

She recognized the markings as German and, from the look of the nose, knew it must be an AGO C.II. For one startled moment, she stared into the eyes of a young man who could be no older than Victoria. He was so close she could see the shock on his face, and for a split second they stared at one another before the other aeroplane pulled away and disappeared into the clouds.

For several heart-stopping seconds she waited for the sound of gunfire ripping through her aeroplane, but all she heard was the sound of her own aircraft and the beating of her heart in her ears. Her paralysis broke and she increased her speed until she came up next to Albert. She pointed above them. For a second he looked puzzled, but then he nodded in comprehension. Glancing around, he signaled for her to fly in a subordinate position. Nodding, she complied, flying slightly lower and to his left. This way, if an attack came from the sky, she would be slightly protected.

Though Rowena's stomach clenched with fear,

her hands were steady on the yoke and her focus sharpened. She put everything out of her mind and concentrated on her surroundings. By the time they made it to Calais, Rowena was both mentally and physically exhausted.

Rowena remembered Calais with fondness. The bustling port city was the first stop in most of the Buxton adventures on the Continent. She, Vic, and Prudence would beg Father to take them to their favorite ice-cream shop for French strawberry waffle cones. He always pretended they were in too much of a hurry, but they always ended up there, sitting outside on the sidewalk, the perfect beginning to whatever adventure they were off on.

The city looked nothing like that now, she thought, falling behind Albert to prepare for landing. A British naval base constructed mostly of tin, wood, and canvas buildings created an ugly counterpart to the otherwise charming city. Many of the Allied efforts were located here because of its strategic importance and proximity to Flanders. She followed Albert's lead and landed smoothly. The moment she braked, she was surrounded by English soldiers eager to get the aeroplane under cover.

Some of the soldiers gave her split skirt strange looks until she pulled off her goggles and helmet and pulled her hair out of the back of her jacket. She'd found it made for less confusion if the men knew right away that she was a woman. Several of them looked shocked, but she supposed they were too polite to say anything. Even dressed in her flying clothes, she looked exactly like what she was: a lady. It was locked into the fineness of her features and the soft fairness of her skin.

Albert hurried back to her. "What did you see?"

"A German aeroplane. I think he was as surprised to see me as I was to see him."

One of the men glanced at her with new respect. "You outflew a German pilot and lived to tell the tale? Not many can say that."

She shook her head. "No, I don't think he even tried to follow."

The man shrugged. "At any rate, you'd best go tell the captain. Thanks for the aeroplanes." He saluted them and went back to his work.

Their debriefing didn't last long because there wasn't much to tell. By the time they were done, Rowena was starving and the captain walked them over to the mess hall.

"We will try to get you on a transport ship taking wounded soldiers back to England, but I'm not sure if there will be room. We'll have someone drive you to the hotel we use for visiting dignitaries after we eat. You can check back with us in the morning and I will have a better sense of availability."

Rowena nodded. They were just entering the tent when a private stopped them.

"Captain, I was told to deliver this to you immediately." He handed the captain a note, his eyes sliding toward Rowena as he did so.

The captain raised his eyebrows as he read the outside of the envelope. "This says it's for Rowena Buxton." He turned to the private. "Did this come by cable?"

The private nodded, and the captain handed the slip of paper to Rowena.

She frowned and her heart rate kicked up a notch. Who could have sent it? Only Mr. Dirkes knew where she was. . . . Her heart slammed into her ribs once again.

Jonathon.

She ripped the envelope open with trembling fingers.

Jonathon found near Flanders. Badly wounded. At the Red Cross hospital at Le Touquet. Possible to check on him? D.D.

Rowena stared at the words trying to make sense of what she was reading. The men were still standing in front of the door. The captain must have read the expression on her face because he asked, "Bad news?"

"Yes, someone, a . . . friend, is badly hurt." She looked at Albert. "They found Jonathon. Mr. Dirkes wants us to check on him."

"Where is he?"

"A base hospital in Le Touquet. Is there any way we can get there? He's a fellow pilot."

The captain hesitated. "It's closer to the front. You know that, right?"

She nodded.

"All right then. I will lend you my motorcar and driver. But please be back by the morning. I would like to have you both on the ship back home. I don't like being responsible for civilians."

It took about ten minutes for the arrangements to be made and included a hastily packed dinner for the road.

"That's British military efficiency," Albert said, taking a bite of a meat sandwich. "You should eat something."

Rowena took a sandwich automatically, but knew she wouldn't be able to force it into her mouth. Her temples throbbed and her eyes burned with the effort to keep from crying. Even though she was praying that she was wrong, her instincts told her that his life was already slipping from him. She must get to him. She couldn't let him die all alone in a foreign country.

She leaned her head against the back of the seat and closed her eyes. Purposefully, she brought up every detail of their time together. Every moment she could possibly remember. From the night she held him in her arms after he had crashed, to visiting him in the hospital soon after. She remembered the first time he'd taken her up in an aeroplane, and the moment when he'd kissed her on the sidewalk in the village, inadvertently setting off the events that would lead to her engagement to Sebastian. She remembered the way he laughed, the blue of his eyes, and the way the sun glinted off the red-gold of his hair.

She remembered those hushed, halcyon hours spent in that hotel room as he made love to her and how she thought she would die of happiness.

She remembered his walking away from her and the last time they had met, when she'd walked away from him. She prayed that she would arrive in time. How tragic it would be if the last words they exchanged were angry.

When they arrived at the hospital, Albert let her go in first. She was fairly sure that he didn't know about her relationship with Jonathon, but Mr. Dirkes had sent the note to her.

She followed an orderly back to a long room with iron beds set in straight rows every four feet. It was dark by then and the room was lit with only a few small gaslights set on low.

A nurse, dressed as primly as a nun in a habit, came to her and asked whom she was there to see. She didn't ask why Rowena had been afforded the privilege of a late-night visit. Many of the men who were in that room wouldn't survive the trip back to England. If someone showed up to say their good-byes, it was allowed.

"How is he?"

The nurse pressed her lips together. "Are you his sweetheart?" she asked in a lilting Irish accent.

Rowena was about to shake her head but changed her mind. "Yes." What other sweetheart did he have?

The nurse briefly touched Rowena's shoulder. "You'd best say your good-byes. He has internal injuries and took a blow to the head that would have already killed most men. I don't know how he managed to burn his aeroplane and walk to safety."

Because he is one of the most determined men who ever lived, Rowena thought as the nurse took her to Jonathon's bedside and brought her a chair. His head had been wrapped in a white bandage, but she could see blood leaking through. His hand lay on the outside of the coverlet, and Rowena picked it up and held it between hers. "Jonathon," she whispered. "I'm here with you now."

She waited but Jonathon didn't respond. *Oh, please, Lord, let him respond. Please let him know I am here.* She sat quietly for a moment, then continued talking as if he could hear her. "I flew over the Channel today. I flew in a Vickers even more advanced than my own. Mr. Dirkes must really believe in my skills if he would have me bring one of those aeroplanes over. Wait until you fly it. It's light as a bird but responds beautifully. Dirkes sends his love, as does your mother." They hadn't of course, but she knew that they did. That even now their love was surrounding them both and would buoy Jonathon on his journey. His hand still lay limp and motionless in hers. Her breath caught and she continued her endless talking, talking, talking.

"Did you know that Cristobel and I ride together when I'm home? She probably never told you that, did she? But we do, and when it's time for her to be presented, I am going to give her my white dress and make sure she has a proper coming-out ball. I know you don't think that's important, but Cristobel does. I think I am going to have her hunt with me next season, she has become quite the jumper. . . ." Rowena ran out of words and covered her eyes with her hand. The events of the day caught up with her and her stomach rolled. She took a couple of deep breaths to calm the dizziness.

Suddenly she felt a tiny movement of his hand within hers. She looked up to find Jonathon's blue eyes trained on her face. They were speaking to her, his eyes, communicating with her without words. She could feel his love and gratitude washing over her. She leaned forward and again brought to mind the memories she had recalled earlier. His mouth on hers. The laughter they'd shared when that silly stick fell out of the aeroplane. She willed the memories to flood his mind, too, and felt that perhaps they were. His eyes drooped and she could feel his pain and exhaustion.

Bending closer, she willed him to stay awake, to stay with her. She felt him trying to rally, and for a moment the determination in his eyes shone, but he was too tired and the pain was too much. His eyes fluttered.

"I love you, Jonathon," she said, her heart breaking all over again. At this moment, nothing was more important than Jonathon's knowing how much she loved him, and how much she would always love him.

Jonathon's eyes dimmed and she knew he was leaving her, and without taking her eyes from his, she knelt and slipped her arms around him. While the thought of a world without Jonathon filled her with grief and loss, all she felt now was an overwhelming sense of thankfulness that she could be here with him.

How many men dying in this war were able to do so in the arms of someone who loved them?

Then he was gone.

Tears streamed down her face as she rested her head against his chest and listened to the last beatings of his heart. The connection she'd had with his spirit evaporated and she felt bereft and utterly alone. She wished Sebastian were with her.

She didn't know how long she stayed that way, with her head pressed against his body, but by the time the nurse came to move her away, her legs were in knots of pain. She staggered with cramps as she got up.

"Is there anything I can do?" the nurse asked gently.

"No," Rowena said, looking at Jonathon's still form. "It's all been done."

CHAPTER TWENTY-ONE

Though she could have slept longer, Victoria's lifelong habit of rising with the sun woke her up early. For a moment, she was disoriented and couldn't figure out where she was. Somehow she'd expected to wake up in her dear little room in the Mayfair house with its beautiful maple furniture and marble fireplace.

Not that she didn't adore this room in her flat. It was clean with white walls and high ceilings, and she'd had the floor refinished and it gleamed darkly. Her fireplace had been replaced with a radiator, and some of the panes in her windows were warped and pitted, but that was all right. She lived much more simply than she ever had before, and it suited her.

She swung her legs out of bed and stretched, then dug her toes into the lamb's-wool rug next to her bed. Before heading to the bathroom, she slipped her feet into the knitted slippers Katie had given her for Christmas. She knew from experience that the tile floor of the WC could be brutally cold. Of course, now that April was finally bringing warmer weather, she didn't burn her feet on the icy floor near so much.

After donning her soft, billowy lawn robe, she tiptoed down the hall to the kitchen to make some tea. Susie wouldn't be up, and Eleanor was already away to one of the hospitals she either worked in or volunteered at.

On the advice of both her doctor and Eleanor, Victoria only worked three days a week at the hospital. Her health just wouldn't stand any more, and she was learning, finally, that she was not indestructible. She had asthma, she would always have asthma, and the sooner she reconciled herself to that, the better off she would be.

She was still working on it.

Lighting the gas range, she put the teapot on to boil and set out cups for both her and Susie. Aunt Charlotte would be aghast to know that Victoria usually made tea for her maid in the mornings, but it wasn't Susie's fault that her mistress liked to wake while it was still dark. Besides, Victoria knew that Susie's beau had visited until late last night. She also knew she would in time be looking for a new housekeeper.

She padded down the hall to the front door to get the milk. It seemed odd not to have a servants' entrance for that, but there was only one way in and out of the apartment besides the fire escape, and Victoria giggled at the thought of the milkman climbing the fire escape to leave milk outside her window.

She opened the door and jumped at the shock of finding a tall man just outside. It took her a moment to realize who it was.

Kit.

She launched herself at him, forgetting everything that had transpired between them in her gladness upon seeing him. He held her for a moment, taking her right off her feet, and a burst of happiness shot through her. He was alive.

But then he firmly set her back on her feet and stepped away from her. Because now, they were just friends.

He was in love with someone else.

Biting her lip, she backed up and motioned for him to enter. "What are you doing here? How are you? Have you seen Colin or Sebastian? And don't forget the milk, if you please."

He laughed, bending to retrieve the cold bottle on her step. "Even a mighty clash of countries can't change the impertinent Miss Victoria. It's nice to know that some things will always remain the same."

The comment vexed her. "Shows how much you know. I have grown immensely since you last set eyes on me. Immensely."

She felt his eyes on her as she walked down the hall into her kitchen. "I don't see it," he finally said.

She bit back a retort, suddenly overwhelmed by how much she yearned for him, that cheeky, insufferable tease. But her longing only made her angrier. She turned away, afraid he would see the depth of her feelings naked across her face.

So Victoria ignored his remark. "I'm sure you would like a cup of tea. Are you hungry, as well?"

"Why? Are you going to whip me up a batch of bloaters poached in cream sauce?" His voice was far too amused for her liking.

"No, you ninny, I was going to offer you a scone that Susie cooked yesterday, but I've changed my mind. You can starve."

"Is that any way to treat a member of the British army?"

She took a deep breath. "You're right. Now tell me who you've seen and I will get you your tea and a scone, but be a good lad and stop vexing me."

He snorted, but changed the subject. "I saw Sebastian not too long ago. He is doing well. I think he will be getting leave in the next couple of weeks. Do you think he and Rowena will be married then?"

"That's the plan."

"It's the strangest relationship," Kit mused. "At first the engagement was fake and then it wasn't, and then the wedding got postponed at least three times, or was it four? It gives me a headache just thinking about it. I can't imagine what it's doing to your aunt Charlotte."

"Or Sebastian's mother." Victoria shuddered as she laid the table for tea. "Makes me glad I don't live at Summerset anymore."

"Yes. Poor Lainey."

The tea water squealed and Victoria poured it carefully over the leaves she had already put in the china pot. Arranging the scones on a plate, she carried it to where Kit had seated himself at the tiny wooden kitchen table.

"I hope you don't mind, I always have my morning tea in the kitchen now. It's warmer than the sitting room."

"No, this is fine."

Victoria sat across from him and took a closer look. He was thinner than she remembered, refining his handsome, clever features. His blue eyes were a bit dimmer, as if the switch that worked the twinkle had been shut off.

How she hoped it wasn't permanent.

He added some sugar to his cup and stirred. "I'm glad we got all that sorted out," he said casually.

"What have we sorted out?"

"Our relationship. Just friends, you know. Like you wanted."

Aching spread through her chest. "Yes. Such a relief, that."

"Yes."

Silence.

"So tell me about that woman." Victoria didn't

want to know about the woman, but if she didn't, he might think she minded, which she did, awfully, but he certainly didn't need to know that.

"What woman?"

Victoria raised her eyebrows.

"Oh, that woman. Yes. She's great actually. Really . . . great."

Victoria stared down into her cup, horrified that she could feel tears coming already. She was going to cry. How could he have loved her so much only to replace her so suddenly with a stranger?

She fought to keep the tears from falling, but one slipped down her face and fell off her chin into her tea.

He cleared his throat and she stared at her cup, unable to meet his eyes. Humiliation bloomed like twin roses in her cheeks.

"Actually, that isn't exactly the truth. There is no woman. I made that up."

Victoria looked up, startled. "Why would you lie about that?"

He shrugged and his foxy face pinched up. "You had made it clear that we were just friends and my pride was hurt. So I lied. But, I've come to decide that if we are to truly be friends, we have to at least be honest with one another."

He looked into her face and frowned. "Victoria, why are you crying?"

Pride and longing warred inside. She ached to

tell him that she loved him, but what if he no longer felt the same way? Hurt over her rejection still bloomed in her chest. "If you felt that way, you could have at least acknowledged my feelings. I poured out my heart and you sent me back that horrid letter, saying that you had found someone else!"

"I apologized for lying, what do you want? And, yes, you poured out your heart very well that night. You were very clear about the fact that you didn't love me. Crystal even."

"What are you talking about?" she demanded. "Not then, you dolt. The letter. I am talking about my letter! You can imagine that it wasn't easy for me to write, and then when I received your reply . . ."

She stood then with her fists clenched rigidly at her sides. How she longed to hit him.

"What letter are you talking about? From you? I never received a letter from you. I stepped up and extended an olive branch from the warfront asking if we could be friends, and you ignored me. May as well have shot me down, as it would have been less painful than your stubborn silence."

Victoria closed her eyes, breathing hard. She couldn't speak. He never received her letter. He didn't know. Would it have made a difference?

There was no help for it. She sat on the chair and began to work at controlling her breathing before it turned into a full-blown episode.

"Victoria?" She felt him kneeling beside her and putting a gentle hand on her knee. "Do you need your nebulizer?"

She shook her head. Even now she could feel her chest loosening. She had to tell him that she had written to him. He might reject her, but if she didn't at least try, she would never know.

It took several more minutes before she could speak, and he waited on his knee beside her, his blue eyes concerned.

"I sent you a letter. About a week after you left that night." She looked down at the ground, gathering her courage. Her father had said there was no gain without risk, and when had she ever been afraid of risk?

"What did the letter say?" he asked gently.

"I told you that I had been wrong. And stupid. That I loved you and was in love with you and I didn't ever want to lose you. Couldn't lose you. And then when you sent that letter to me . . . I thought I did."

She looked into his eyes and saw that he was beaming. "Oh, my dear. You could never lose me. I don't know why or how you could love someone like me, but I won't question it if you are sure it's true. Please say it's true. I can't take much more being played with."

The hope in his voice set her heart soaring. She reached up and touched his cheek. "My darling Kit. I would never play with you. Not anymore. I am so sorry it took me so long to understand, but I am rather a late bloomer, you know. And I have been known to be stubborn."

He snorted and she gave him a pinch. "But it's true, I love you so, I can hardly breathe. It was thoughts of you that kept me alive while at the front, even just thoughts of our friendship. Please say you love me back and you still want to marry me. Because I would very much like to marry you, as long as we would be equal partners and you would give me equal say, no matter what the conventional mandates of marriage would imply . . . and only if you will let me win *at least* every other argument."

He stood and pulled her up against him. "Where is a vicar? I want to marry you before you change your mind!"

She rapped him on the head with her knuckles. "It's too late to change your mind. If you do, I will tell Aunt Charlotte and your mother."

"God forbid," he breathed reverently, and bent to kiss her lips.

His mustache tickled her upper lip enticingly, and heat rose from Victoria's toes and swept through her entire body. She broke away, gasping again. "I can't breathe!"

His eyes gleamed at her. "I can't either. Your asthma must be catching."

Tenderness filled her and tears came to her eyes again. "I do love you so, Kit."

He grinned down at her, a smug look crossing his face. "You know this means I was right all along, don't you?"

It seemed appropriate that the wedding would take place in the rose garden their father had redesigned. They had planned on having the ceremony in the conservatory if the weather hadn't held, but the day had dawned clear and the spring rains had been held at bay.

Rowena wore a simple dress of burnt umber that didn't quite reach her ankles. Instead of an ornate veil, she had twisted her hair up, and Victoria had adorned her with lilies, their father's favorite flower. Victoria stood by her side, and Colin had managed to get leave at the last minute and had joined the wedding party to stand for Sebastian. Kit hadn't been able to come and Victoria had been crushed.

Rowena glanced at her baby sister while the vicar nattered on and on. Victoria simply glowed with love. She and Kit had broken everyone's heart by getting married hastily the last time he was on leave. Aunt Charlotte had been so grateful that she was actually going to get to attend Rowena's wedding that she hadn't made much of a fuss over the arrangements. Maybe even Aunt Charlotte could see that things were changing.

Just as Rowena's father had said they would.

Prudence couldn't make it because Maggie Rose

was still too young and too tiny to be out and about. Besides, Prudence and Andrew were so wrapped up in one another that they couldn't be bothered. Soon Andrew would be at school and Prudence would be busy with her duties keeping house for Andrew and taking care of her baby. The role fit Prudence far better than she ever thought it would. Rowena could feel Prudence's love and blessings all the way from London.

A bee, no doubt attracted to her lilies, buzzed around her for a moment before being lured away by the sweeter scent of the roses surrounding them.

It was funny how quickly even a society wedding could be arranged if the participants brooked no opposition to their plans. Sebastian had written Rowena two weeks ago, telling her he would be on leave, and she wrote back telling him to come prepared to be married. The cable he sent back said simply, *I am always ready to marry you.*

She caught Sebastian's eyes and smiled. Contentment settled in her heart like a curled-up cat. She loved this man. She might not love him in the same wild way she had loved Jonathon, but this love would not burn out like a firework; the love she shared with Sebastian was steady and sure and full of hope for a good life and future.

Her voice as she repeated her vows was strong, for she had never been more sure of anything in her life, except perhaps her passion for flight. Mr.

and Mrs. Dirkes stood behind her in the crowd as did Cristobel. At first, Rowena was hesitant to ask Jonathon's mother to attend, but Mr. Dirkes assured her that she would be touched by the gesture. Their presence here on Summerset land told her more than anything else how things had changed. The new Mrs. Dirkes had even treated her uncle cordially, though Cristobel had been much more reserved in her greeting. Rowena understood. The pain of losing one's father never went away.

But today, Rowena almost felt as if her father were with her, especially as she gazed over the garden, the early roses just now blooming with color.

Sebastian turned to her and she realized she had been daydreaming and it was now time for him to kiss her. His lips met hers and she thrilled at his touch. She would have a good life with this man. He pulled away, his dark eyes smiling deeply into hers. Then they turned to the small gathering to the sound of applause.

Just then another sound caught Rowena's ear, and she glanced upward automatically. It sounded like one of the new, experimental SPADs Mr. Dirkes was collaborating on.

"Merciful heavens!" Aunt Charlotte cried. "It's an air raid!"

"I hardly think it's an air raid, dear," Uncle Conrad said mildly. He seemed pleased with himself, and she turned to Mr. Dirkes, who put his hands up in the air. "It's not an air raid, folks, don't be alarmed. It's a little surprise for Rowena."

"I told you people would be alarmed," Rowena heard Mrs. Dirkes say.

The air filled with the sound of aeroplanes as three new SPADs flew low over the wedding party, sharply lifting over the high roof of Summerset. Rowena shaded her eyes as they circled around in unison.

Cristobel clapped her hands. "How wonderful!"

"What a fabulous idea!" Elaine agreed.

Rowena turned to Mr. Dirkes, whose broad face held a pleased smile at the success of his surprise. "You did this!"

"I thought you would like that," he said. "It was partly Albert's idea, but it took some finagling to get the timing right. They'll be heading on to Dover after this."

Tears filled Rowena's eyes. "Thank you so much. I can't tell you how much this means to me."

Mr. Dirkes pointed to the sky. "Watch now."

All turned their gazes upward as the planes swooped to make another low pass, then gasped as the three aeroplanes seemed to wave their wings at the wedding party.

Sebastian's arm tightened about Rowena's shoulders, and she watched as the aeroplanes flew off into the distance.

AUTHOR'S NOTE

I cried when I finished writing *Summerset Abbey: Spring Awakening*. When authors spend as much time with their characters as I do—especially when those characters and storylines span an entire trilogy—we become incredibly attached to them. This was especially true for me. You see, shortly after signing the contract for the *Summerset* books, I was diagnosed with throat cancer and underwent treatment and recovery while writing these stories. So Rowena, Prudence, and Victoria will always be very special to me. Whenever life became too overwhelming or I was in too much pain, I would immerse myself in their lives to escape from my own. I was transported over and over to Edwardian England to spend time in the gracious manor houses, luscious green fields, and chic London salons that define the landscape of these women's lives. My heart ached when Prudence realized that her life had irrevocably changed following Sir Phillip's death, and I rejoiced when her baby was born safe and sound. I feared for Victoria when she was imprisoned and cried when she realized that Kit was her true love only after sending him away. And finally, I sobbed with Rowena as she said goodbye to her first, passion-filled love and instead married the man she would grow old with.

These young women became a treasured part of my life and I will never forget them. Thank you for allowing me to tell you their stories. I hope you loved them as much as I did.

READERS GROUP GUIDE

SUMMERSET ABBEY: SPRING AWAKENING
T. J. BROWN

Sisters Rowena and Victoria Buxton and Prudence Tate, who was raised as their sister, are all trying to understand where they fit in their newly reshaped family and in Edwardian England when World War I breaks out and changes everything. Prudence's husband, Andrew, is shipped off to war just weeks before she discovers she's pregnant with their first child; Rowena accepts a daring mission transporting planes for the British government as a female pilot and crosses paths with a former lover who makes her question her engagement to Sebastian; Victoria is pushed to her limits when she's sent to an active combat zone in France as a volunteer nurse—and when she realizes she's made a terrible mistake in sending Kit away. Their independent spirits are tested and their lives changed as war alters everything they thought they knew about life . . . and about love.

TOPICS AND QUESTIONS FOR DISCUSSION

1. Has anyone in your group read the two previous novels in the Summerset Abbey series? Is there anyone who has not? Did you

find it easy to follow the story without the first two books for context? How does it enrich the experience to have read them? Discuss how the reading experience changes when you are reading a part of a series.

2. When Rowena is waiting for Sebastian in Brighton, she wanders into a bookstore, thinking that "losing herself in a book would be a welcome distraction." (p. 155) Have you ever felt that way about reading? What is it that drives you to read? What role do books play in the characters' lives, especially given the lines from literature they quote throughout the story?

3. "This is the way it had always been done and the way it will always be done," (p. 244) Elaine says of the Christmas gift-giving at Summerset Abbey. How do you see this reverence for tradition in other areas of the characters' lives? In what ways is this changing in the timeframe of the story, and why? Do you see any of the characters successfully breaking free from tradition? Are there ways they choose not to?

4. How do the different settings for this story enhance and even define what occurs in them? Think about how scenes set at the different locales—Summerset Abbey, Victoria's single-girl London flat, Prudence's small city apartment, Brighton—are influenced by the

rooms and worlds in which they take place. How does the absence of the Mayfair House loom over the characters and their actions?

5. In many stories about war, the men go off to fight while the women stay home and keep the home front running. That model is upended here—Rowena flies war planes and even faces down enemy aircraft, while Victoria heads to the front to nurse the wounded. In what other ways do the characters defy our expectations in this story? What do you think the author's intentions were in writing nontraditional roles for her characters? Is it effective?

6. "She'd proven her worth and her skill, and yet she was still being held back because of her sex," (p. 195) Rowena stews when Mr. Dirkes tells her she can't fly across the channel. Rowena is not the only character facing discrimination because she is a woman, though. What roadblocks do the other characters face? How do they react?

7. Do you think the men in this story are limited by the roles they are approved to play, much as the women are? Almost all of the young men in the story join the war effort. How many of them do you think chose that role, and which were conscripted into service because that was what they felt they had to join up? How much freedom do any of the

characters—male or female—really have over their lives?

8. Rowena likes flying because, "up here she was in control of her own destiny." (p. 107) But is she? She is reliant not only on having the aircraft available to her—the plane her uncle bought for her; the planes Mr. Dirkes allows her to fly—but also the functioning of that equipment and the weather, both of which are out of her control. Do you think Rowena is deluding herself? Or do you think she is grasping at the small bits of power she is allowed to have? In what ways do we sometimes keep from admitting the whole truth about our motives?

9. "I would very much like to marry you, as long as we would be equal partners and you would give me equal say, no matter what the conventional mandates of marriage would imply," (p. 338) Victoria tells Kit. As readers, we love her strong, spunky view of the institution. But her idea of marriage seems to reflect modern attitudes. Do they seem at all anachronistic to you? Does it matter to you if they are? How much do we necessarily read our values into a text, and how do you think that changes our understanding of a character?

10. In light of the feminist themes throughout the book, what do you make of the fact that everyone assumed Prudence's baby would be a boy?

11. Rowena admits she will always love passionate, volatile Jonathan, even as she falls for and prepares to marry steady, strong Sebastian. Which man do you think she ultimately loved more? Which do you find more appealing, and why?

12. What do make of the title *Spring Awakening*? How do you see themes found in imagery of spring—new life, blooming, resurrection—throughout this story? Do you see awakening as an apt illustration for what happens to Victoria, Rowena, and Prudence? The book shares its title with a controversial play and also echoes the title of Kate Chopin's novel *The Awakening*, both of which focus on themes of transgression. Do you see any echoes of that in this story?

13. By the end of the book, Rowena is married to Sebastian, Victoria is engaged to Kit, and Prudence and Andrew are married and have a baby. Through the course of the series—and, in fact, through the course of this book—each pair took a roundabout road toward love. Which sister do you think is the happiest with her choices by the end, especially as they relate to marriage?

14. Despite the modern ideas about marriage and family threaded through the story, this book ends with all three sisters married or on the road to marriage. Do you think it could have

ended any other way? Would you have been disappointed if it did? What makes it so satisfying to us to see the characters fall in love? Do you believe that readers always want a happy ending, and if so, what do you think it says about our desires?

ENHANCE YOUR BOOK CLUB

1. If you haven't read the previous books in this series, *Summerset Abbey* and *Summerset Abbey: A Bloom in Winter*, read them, or check out the book pages on Simon and Schuster.com (where you can read summaries, reviews, and excerpts): http://books.simonandschuster.com/Summerset-Abbey/T-J-Brown/9781451698985 and http://books.simonandschuster.com/Summerset-Abbey-A-Bloom-in-Winter/T-J-Brown/9781451699050

2. Both Rowena and Victoria help directly in the war effort in this book. Women often have been more involved in war than many people realize, and women's roles in fighting wars have often gone overlooked. There have been several excellent movies about women and their role in war efforts, including *V for Victory: Women at War* (1988), about women in World War II, and *Lioness* (2008), about a group of women sent into combat in Iraq. Together, watch one of these films and discuss. Do you think women's contributions

to wars and roles in military life have become more accepted since World War I? Why or why not?

3. Prudence, a notoriously bad cook, is instructed to bring a premade plum pudding to her Christmas gathering. A traditional plum pudding does require some work, but it is a traditional English treat that your whole book club will enjoy. One member of your group can start making the puddings a few days ahead of time, and then, when you all get together, do the last few steps together. You can find a recipe here: http://www.epicurious .com/recipes/food/views/Superb-English-Plum-Pudding-20010

4. "The reality of death made me think hard about what's actually worth fighting for in this world," (p. 274) Jonathan says as he tried to win back Rowena. In your group, discuss what each member thinks is worth fighting for. Would it take the specter of war to make you stand up and claim them? What is one thing you could purposefully choose to work harder on or toward? Commit to each other to make that a priority.

Center Point Large Print
600 Brooks Road / PO Box 1
Thorndike ME 04986-0001 USA

(207) 568-3717

US & Canada:
1 800 929-9108
www.centerpointlargeprint.com

UPPER DARBY LIBRARIES UPPER DARBY, PA

3 5920 1015 1416 2